ASK ME TO
STAY

OTHER TITLES BY TERRI OSBURN

Shooting Stars Novels

Rising Star
Falling Star
Wishing on a Star

Ardent Springs Novels

His First and Last
Our Now and Forever
My One and Only
Her Hopes and Dreams
The Last in Love

Anchor Island Novels

Meant to Be
Up to the Challenge
Home to Stay
More to Give

ASK ME TO
STAY

TERRI OSBURN

Montlake
Romance

Published by Montlake Romance, Seattle

www.apub.com

Amazon, the Amazon logo, and Montlake Romance are trademarks of Amazon.com, Inc., or its affiliates.

ISBN-13: 9781503903470
ISBN-10: 1503903478

Cover design by Caroline Teagle Johnson

Printed in the United States of America

For Dewees Island
for igniting the spark of inspiration that brought this
story to life.

Chapter 1

There must be a hundred places to hide a body on this island.

This morbid thought exemplified a lesser-known problem of being blessed with a writer's mind—the overactive imagination that came with it. Standing beneath a weathered structure on the edge of remote Haven Island off the South Carolina coast, Liza Teller couldn't help but wonder whether she'd volunteered for a ghostwriting gig *or* to be the featured victim on one of those overly dramatic true-crime shows.

"No one would find me out here," she muttered, surveying the landscape.

Liza had seen beaches before, but Haven Island looked more like a forest with sandy edges. Rooftops peeked through the leaves in two or three places, but the rich green canopy dominated the view, seeming to float right up to the horizon line.

Even the salt-scented air smelled cleaner than any place she'd ever been. An entirely new experience for a city girl like Liza. A city girl with no survival skills to speak of and not a soul back home who would even notice she'd gone missing. Vanessa Dunsmore, her agent and only friend, would eventually miss her, but not before the dreaded deed was done and Liza's mutilated body lay buried in some dark corner of this junglelike island.

A morbid thought yet a promising premise. Maybe this crazy adventure would pay off in more ways than one. She could complete the memoir she'd come here to write and go home with a suspense plot or two that her agent could hopefully sell.

As Vanessa had reminded her several times over the last six months, she couldn't sell a product that didn't exist. But after Liza's debut work of fiction had leaped unexpectedly onto the bestseller lists nearly a year ago, her idea well had run dry, hence the no-product problem. Liza had never liked the term *writer's block*, nor had she really believed in the phenomenon itself, but as the cliché went, karma was a bitch, because she was definitely blocked.

One would think that living in New York City would be enough to fill a notebook full of plots, but Liza had tried everything from reading the papers to people-watching several days a week. Still nothing. If only being a bestselling author equated to being a highly paid one, then she wouldn't be putting her life in danger just to stay financially afloat.

"No one is going to kill me," she said, as if speaking the words aloud might convince her brain to nix the ridiculous notion. Though she had to admit, "Woman Lured to Remote Island"—and stupid enough to actually go alone—had "Destined to Be a Movie" written all over it. Liza withdrew her phone to make the note for later cogitation.

Since her phone was out, she double-checked the arrival instructions she'd received that morning. The original email said to locate the golf cart with her name on it and follow the enclosed map to her destination. Surveying the long line of carts parked down the narrow wooden walkway that extended from the covered landing, she considered the chance that one might actually have her name on it.

But the revised instructions said to wait for her escort at the landing dock. Since she hadn't received any new messages, Liza resolved to wait, resisting the urge to wave back the ferry that was quickly disappearing in the direction it had come. Not that they were likely to see her anyway.

Eyeing a fragile-looking bench, she left her suitcases where the boat captain had set them and settled in to wait. Though leery, she had to assume that if the bench could withstand a hurricane, as it surely had at some point in its life, it could sustain her 125 pounds.

Perching on the edge with a sigh, she mumbled, "Please, let this *not* be a mistake." And she didn't mean the bench or the murder fears. A journalism degree and one successful novel did not qualify Liza to write a memoir. The client, who Vanessa had assured her wanted his story told in narrative form, had insisted that Liza was the only person who could tell it.

Turning down the offer would have meant returning to her previous career as a reporter, and chasing down stories in the hope that some internet news site might carry them hadn't proved any more lucrative than writing fiction. If Liza's contrary writer's brain refused to cough up a workable idea, then writing someone else's story was better than not writing anything at all.

Bright-white Keds, bought days before departing for this trip, tapped out a rhythm of impatience as Liza waited. The sun would set soon, and there were no streetlights in sight. She doubted the flashlight on her phone would penetrate far and didn't want to think about the wildlife she might encounter. Birds were abundant in the distance, but what might be lurking in the brush was a mystery she had no desire to solve.

Maybe the first email had been the right one, after all, but the moment she considered checking the line of carts, the sound of a motor cut through the cacophony of chirps and caws echoing from the trees. A beige-and-green cart raced toward her, and through the cloud of dust, she could make out only the driver's shape.

His very large shape.

Like a grizzly bear riding a tricycle, the driver looked ridiculous. Shoulders filled the width of the cart, which she was certain would accommodate two normal-size individuals, and he was so tall that his dark mop of hair nearly brushed the covering above his head. One of the few facts Liza knew about her client was his age. The giant racing her way was nowhere near ninety-plus years old.

"So this is how I die," Liza mumbled, debating whether two years on her high school swim team had prepared her for a swim back to the mainland.

❦

Great. His cargo had missed the boat.

Kendall James drove his cart to the end of the walkway and parked in front of the covered landing, hoping the guy hadn't just missed the boat, but that he wasn't coming at all. A memoir? What the hell was Ray thinking? After thirty years of making himself invisible, why would he want to put his life story on paper for all the world to read?

Stubborn old man.

He didn't know much about this L. R. Teller guy, but Kendall didn't plan to make him feel overly welcome. The writer was going to have Ray's life in his hands. Literally. And there was a good chance that after the book was released, he'd also have his subject's blood on his hands.

The ferry wouldn't return for nearly an hour, and Kendall had no contact information to call and check on Teller. He could hope for the best, return to the struggle of fixing the nonrunning cart that was giving him fits, and then come back again to see if the writer showed up.

A lot of back and forth, but better that than sitting here doing nothing. Kendall didn't like doing nothing.

Swinging the cart to the left to turn around, he spotted a beautiful woman perched on a bench under the covering. She was staring off across the water, curls dancing in the wind and the hem of her dress fluttering along the top of her knees. The image could have been from a magazine ad or a postcard beckoning visitors to a tranquil location.

When she shifted, swinging her gaze toward the island, he noticed the divot between her brows. Concern? Confusion? The stranger looked down at her phone, lips tight as if she were trying to solve a mystery. When her eyes cut again to the horizon, Kendall recognized the expression. Fear.

Whatever she was afraid of, he couldn't leave her there to fend for herself. After locking the brake and cutting the motor, Kendall spoke to the dog in the back seat. "Stay here, buddy." Exiting the vehicle, he pasted on what he hoped was a neighborly smile.

His heavy work boots thudded on the weathered planks, and he noticed the woman's grip tighten around her phone. Though she was smiling, she couldn't hide the suspicion in her intelligent blue eyes. Not wanting to spook her, Kendall stopped near the edge of the covering.

"Hi there," he said, keeping his body loose so as to appear less threatening. Not an easy task for a man his size. "Welcome to Haven Island."

Honey-blonde curls framed her slender face. "Thank you." Her eyes cut away as she exhaled, but her shoulders didn't relax.

Normally, Kendall didn't pry into other people's business, but this case clearly called for further investigation. Tourists weren't provided escorts from the landing, so she had to be a guest of one of the locals.

"Are you waiting for someone?"

Her nod was nearly imperceptible. "Yes."

To ease her tension, Kendall let her know why he was there. "I was expecting someone on the ferry, but I guess he must have missed it. Did you see anyone on the other side when you boarded?"

"There was no one else waiting when we left the dock." She lifted a large purse from the seat beside her and hugged it to her chest. "How often does the ferry run?"

"Top of the hour on the other side. On the half hour over here. Unless there's no one waiting, and then they wait for a call."

"So there's a way to call them back?"

If he didn't know better, Kendall would think this visitor didn't want to stay. Odd, since someone must have been waiting for her.

"You can, yeah, but this time of day, they run pretty much on schedule."

Leaning his shoulder on a post, he considered who she might be visiting. On such a small island, everyone knew everyone else, and he hadn't heard mention of any impending company. The tourists came through regularly but always with plenty of provisions, since Haven lacked any sort of store or restaurant. A quick check of the area revealed two purple suitcases but no groceries or beach supplies.

If she was a tourist, she was going to starve.

Her eyes cut back to the distance, and Kendall dragged the phone from his pocket to appear distracted. From beneath his lashes, he assessed the stranger. She looked close to his age, which put her around thirty. A bit prim, based on the set of her lips and the way she held her shoulders. Feet flat on the floor, back stiff, and that tiny dimple still hovered between her brows.

"You been to the island before?" he asked, his voice casual.

She nearly jumped when he broke the silence. Kendall was big, but he wasn't *that* scary. This woman really needed to relax.

"No, this is my first time." Pulling the purse tighter against her chest, she looked ready to jump over the side of the landing to get away from him.

Taking the hint, Kendall shifted to his full height and slid the phone back in his pocket, planning to drive on up to the Welcome Center, where he could keep an eye on her without causing her any more stress.

"I hope you enjoy your visit." He spun to head back to the cart, but she stopped him with a question.

"You're certain the ferry will come back?"

"It'll be back," he replied, "but didn't you just get here?" No one boarded the ferry without their name showing up on the list, so she couldn't have made the crossing by mistake.

"I did, yes." Chewing the inside of her cheek, she scanned the distance. "But it's late, and the person picking me up doesn't seem to be coming. Maybe I should go back to the other side and try again tomorrow."

This was an easy enough problem to solve. "Who's supposed to pick you up? Do you have a number to call them?"

A white-tipped thumbnail slid between her teeth as she hesitated to answer. Surely she knew who would be looking for her.

"I'm not sure who is supposed to meet me, and I don't have a number."

This was not how the island worked. Tourists were sent pages of information before arriving, about everything from transportation to garbage disposal. And Kendall doubted any of the residents would bring someone in without providing at least a contact number.

"Do you have any name at all?" he asked.

The blonde glanced down to her phone. "I'm here to see Ray Wallis."

Kendall's jaw tightened as realization dawned. His cargo hadn't missed the boat. He was the wrong damn gender.

🦋

As she contemplated her escape options, the inquisitive islander's expression changed. The casual demeanor vanished, and his hands landed on his hips.

"Are you L. R. Teller?"

He said her name as if it tasted rotten on his tongue.

"Yes," she replied, more anxious than before. "But I go by Liza."

The brute shoved a hand through his hair as an audible growl crossed his full lips. He was obviously her escort, yet she was not the person he'd expected. Seconds passed as he glanced from the inlet, to his cart, and back to her. Liza feared he might leave her there, but then he muttered a curse and pointed to her suitcases.

"Are those yours?"

"Yes, they are."

The stranger snatched the hard-shell cases and stormed back to his cart without inviting her to follow. How amazingly rude. Having lived in New York City for the last eight years, Liza was well acquainted with the most hostile of their species, but grumpy New Yorkers had nothing on this . . . Neanderthal.

Though he'd been nice enough before learning her name.

Loading up her purse and laptop bag, one on each shoulder, Liza strolled off after him, only to stop dead several feet from the cart.

"What is that?" she asked, feet frozen to the sandy path.

The man tossed her suitcases onto the back of the vehicle. "A golf cart."

He could shove the smart-ass reply where the sun didn't shine. "I mean the beast *in* the cart."

Deep-brown eyes looked her way. "That's Amos. He's a dog. Don't they have dogs where you come from?"

She didn't dignify that with a reply.

Liza had never lived with any dogs, nor did she seek them out. When she'd inherited her grandmother's tiny apartment in the Bronx, she'd been relieved to find herself in a no-pets building. It wasn't that she didn't like them, necessarily. She'd simply lacked the dog-loving gene that compelled normal human beings to canoodle with every canine that crossed their paths.

"He won't hurt you," the dog owner said as he squeezed his stocky frame into the cart. Muscles bunched, pulling the stained gray tee tighter across his shoulders. When Liza didn't move, he leaned his elbows on the steering wheel, his full lips flattening into a line. "What are you waiting for?"

"An animal-free option."

"You allergic?"

"No." Unless fear could be categorized as an allergy.

"Then what's the problem?"

Stalling, she said, "Where am I supposed to sit?" Even if the black-and-white pit bull hadn't been occupying the entire back seat, tongue hanging to the side like a slobbery pink noodle, the driver's broad shoulders and denim-clad tree-trunk thighs left little room in the front.

Moving his right leg one inch to the left, he nodded toward the minuscule patch of stained white vinyl beside him. "Right here."

Unconvinced, Liza crossed her arms. "I'd rather walk."

"It's too far to walk. Now get in. Ray is going to wonder where we are."

The dog barked as if to back up his owner, and a flock of birds burst from the trees at the same moment Liza nearly leaped out of her skin.

"Quiet, Amos." The words were said with kindness, the gentle tone calming woman and beast.

Telling herself the sooner she climbed into the cart, the sooner she could climb back out, Liza approached the vehicle anticipating a growl, though she couldn't say from which occupant. Pulling her shoulder bags in front of her, she edged one butt cheek onto the seat, careful to keep as much distance as possible between herself and the Goliath who still hadn't bothered to introduce himself. A woodsy scent carrying a hint of sweetness filled her senses as heat radiated from his big body. A quick glance to her left and the scent changed to dog breath, so Liza locked her eyes straight ahead.

"You in?" he asked.

Grasping the chrome pole with one hand, she locked the bags onto her lap with the other. "Yes."

Without another word, her driver hit the gas and made a hard right turn, sending Liza crashing against his side. She'd never been hit by a truck before but imagined the sensation would be similar. As the wind whipped through her hair and hot breath filled her left ear, she prayed whatever hut they'd put her name on wasn't far away.

❦

Where did this writer get off being a woman?

Kendall was supposed to drive to the pier, find the writer guy, and take him back to Ray's. The last thing he'd expected to find was a woman—especially a beautiful one who looked as out of place sitting on that bench as a prairie dog would popping up through a manhole in Manhattan. In the weeks since Ray had shared this foolish idea, Kendall had toyed with a plan to intimidate the writer into backing out. A plan that was now dead in the water.

In the eight years since he'd returned from the service, Kendall had never given two thoughts to the size of the golf carts he drove every day. With Liza Teller pressed along his side, he might as well have been driving a little red wagon. The frilly blue dress fluttered in the wind, revealing enough skin above her knees to be more than a little distracting.

Maybe Francine was right. He'd been living like a hermit for far too long.

Not that women never showed up on Haven Island, but Kendall rarely paid them much attention. The majority were either newlyweds or moms hoping for some peace and quiet while their husbands entertained the kids in the sand. The locals were all married, and on the rare occasion single women stepped off the ferry, Kendall made a point to keep his distance.

No sense in starting something that was always guaranteed to end.

"You know, most people wouldn't do this," she said, raising her voice to be heard above the wind.

Kendall looked over, but her eyes remained on the path. "Do what? Ride in a golf cart?" He'd had the misfortune of riding in a New York City cab. There was no way this cart was more dangerous than that.

She turned his way, one brow arched high. "Step onto a remote island and get into a cart with a stranger the size of an NFL linebacker. You could kill me, and I wouldn't even know the name of the man who'd turned me into fish food."

He considered listing the myriad ways he *could* kill her, but feared she'd leap out of the cart and run back to the pier. Then he'd have to explain to Ray why the ghostwriter had changed her mind before she'd even met her subject. A conversation that was bound to go poorly.

Instead, he shared his name, hoping the info would allay her fears and they could go back to riding in silence.

"Kendall James. And I haven't killed anybody in nearly a decade." A true statement, but one he had no intention of elaborating on.

With annoyance in her smoky voice, she said, "Is that a joke?"

He met her dark-blue eyes. "Nope."

"Right." She faced forward again. "I feel *much* better now."

As he'd hoped, the conversation died, though he continued to assess his passenger. A blush emphasized her high cheekbones, and she held her chin in a regal way, like a queen out for a ride to visit the peasants.

They cleared the trees, running headlong into the wind off the salt marsh. Loose curls whipped across her face, forcing his passenger to release her hold on the chrome post. And because Kendall was too busy looking at her to watch the road, he had to make a hard left turn at the last second.

Physics took over. In a matter of seconds, her scream cut through the air as her body was nearly flung from the cart. Kendall caught her in time, pulling her tight against his side and clamping his arm around her shoulders to keep her there.

"Hold on!" he yelled as he made a hairpin right before pulling the cart to a stop in a small patch of grass beside the trail.

Hair still covering her face, the writer's body remained rigid beneath his touch as they sat in silence for several seconds. As if to remind them that they weren't alone, Amos barked, snapping his owner back to reality.

Shrugging off Kendall's arm, his passenger cleared the hair from her eyes and stepped out of the cart.

"Who taught you how to drive this thing?"

Did she really think there was a golf-cart driving school?

"Get back in. It's getting dark and Ray is waiting."

Hugging her purse and what looked like some kind of briefcase to her chest, she shook her head. "I'm not going through that again. I'll wait here until you send someone else."

She'd been the one to let go. How was that his fault?

"There *is* no one else." Not technically true, but Kendall couldn't leave her standing out here while he hunted up Francine or Larimore. Bruce could show up at any minute, and then she'd *really* be running back to the ferry. "Get in."

The stubborn woman took a step back. "Give me directions and I'll walk."

Ray would kick his ass if Kendall obeyed that order. Instead, he turned to the back seat. "Come on, Amos. Up front."

The dog hopped over the seat, filling the vacant spot.

"Good boy," his owner said before returning his attention to the pain-in-the-ass writer. "Now you can sit in the back. Put the bags between your feet, and hold on to this bar." Kendall tapped the chrome handrail that ran along the top of the seat.

Accepting this new arrangement, she followed his suggestion, securing the bags between her ankles and locking a death grip on the bar. "Okay, I'm ready. But if you throw me out again, I'm not getting back in."

He hadn't thrown her out at all. "Fair enough."

Kendall stepped on the gas, grateful to have her out of his line of sight. Now he could concentrate on reaching their destination without thinking about pale thighs, honey-gold curls, and whether her skin would feel as soft as it looked.

Chapter 2

Liza's hair must have looked as if she'd used Aqua Net in a wind tunnel. During their race down narrow dirt paths, she'd spotted a sign that said SPEED LIMIT **17 MPH**. If the cart had a speedometer, she couldn't see it past the behemoth in the driver's seat, but Liza felt confident in saying he had *not* obeyed the limit.

Holding on tightly, she took in the constantly changing scenery along the way. Dense woods for one stretch. Marshland for another. Palmettos and pines arched over the path and then fell away to reveal wetlands as far as the eye could see. Slender birds of white and gray and muted blue stood among the reeds, fishing for their suppers and enjoying the waning light.

In the city, birds flitted here and there, dodging imminent peril, but these creatures appeared completely confident in their surroundings. Not a ruffled feather to be found, as if they felt secure in the knowledge that no threats lurked around the corner. In fact, there were no corners. Just nature, in all its curves and colors and endless splendor.

Whatever she'd expected from this trip, an immediate sense of peace had not been on the list. Though she'd feel more at peace once this mad dash ended.

Blessedly, Kendall slowed and eased the cart down a narrow drive on their left. From the corner of her eye, Liza spotted the white tail of a deer darting off through the trees and hoped she'd get a better glimpse another time. Dead limbs leaned against sturdier trunks as the cart traveled deeper into the forest, until a set of stairs appeared straight ahead.

The one or two buildings she'd spotted along the way had been built high off the ground, which made sense in this part of the world. Storm surge must come in high during bad weather. This house was built the same way, but she hadn't been prepared for the sheer size of it.

Hut had clearly been the wrong assumption for where she'd be spending her time. Nestled in the trees stood a beautiful buttery-yellow home with dark wood shutters and a wraparound porch right out of *Southern Living*. Two stories soared above the pillared foundation, wide and gabled and seemingly plucked from some affluent suburban neighborhood.

Busy staring at the impressive home, Liza hadn't realized they'd come to a stop.

When Kendall climbed out and stepped around to retrieve her suitcases, she found herself staring into the furry face of his sidekick. To her surprise, the dog appeared to be smiling. Liza smiled back—a sure sign that this unpredictable island possessed some sort of magical powers. When the dog licked her face, she returned to her senses.

"There will be no licking," she admonished. The pooch continued to smile, unaffected by the scolding. "That cute face might work on other people, but not me, buddy. As they say where I come from, fuhgeddaboudit."

Amos barked, whether in protest or agreement, she couldn't say, and leaped from the vehicle to follow his master up the wooden stairs. Once again, Kendall didn't invite her to follow. The man seriously lacked people skills.

"How many people live here?" Liza asked when she caught up.

"Just Ray since Daphne died." He conveyed this information with no more emotion than if he were giving a weather report.

"Was Daphne his wife?"

14

"His parrot."

She couldn't have heard him right. "His what?"

"Parrot." Kendall reached the porch landing and set the suitcases on their wheels. "You know. A bird."

"Yes, I know what a parrot is." She simply hadn't expected one to be talked about like a spouse or roommate. "This is a large house for one man, with or without a parrot. Does he entertain guests?"

"Not until you." Kendall's tone carried a distinct note of disapproval.

"Mr. James," she said, "is there a reason you don't like me?" He'd been nice enough until finding out who she was.

Dark brows drew tight over a perfectly triangular nose. "I don't know you well enough not to like you. I just don't like the reason you're here."

Liza was there to write a man's memoir. Why would anyone disapprove of a man telling his life story? Before she could ask that very question, Kendall carried her suitcases into the house, holding the door for the dog but not for her.

The man needed a serious lesson in manners. She rolled her eyes as she let herself in, contemplating possible reasons Kendall would oppose this project. Maybe Mr. Wallis wasn't healthy enough. He was in his early nineties, after all. Liza never imagined she'd be interviewing her subject from his deathbed.

Or maybe he was relatively healthy but had lived a difficult life, and the younger man didn't want him reliving a traumatic past. If that were the case, Liza wouldn't feel comfortable moving ahead with this endeavor, either.

"There's my guest of honor," exclaimed a slender man shuffling around Kendall to reach her. A sagging, round face smiled from beneath a dapper fedora. A sport jacket of vertical stripes in black and gray contrasted with white trousers that tapered above a pair of bright-purple tennis shoes.

Ray Wallis looked like a flamboyant, shell-less turtle. In a hat.

"I thought maybe you'd missed the ferry," he said with great concern, pulling her farther into the house. "Or Kendall had scared you away." Squeezing Liza's hands, he asked, "Was he nice to you?"

Ray Wallis was definitely not on his deathbed. "No, he wasn't," she replied, honesty winning over tact.

Flashing the kindest smile she'd ever seen, Ray leaned in close to whisper, "That's just Kendall. You'll get used to him."

Liza doubted that but refrained from saying so. Just to verify her assumption, she said, "You are Mr. Wallis?"

Light-blue eyes scanned her features. "I am. And you look exactly as I'd imagined."

Since her picture appeared on the website Vanessa had insisted she establish, Liza had assumed he'd looked her up. Apparently not. Maybe he was one of those people who liked to be surprised.

"You have a lovely house," she said, setting her purse and laptop bag on the floor near her feet.

"Thank you, my dear. I'll give you the full tour after dinner, but first we need to get you settled in." Ray turned to Kendall, who lingered near the expansive island centered in the contemporary white kitchen. "Show Ms. Teller to her room while I set the table. And don't go far. The clams will be ready any minute, and I expect you to eat with us."

That's what smelled so familiar. Liza loved clams but couldn't remember the last time she'd had them. Living on a budget didn't allow for meals out, especially in New York City, and her cooking skills were not at the clam-dish level.

Since reaching her room would provide an opportunity to brush her hair and shake off the harrowing ride to get there, she retrieved her bags and willingly followed Kendall through the living room to a sweeping wooden staircase that did a full turn on its way to the second floor. The landing at the top was open to the living area, and a row of windows provided breathtaking views in every direction.

No wonder the houses sat up so high. If Liza weren't seeing the wonders of this island with her own two eyes, she would have never believed that a place this untouched existed. At least not in the US.

"You're down here," Kendall called when she lagged behind.

Following the path he'd taken, Liza was surprised to find herself in front of a screen door much like the one at the main entrance. She stepped through it to find a small replica of the kitchen downstairs as well as a cozy living room nearly as large as her entire apartment back home.

Confused, Liza lingered on the threshold, wondering if she'd made a wrong turn. Afraid she'd rudely invaded someone else's space, she retraced her steps, hoping to track down the man with her luggage.

"Where are you going?" Kendall asked.

Liza spun as if caught in the act of breaking and entering. "I thought I was in the wrong place."

"No. This is your apartment."

"Apartment?"

"You've got everything you need, though we weren't sure what kind of food to get. You can make a trip back over to Isle of Palms tomorrow if Francine got the wrong stuff."

"Francine?" The information was coming too fast for her to keep up.

"You'll meet her." Kendall pointed to a door at the opposite end of the living room. "You have your own entrance, and I'll get your cart repaired and parked downstairs sometime tomorrow. There's a map taped to the windshield, so you can find your way around. Not that there's much to find." Indicating the door to her right, he added, "The bedroom and bath are back there. Your suitcase is on the bed. Read the recycle info on the side of the fridge, keep the showers short, and put the emergency number that's on the wall in your phone, so you can reach me, if necessary. Any questions?"

Blinking, she struggled to process the flurry of instructions. "I guess not."

"Then I'll see you downstairs."

Eyes down, he stomped past her like a charging pine, in both scent and size, leaving Liza alone and befuddled. Rooted to the spot, she took in her surroundings. The leather sofa. The cheerful curtains. The gleaming hardwood floors. She'd expected to have a small room with a bed and maybe a desk to work. But then nothing so far had been as she'd expected.

"An entire apartment all to myself. Huh. What will they throw at me next?"

❦

"Did you know that woman wasn't a man?" Kendall would have appreciated a little warning.

"That was evident the moment she walked in," Ray replied, ladling clams and sauce into a large serving bowl. "But I wouldn't be surprised if *you* failed to notice."

Kendall was a hermit. He wasn't dead. "I mean, did you know when you hired her?"

Tipping his hat back, the old man flashed a mischievous grin. "Yes, I did."

"You could have told me before I went to the dock looking for a dude in loafers and dark-rimmed glasses."

"That's a stereotypical assumption on your part. I never said she was a man, and you never asked." Lifting a stack of empty bowls, he nodded toward the clams. "Carry that to the table for me, please."

Without hesitation, Kendall completed the task and then crossed to the fridge for a beer. Other than the fact that he couldn't intimidate her out of writing the book, at least not the way he'd planned, why the writer's gender bothered him, he didn't know. There was just something about her. The way she'd appeared scared and uncertain when he'd first found her on the bench but then called him to task for his curt behavior. A combination of innocence that brought out his protective side and a toughness that said she didn't need his protection at all.

"Did she like the apartment?" Ray asked, dragging Kendall back to the present.

"Seemed to."

Not that he'd stuck around long enough to find out. Being near Liza Teller made his palms sweat, and that hadn't happened since he'd asked Mira Dobrowski to the senior prom.

"Good. I want her to be comfortable." Ray set the last bowl in place. "She's a pretty thing, isn't she?"

Pretty didn't begin to cover it. "I guess so." Kendall kept his eyes on his beer bottle. "But you need to be more worried about whether she can write. Why don't you send her home and call this whole thing off."

Ray rolled his eyes. "We've been over this enough now. I'm telling my story, and that's that."

"How much detail are you going to give? What if the wrong people see it?"

"The wrong people died years ago."

He could not be so naive. "That doesn't mean the threat is gone."

With endless patience, Ray patted Kendall's cheek on his way to the kitchen. "You're just like your father. You worry too much."

Being cautious had saved Kendall's ass on more than one occasion. And whether Ray liked it or not, he was the closest thing to family that Kendall had left on this island. Other than Amos.

"Just leave out some details," he urged. "What could it hurt?"

"Don't worry." The older man withdrew napkins from a drawer. "Names will be changed to protect the guilty."

Footsteps sounded on the stairs, and both men turned to watch the new houseguest glide gracefully across the living room. Hair tamed and smile in place, she looked like a goddess in a frilly blue dress and shiny white tennis shoes. Kendall's chest tightened as his palms dampened once again. He'd clearly lost his mind, because all he wanted to do was sweep her into his arms and march right back up the stairs.

"Sorry if I kept you waiting," she said, lacking the typical New York City accent Kendall expected. Other than sounding clearly northern, there wasn't much of an accent at all. "I needed to freshen up after the death-defying ride here."

Ray glanced to Kendall with one gray brow arched high. "This girl is going to be a match for you."

Kendall didn't dignify that with a response.

"Come." Ray withdrew a chair from the table. "Let's eat."

The writer took the offered seat with a nod of gratitude and shook out her napkin before spreading it across her lap. "The food smells wonderful. Reminds me of a dish my grandmother used to make."

"Used to?" Ray queried as he shuffled around to his own chair.

The writer nodded. "Grandma Teller died five years ago. I still miss her, but she left me her apartment, and every now and then, I find some little treasure from her past."

Their host sank into his chair.

"Ray?" Kendall set his beer on the table. "You okay?"

The older man dismissed his concern. "Yes, I'm fine. Just had a dizzy spell is all."

The doc had advised Ray to slow down, but he wouldn't listen. When they'd argued about it, the old man had tossed out a comment about slowing down when he was dead. Kendall hadn't appreciated the joke.

"I forgot the wine."

"I'll get it." Kendall moved into action before Ray could rise from his chair. The stubborn man was going to be the death of them both.

"Mr. Wallis, I appreciate your putting this meal together, but I don't expect to be entertained," the writer said. "I'm here to do a job, and there's no need to exert yourself on my behalf."

Ray waved her words away. "Don't let my age fool you, Ms. Teller. I'm as spry as I ever was. A little cold last week weakened me a bit, but I'll be back to full strength in no time."

Kendall couldn't remember the last time Ray had a cold, but loyalty kept him from saying so.

"Regardless"—she clasped her hands on the table as Kendall returned with the wine—"I don't want any special treatment. And please, call me Liza."

"And you must call me Ray. So the *L* in L. R. is for Liza? Can I ask what the *R* is for?"

"Ruth," she replied. "A bit old-fashioned, but it's another inheritance from my grandmother."

"You two must have been close."

Her expression faltered. "Sadly, no." Sitting up straighter, she crossed her arms on the table. "The clams really do smell wonderful. Should we eat before they get cold?"

Disappointment shone in Ray's eyes before he said, "You're absolutely right. Let's eat." He swung the ladle around her way before setting his glass closer to Kendall. "Pour the wine, my boy."

Kendall did as asked, surprised by the sudden tension hovering around the table. Ray wasn't used to being shut down, nor did he take well to being rebuffed. In truth, the man was nosy to a fault, and most folks went along either out of deference to his age or because he simply charmed them into submission.

Liza did not seem affected by either of those options, making for an auspicious start to their impending professional relationship. Kendall smiled for the first time since learning the writer's identity. At this rate, Ray would abandon this ridiculous book idea in no time at all.

Chapter 3

Navigating this visit was going to be tougher than she'd expected.

Liza longed to be one of those women who exuded confidence in any situation, but she wasn't. In fact, throughout her entire life, she'd fought insecurity, which had sharpened her acting skills at an early age. Between her last name and her nose, there was no hiding her Jewish heritage, but she'd grown up with little knowledge of the religion or that side of her family.

Her Irish mother had been raised Catholic, and despite walking away from the faith long before Liza had come along, Mary O'Dowd had still put her daughter through twelve years of Catholic school. It hadn't taken long for Liza to consider herself a fish out of water. She didn't fit in with her classmates, nor did she belong with the family she rarely saw.

In essence, she'd been a book-loving, introverted child who'd honed the necessary coping skills to survive basic human interactions when necessary. As an adult, Liza had embraced the power to avoid social situations as much as possible. Then again, a lack of friends meant few social invitations. A fact that suited Liza just fine.

The remoteness of Haven Island had been a plus when she'd debated taking the job. No cars, stores, or restaurants had to mean no social requirements. That would leave her with the simple and peaceful task of typing up an old man's story. If she was lucky, he'd hand over a stack of journals, and she could spend the monthlong visit huddled over her laptop, writing away.

Dinners that included her genial client and his surly sidekick, who'd made his objection to her presence abundantly clear, had not been part of the plan. *Just smile and nod,* she told herself. *How hard could this be?*

"Why don't you have an accent?" Kendall asked as Liza sipped her white wine. She didn't particularly like wine but hated to offend her host, who'd boasted of the vintage as Kendall had filled her glass.

"What accent did you expect?" Did he assume every northerner sounded like a Kennedy?

"New York City. That's where you're from, right?"

Ray stirred his clams but didn't seem interested in eating them. In fact, his enthusiasm had dropped significantly since they'd sat down to dinner. Keeping an eye on her subject, she answered Kendall's question. "That's where I live now, but I grew up in Rochester."

Pale-blue eyes met hers. "But you were born in the city." A statement instead of a question. Liza had to wonder how much information her agent had shared with her new employer.

"Yes, I was born in New York City, but my mom moved us to Rochester when I was two. I didn't move back to the city until eight years ago." Why she'd moved back was her own business. "Ray, how long have you lived here on Haven Island?"

"It'll be thirty years this fall," her host replied, eyes locked on her face as if he were trying to memorize her features.

Liza tried not to squirm. "And where did you move from?"

"I'm a New Yorker, too."

"Really?" she asked. "What part?"

"The Bronx. You say your family moved to Rochester?"

"My mom and I, yes. In what part of the Bronx did you live? My family has been there for decades."

"Allerton," Ray replied. "Did your father not move with you?"

Liza didn't like sharing the details of her family, especially not with virtual strangers, but if she was going to learn the intimate details of Ray's life, she supposed it couldn't hurt for him to know a little of hers.

"No. My parents divorced shortly before the move. But my father's family is from Allerton, and that's where I live now. Did you know the Tellers? My great-uncle had a dry cleaning business right on Allerton Avenue."

Ray gave a halfhearted smile. "The memory isn't what it used to be." A worrisome answer considering the task ahead. "I'm sorry to hear about your parents," he added. "Did you get to see your dad often?"

"I didn't, no."

Her father had made little effort to remain in his daughter's life, instead choosing to blame her mother for the separation, claiming the move kept them apart. Sometime during high school, Liza had realized the ridiculousness of that claim, but as he was the only parent she had left, she'd made the conscious choice to forget the past and build a new relationship with the man she hardly knew.

That didn't mean she wanted to talk about him with strangers. Ephrem Teller hadn't only neglected his daughter; he'd taken every opportunity to make her mother's life miserable. One June while she was still in college, Liza had gone shopping with a couple of friends. During the excursion, they'd stopped to buy Father's Day cards.

The sentiments were all the same—sincere, sappy messages about how much he'd taught her and been there for her and how she hoped to find a man just like him. None of them ever fit Liza's situation, so she did what she'd always done—edged down to the humorous section and bought a card with no sentimental meaning at all.

Eager to change the subject, Liza turned her attention to the silent guest to her right. "How about you, Mr. James? Where were you born?"

"Add me to the New York City group, but I've been down here since I was four." He dropped a spoon into his nearly empty bowl and reached for his drink. "Why didn't you get to see your dad? Rochester isn't that far from the city."

Anyone who said women were the nosy ones hadn't met these two. "Distance wasn't the only obstacle." Liza didn't elaborate and hoped her silence would deter further questions.

"We didn't mean to pry, Ms. Teller," Ray said, his voice heavy with regret.

Now she felt bad. "It's fine, really. And please, do call me Liza."

The conversation faded as Kendall grinned into his beer. What he found amusing, she didn't know. To end the uncomfortable silence, she searched for a safer topic and chose their current location.

"I've been fascinated by this island since my agent told me where I was going. Are there really no cars?"

"There are trucks, but only the wildlife caretakers use them," Kendall replied. "We also have a full-size fire engine. Just in case."

A reality she hadn't considered, but it was good to know that should there be a fire, emergency equipment was close by. Though who exactly manned this truck?

"Are there enough people on the island to operate something like that?"

Kendall shrugged. "We get by."

Not the most reassuring answer. Liza opted to ignore Mr. Difficult and returned her attention to her host.

"Do all of the houses on the island come with apartments like the one upstairs?"

"Each house is unique. Mine was a *Field of Dreams*–type thing. I hoped that if I built it, they would come."

"Who would come?" Liza asked, noticing Kendall's confused expression.

Ray leaned back with his wine, the clams still untouched. "Whoever normally comes to visit."

The answer told her nothing at all, and she once again wondered about his state of mind.

"Most of the other homes are rentals," he said. "Some throughout the year and some limited to the main tourist season. Only a few of us live on the island year-round."

Liza enjoyed her solitude, but even she couldn't imagine living so remotely all the time. "That must keep things very quiet."

"Quiet may be a bad thing to you city people," Kendall cut in, "but we like it this way."

Despite the thought that had just raced through her mind, Liza narrowed her eyes as she turned his way. "You're good at making assumptions, Mr. James, but not every New Yorker thrives on noise and energy. Peace and quiet are high on my list. Right behind civility and kindness. You should try them sometime."

Her rebuttal brought a grin to Ray's face. "You're going to work out just fine, Liza Ruth. Just fine, indeed."

No one had called her Liza Ruth since Granny T had passed away, but she didn't mind Ray doing so. The names sounded right together coming from his lips. Relieved she'd managed to turn things around, Liza ignored Kendall's childish pouting and returned her host's beaming smile. "Thank you, Ray. I'm glad you think so."

❦

Kendall could be civil. *Dammit.*

After scraping the last dish clean, he flipped on the faucet and sent water splashing across the front of his shirt. "Shit," he mumbled, stepping back from the sink to survey the damage. A drop of water slipped from his shirt and landed between his feet on the mat. "Great."

Kendall stripped off the shirt to wring it out over the sink. Once it stopped dripping, he hung it over the back of a chair and returned to finish the dishes. On an island like Haven, water came at a premium, which meant running the dishwasher only happened on rare occasions. Kendall had insisted Ray sit while he cleaned up. The writer offered to help, but Ray had dragged her off for the promised tour of the house. Fine by Kendall. She'd probably lecture him on how to properly do the dishes anyway.

As he put the last glass away, Liza stepped in from the back deck where she and Ray had ended the tour. "Two more glasses," she said before coming to a stop at the edge of the kitchen. "Oh. I'm . . . Ray wanted me to . . ." As she hovered with two wineglasses in her hands, her eyes lingered on Kendall's torso. "Where's your shirt?"

A heat he hadn't experienced in far too long simmered to life in Kendall's gut. "I got it wet."

Blonde curls swayed as she nodded. "I see." She continued to stare, and against his better judgment, he let her. One pearly-white tooth sank into her bottom lip as she slowly crossed the room to set the glasses on the counter. Not until they stood a foot apart did she finally meet his eyes. "There are the glasses."

"Thanks," he mumbled, voice heavy as her scent surrounded him. She must have splashed on something sweet before dinner. "Did you want anything else?"

Blue eyes darkened, and he knew exactly what she wanted. He may have been out of the game for longer than he liked to admit, but Kendall recognized raw desire when he saw it. Sadist that he was, he held his ground, waiting. For what, he didn't know. His brain said to back the hell off, but his brain was no longer in charge.

"I should go back outside." She didn't move.

"Yeah, you should." His grip tightened on the towel to keep from reaching for her.

"Sorry about your shirt." She was a terrible liar. "Ray said you should come outside when you're finished."

Kendall leaned a hip on the counter and crossed his arms. "I'll do that."

A sigh escaped her lips as her gaze dropped to his chest. At a breaking point, he said, "Walk away, Liza."

As if the words had snapped her back to reality, she blinked several times, blushed a pretty pink, and hurried from the room. Muscles tight, Kendall turned to brace his hands on the edge of the sink, needing the cool porcelain against his palms. He'd never been set on fire by a look before. If the woman ever actually touched him, he might go up in flames.

No one will be touching anyone, he told himself, but his body still simmered. If Liza had been a tourist passing through, he'd have taken her up on the unspoken offer. But she wasn't passing through. She was there for Ray, to do a job Kendall didn't approve of, and her sudden flare of desire didn't negate the fact that she didn't even like him.

Annoyed by his lack of control, Kendall left the glasses where she'd set them and charged off to fetch a jacket from his cart. When Amos leaped up from his spot near the fireplace, his owner held up a hand. "I'm not leaving, buddy. Go back to sleep."

Amos whimpered but followed the order. The cool breeze hit Kendall in the chest as he stepped onto the front porch, but it did little to cool his body. A quick jaunt down the stairs and he snagged an old sweat jacket from beneath his back seat. Zipping it up, he cast his eyes to the star-filled sky.

"Forget it, James. You don't need that kind of trouble."

A few deep breaths and he headed back upstairs to say a quick good night, ignoring the voice in his head that argued a little trouble might be just what he needed.

🦋

Liza was grateful for the darkness that prevented Ray from seeing her face. Her cheeks were hot, as were other parts of her body. Parts neglected for far too long if she could be so thoroughly turned on by a bare chest. And sculpted abs. Shoulders that went on forever and a jagged scar above his left nipple that made her fingers itch to touch it.

Not helping. Not helping *at all.*

To be fair, she'd never seen a man like Kendall James in the flesh. There had been athletes in college, but Liza's nose had been too buried in her books to notice them, clothed or otherwise. The few men she'd dated over the years had run lanky to svelte. Academics who lifted little more than a leather briefcase and a latte. Which made her wonder what Kendall lifted. Tree trunks, perhaps?

"Don't worry," Ray said. "Kendall will warm up to you."

He'd warmed up all right. And warmed her up in the process.

"Maybe," she replied, hoping Ray wouldn't notice the tremor in her voice.

"Give him time. He isn't happy that I'm doing this book, and he's taking that out on you. He'll come around."

Again, what could be so bad about Ray telling his story? Liza wouldn't normally pry, but considering her reason for being there, she needed to know why Kendall would be working against her. "Why doesn't he want you to do the book?"

Ray turned her way, the fedora shading his eyes from the porch light. "That answer is better left until later in the story."

When presenting the project to Liza, Vanessa had provided the few minor details that Ray had shared. He had been born in the 1920s, served in World War II, and afterward cashed in his GI Bill before meeting his wife shortly after college. That's where the information had stopped. If she were being honest, Liza had to admit that the questions left unanswered were what drew her to the project. Other than the money, of course.

Having grown up without grandparents—Granny Teller hadn't been very talkative during the few years Liza had had with her—she'd often longed for the opportunity to hear stories of yesteryear. Not just in books and movies, but real-life accounts from the people who were there. That had been a big reason she'd pursued a degree in journalism with a minor in history. Liza felt no draw to report on the present or what might happen tomorrow, but give her a good story involving a sprawling steamliner or the first transatlantic flight, and she was happy.

This memoir was promising to be an in-depth historical article on steroids. Born before the Depression, Ray had seen nearly three-quarters of the twentieth century, and before long, his generation would be gone. Firsthand accounts like Ray's would be all the world had left of such an important time in history.

A reality that sharpened Liza's determination to get this right.

"I asked my agent to make sure you understood that I've never written a memoir before. I appreciate you still giving me this opportunity."

"I wouldn't trust anyone else with my story."

Flattering, but Liza had done nothing to deserve such faith. "There are countless other writers with experience in this genre. Why me?"

Ray slowly rose from his rocker. "Because *you* are bestselling author L. R. Teller."

Liza debated whether to correct him with the truth—that she was a broke writer who'd gotten lucky with her first book and didn't deserve one ounce of his misplaced confidence. But then she remembered how badly she needed this job and kept her mouth shut.

"I'm heading out," said Kendall as he stepped onto the back deck. "Ray, Francine is picking you up at eight thirty for your appointment in Charleston."

Liza was relieved to see he'd found a jacket. Even so, enough skin peeked out above the zipper to remind her how good he'd looked without it. Keeping her gaze locked on the distance, she failed to see the dog trotting her way until he landed in her lap.

An oomph escaped her lips as his weight settled on her thighs and his hot breath hit her in the face. The two men continued to chat as if she wasn't being accosted by a furry beast.

"I'll be ready," the older man replied, shuffling past her chair. "I want you to show Liza around the island tomorrow."

"What?" she said, struggling to keep her face a safe distance from the dog's tongue. She'd tried pushing him off to no avail, and dang if he wasn't smiling at her again. "I don't need to be shown around."

"Ray, I've got things to do," Kendall added, clearly not liking the idea any more than she did. "Including fixing her cart so she can show *herself* around."

With an impressive air of authority, her host stood firm, if slightly bent, and flashed a stern look. "Nonsense. I want her to feel comfortable here, and riding around with some simple map isn't going to tell her anything about the island. You know Haven better than anyone, so you should give her the tour."

Kendall's eyes met hers in a clear plea to back him up, but she wasn't about to argue with her employer before they'd even started working together. If nothing else, they could drive down the road and back and let Ray think they'd covered more ground.

"And don't drive her in a circle and bring her back," Ray said, as if reading Liza's thoughts. "She needs to know where she can go and what parts to avoid while she's here."

There were parts to avoid? Liza didn't like the sound of that.

"Come on," Kendall pleaded. "Let Francine take her when you guys get back."

"You'll take her in the morning, and that's that." Tilting his hat back, Ray looked down at Liza. "I see at least one of them has taken a liking to you. Amos doesn't approve of everyone, and he's obviously a fine judge of character. Can't say the same for his owner."

Without another word, the older man shuffled into the house, leaving Liza alone with the beast and his dog.

"I'm sorry," she said, feeling bad about the situation. Regardless of whatever seemed to be going on between them, Kendall shouldn't be forced to spend time with her. "If you want to tell me the areas to stay away from, I'm willing to pretend I had a tour."

He sighed in surrender. "It's fine. I'll be here before nine." To her surprise, the corner of his mouth tilted up as he watched her. The hint of a grin had an odd effect on her ability to breathe. "I thought you didn't like dogs."

Liza followed his gaze to the pit bull in her lap. She was scratching behind his ear as his eyes rolled shut in doggy bliss. "I don't." The reply was in direct conflict with her actions. "But I guess he's kind of cute."

"Ray was right. Amos doesn't like a lot of people."

"Then I'll take this forced proximity as a compliment." The words made her realize that's exactly what the impending tour would be—forced proximity. If the encounter in the kitchen was any indication, time alone with Kendall James would not be good for her peace of mind. Though it would likely be good for her other parts. "I'm serious about tomorrow. You don't have to take me anywhere."

He slid his hands into the jacket's pockets. "Don't worry. So long as I keep my shirt on, we should be okay. Come on, Amos."

The dog leaped off her lap to obediently follow his master, while Liza stared at the empty doorway. Was he implying that she might *jump his bones* if he went shirtless again? That what had happened in the kitchen had been one-sided, and he'd merely been an innocent, shirtless victim? *Bull. Crap.* He'd been just as aroused as she'd been, and Liza hadn't been the one traipsing around half-naked.

The only thing bigger than this man's muscles was his ego, and by the end of their tour, she'd make it very clear that his delicate virtue was in no danger from her.

Chapter 4

Kendall pulled up to Ray's place at eight forty-five to find Liza waiting on the front stairs. He was relieved to see that her gauzy dress reached her ankles, so there would be no thigh sightings to distract him.

He'd taken a long cold shower before bed and gotten little sleep before the sun penetrated his bedroom windows. Dragging ass, he'd hiked down to the beach for his daily run before showering again, feeding Amos, and then heading to the garage with his coffee to work on Liza's cart. After less than an hour of getting nowhere, he knew the battery was the problem. He put in a call to a parts shop in Mount Pleasant and sent a text to Francine with the pickup information, and then Kendall found himself with nothing to do.

Idle hands meant plenty of time to mull over the new thorn in his side. Liza Teller was as smart as she was beautiful, with eyes like sapphires and a mouth that could put him in his place one minute and make him want to taste it the next. Spending a couple of hours with her pressed against his side would be a true test, but Kendall didn't see any way around it. Ray wanted her to see the island, so she'd see it. But as soon as his tour-guide duties ended, she was all Ray's.

"You're ready early," he said, turning in his seat to rub Amos's head.

"You said before nine." She rose to her feet and brushed off her dress. "That wasn't exactly specific." The navy-colored dress, covered in pink-and-blue flowers, wrapped around her long legs as she removed a wide-brimmed hat from her head. "Are you going to put the dog up front?"

"I can't tell you about the island if you're in the back seat." This excursion would take forever if he had to spend the whole time yelling over his shoulder. "I'll take it slow."

Liza looked doubtful but tugged the simple white sweater tight across her chest and silently climbed aboard. Her stark-white tennis shoes looked tiny next to his dirty old boots. Then again, all of her looked tiny next to his bulky frame. Hat secured in her lap, she nodded like a bull rider ready to leave the chute. "Okay, I'm in. Let's get this over with."

Kendall fought the urge to shove her high-and-mighty ass right back out. He was the one doing her a favor here. Not the other way around.

"I'll keep it short and sweet."

"I appreciate that."

Jaw clenched, he circled around and headed up the driveway, making a right onto the main path back toward the ferry dock. He kept his speed down as they came through the trees into a clearing.

"You might see a white-tailed deer or a raccoon," he said to start the tour, "but otter sightings are rare."

She nodded, taking in the scenery.

"If you hear howling at night, that's the coyotes. They don't bother people much, but folks need to keep a close eye on their dogs when they're outside."

That got her attention. "Coyotes?"

"Like I said, you'll hear them, but you aren't likely to see one." Kendall pointed to their right. "This is the impoundment. You might call it a reservoir. Popular with the bird-watchers." They passed a couple of canoes sitting on the bank of the water. "You're welcome to try out a canoe—just wear a life jacket. Ray has some in the storage space under his stairs."

"I'm not much of a canoe girl," she said, checking out the small dock that was big enough for a bench and not much else. As they passed, she read the warning sign and instantly turned his way. "'Dock closed when alligator present'? Is that a joke?"

"No, ma'am. Last count we had about thirty-five, but mostly babies."

"You don't get babies without the full-grown variety."

"Pay attention to the warning signs, and you should be safe." There hadn't been an incident in at least three years. And they'd been able to save the tourist's foot, so it had turned out fine. "I'll show you where you can refill the water jug in your fridge up here at the Welcome Center."

Minding his speed, Kendall made the left into the gravel parking area and backed the cart into an open space. After engaging the emergency brake, he stepped out. Amos leaped out behind him and trotted toward the building. Halfway to the stairs, Kendall noticed Liza wasn't with him and turned to find her still sitting in the golf cart.

"You coming?"

She crossed her arms and glared in silence. Marching back to the pouting woman, Kendall heard Ray's voice in his head saying, *Be nice.*

"What's the matter?" he asked, his effort to speak in a friendly tone failing miserably.

"That's the third time you've lumbered off, expecting me to follow you like that dog of yours."

Kendall ignored the lumber part. "I just said I'd show you where the water is. Seems like the follow-me part is a given after that."

"A lot of things seem to be a given with you," she mumbled, finally getting to her feet. "From now on, if you want me to go somewhere, say so."

She could go somewhere, all right. "Fine. Follow me."

Her royal pain in the ass plopped the hat on her head and sauntered off toward the stairs where Amos waited. Gritting his teeth, Kendall followed behind. If he survived this tour without throwing himself off the pier, he'd consider the day a success.

🦋

Liza didn't enjoy conflict, but she'd learned long ago the importance of defending herself. When the bullies had made her a target in third grade, Mom had assured her that handling them on her own was the best approach, despite Liza's plea for parental intervention.

When her classmates weren't picking on her nose, it was her curly hair. Or her practical shoes and sagging knee socks. Reaching her limit, Liza chose a cool day in mid-October to stand her ground, and to her surprise, the teasing stopped. Mom had been right. The bullies weren't brave and confident. They were scared little kids, many with older siblings who tortured them mercilessly at home.

By picking on someone their own size, they could make up for constantly feeling powerless. Of course, with a nose like Liza's, she'd been a target many more times over the years, but that day in third grade had provided a lesson she never forgot. More times than not, setting boundaries early had served her well.

Using the long-practiced tactic with Kendall James had been second nature, though she hadn't expected such satisfactory results. The moment he joined her at the base of the Welcome Center stairs, he'd been almost cordial.

"Access to the water is under the building, over this way." He reached a set of screen doors behind the stairs and held one open. "After you."

Liza hesitated, surprised by the sudden change in both tone and demeanor, but manners took over, and she stepped through the opening into a dirt-floor area lit by scattered beams of sunlight. To her left was what looked like a storage room. She could see empty shelves, stacks of boxes, and a collection of broom handles through the wooden slats that ran horizontal from floor to ceiling.

Kendall flipped a switch, and a bare bulb illuminated the area. "The tap water on the island is safe but doesn't taste great. The water that comes from this spigot is filtered, so most people prefer to use it, at least for drinking." Flipping off the light, he said, "Upstairs is the closest thing to a store we have. Souvenirs and stuff for the tourists. You want to go up?"

"Sure," she replied, shocked to be asked instead of ordered about. "I'd like to see it."

"Okay, come on."

Once again, he held the door for her to pass, and then followed her up the stairs. Amos waited at the top landing, tongue hanging out as usual.

"Does he always stay where he's supposed to?" Liza had assumed that a dog off leash would run away.

"Pretty much." A bell jingled as Kendall opened a solid glass door. "Watch your step."

"Thank you." She lifted the hem of her dress to make the small step up into the building and found herself staring into a squat, square tank of water. Perched atop a dark rock sat a small turtle, which dove headfirst into the murky depths when Liza took a step closer. "Sorry, little one. I didn't mean to startle you."

"Don't mind Gus. He's afraid of his own shell." A curvy brunette smiled from behind a tiny brown desk. "Welcome to Haven Island, darling. We're happy to have you. My name's Doreen, and if you need anything at all, don't hesitate to holler."

Liza nodded, charmed by the woman's ready smile and pretty green eyes.

"Hey there, sugar," Doreen purred as Kendall stepped in next. "Haven't seen you in a month of Sundays. Where you been hiding yourself?"

"I've been around. How are you doing, Dor?" Crossing the short distance to the desk, Kendall hiked his hip onto the wooden surface and smiled down at the woman, who was watching him like a hawk about to swoop in for her prey. "Tourists keeping you busy?"

"Not too bad, but I've always got time for you, handsome. You know that." Leaning forward, Doreen showed off the ample breasts God had granted her. Liza glanced down to her own nonexistent cleavage and tried not to feel inferior. "I just got a new case of wine last week. Why don't you come over and help me drink a bottle or two? We haven't done that in far too long."

Starting to feel like a third wheel, Liza wandered around the room, pretending to examine the various mugs, key chains, and T-shirts available for sale.

"I'll see if I can find the time."

She bet he would. Liza sized up the flirtatious woman through a postcard display stand. Early fifties was her best guess, but with the allure of a woman half her age. The coral-colored blouse gleamed against Doreen's tanned skin, and purple-tipped toes encased in sparkling silver sandals peeked out from beneath the desk.

Distracted by the couple across the room, Liza nearly toppled the display.

"You all right over there, honey?" Doreen asked.

Liza waved the set of duck-themed cards she'd managed to catch before they hit the floor. "I'm fine," she answered, voice much too chipper. "Just looking at the cards."

"They're ten dollars per pack, and all designed by one of our former resident artists, Preston Piccadilly. He was crazy as the day is long but a genius with a paintbrush."

Placing the cards back in the rack, Liza smiled and moved on to the bin of drink koozies.

"I'll be taking my lunch around eleven thirty," Doreen said to Kendall. "We could break into a bottle and enjoy the breeze in the gazebo."

The woman clearly wanted to enjoy more than the breeze.

"Afraid I can't." Kendall shifted off the desk. "I'm giving Liza a tour of the island."

"Liza?"

"Yeah," he said, pointing toward the koozies. "This is Liza Teller."

"Oh." Rising to her feet, Doreen stepped around the desk, revealing long, slender legs sheathed tightly in white linen capri pants. "I thought y'all just happened to come in at the same time. So you're together?"

"Only for the tour," Liza answered before Kendall could speak. Unhappy with the unexpected wave of jealousy flooding her brain, annoyance crept into her next statement. "After that, he's all yours." Jaw tight, she addressed her tour guide. "I'll wait outside while you finish in here."

Without waiting for a reply, she exited the building, hoping the fresh salt air would restore her wayward sanity. Removing the hat, she used it as a fan as she dropped into an Adirondack chair to the left of the entrance. Amos plopped his big head on her knee.

"I don't know what you see in him," she said to the dog. "He's moody, taciturn, and far too arrogant."

Amos's brows shifted up and down as if he understood every word. Liza took the gesture as a sign of agreement.

"You have my sympathies for having to live with him. I certainly couldn't do it." Remembering the scene in the kitchen, she added, "Granted, he is nice to look at, but personality matters much more than looks. I need to remember that from now on."

The dog nudged her hand, as if to say, "Forget about him. What about me?"

"I guess you aren't so bad." Liza rubbed his soft head, and the dog's expression softened. "Not that I want to live with you, either, but if I had to make a choice, you'd be it, buddy."

With a sigh of contentment, Amos leaned his weight against her leg and closed his eyes.

❦

Trying to follow the many moods of Liza Teller was going to drive Kendall to drink. He'd gone out of his way to play nice. He'd even opened the door for her. Twice. Yet thirty seconds later, she was pissy all over again.

"If I didn't know better," Doreen said, "I'd say that woman has taken a liking to you."

A statement that proved all women were out of their minds. "If that's a liking, I'd hate to see how she treats people she can't stand." Crossing to the exit, he spotted her sitting outside the door with Amos all but sleeping in her lap. At least she'd learned to tolerate one of them. Kendall glanced back at Doreen. "I don't suppose you'd be interested in taking over tour-guide duties?"

Doreen dropped back into her chair. "Oh no, honey. I want to see how this turns out."

Kendall didn't have the time or inclination to untangle that one. He stepped outside and loomed over the temperamental woman. "What was that about?"

She tipped her face up, flashing the smile of an angel. "What was what about?"

"In there," he said. "Where'd that come from?"

Tilting her head, she frowned. "I don't know what you mean. I was finished looking around and didn't want to rush you, so I came out here to wait."

Now she was messing with him. "You weren't pissed when you walked out here?"

"Why would I be angry?"

Kendall noted her change of phrasing. "You tell me."

Rising gracefully from the chair, she placed the floppy hat back on her head and met his gaze. "I truly don't know what you imagined, but I'm fine. Should we move on with the tour? Or did you want to visit a little longer with your lady friend?"

Something about how she said *lady friend* set him on edge. "I'm ready if you are."

"Are you sure? Doreen seemed very happy to see you. Don't cut your visit short on my account."

Kendall wondered if he'd hit his head somewhere between showing her where to find the water and entering the center. "We're only here on your account. If you're done looking around, then we'll go."

"Okay, then. You're in charge." Halfway down the stairs, she added, "We can probably wrap this up well before eleven thirty, so you can make that lunch date."

"What lunch date?"

"With Doreen."

"Why do you keep talking about Doreen?"

"You're right." She held up a hand in apology. "Your private life is none of my business. But if you're trying to keep your relationship a secret, you probably shouldn't flirt like that with an audience."

Flirt? *What the . . .*

"Hold up." He marched down the stairs to catch up to her. "First off, Doreen is married. And second, I grew up with her son. The woman is old enough to be my mother."

"You don't have to defend yourself to me."

"Who's defending?"

"Kendall, your yelling is scaring the birds."

Clamping his jaw shut, he ran a hand through his hair and stared hard at the woman pushing his buttons. "Get in the damn cart."

She stayed put. "I'm not sure that's a good idea. You're upset."

"I'm fine," he growled.

"You don't seem fine. Maybe we should do this tomorrow."

No way in hell was he going through this two days in a row. "Get. In."

Amos barked from the back seat of the cart, and Liza jumped into action. "I'm coming. I'm coming."

The words were aimed at his dog, but Kendall didn't care, as long as she got in the damn cart. And if she ticked him off again, he'd conveniently stop at one of Bruce's hangouts and let him take care of her.

Chapter 5

Despite her lack of enthusiasm for this tour, Liza found herself enjoying it. Quite possibly due to how much fun it was to drive Kendall up a wall. She'd planned to play innocent outside the Welcome Center, but watching the utter confusion on his face had been much more entertaining than expected.

The revelation that Doreen had a husband also lightened her mood, although Liza would never admit as much aloud.

As they traveled the bumpy island roads, Kendall pointed out various species of birds, the one cleared field available for helicopter landings, and the firehouse, which she could have recognized on her own. The gleaming red-and-white engine inside the open garage looked much too large to navigate the dirt paths she'd seen so far, but they must have a way to make it work. The truck *had* reached the firehouse, after all.

They passed a series of homes, all different in size and style. Each was set back in the trees as if it had sprouted from the earth alongside the oaks and pines. One stood four stories tall, while another was comprised of two three-level homes joined together. Like Ray's house, they were all built on stilts to keep them high off the ground.

Kendall had explained that many of the owners spent only weekends or summers on the island, leaving the homes available as rentals to tourists for the rest of the year. He stopped at the end of one driveway to point out the unique structure ahead.

"This is Francine's place. She's a mostly full-time resident, like me and Ray."

The home consisted of two structures, one larger than the other, connected by a short walkway. The odd shape set them apart from the rest of the homes.

"Are those round?"

"Octagons," Kendall corrected. "Symbolizes good luck in China. That's where her family emigrated from."

Liza pulled out her phone to take a picture. "Do you think she'll mind?" she asked.

"People take pictures all the time. She's used to it."

"I've never seen anything like it." After capturing the shot, she put the phone back in her sweater pocket. "Do you think she'd show me the inside?"

Kendall set the cart into motion. "She'll probably insist. Just be prepared. Francine likes to talk."

"So she's the opposite of you."

His eyes cut to hers, brow furrowed, until he spotted her smile. "I'm talking now, aren't I?"

"Yes, you are." Liza realized they'd been getting along for a good fifteen minutes. A record for their short-lived acquaintance. Maybe they could find common ground, after all. "Considering our rocky start, I appreciate your taking me around like this. Bringing Ray's world to life on the page will be easier after experiencing it myself. At least as much as I can during the month I'm here."

The body beside her tensed at the reminder of why she was on the island.

"You said last night that you don't want Ray to do this book. Why is that?"

His sigh blended with the wind. "Some things should stay in the past, that's all."

"I don't agree." Liza ignored her driver's eye roll. "History is important. Without people like Ray sharing their stories, so much would be lost. He was born in the 1920s. Can you imagine living through all of the progress that came after that?"

They reached a fork in the road, and Kendall once again brought the cart to a stop. "The point isn't what he's lived through but that he keeps on living." A cryptic reply that heightened Liza's curiosity. "Besides," he added, "nothing comes from looking backward. You can't change what's happened, so why dwell on it?"

"Well . . ." Liza struggled to find a rebuttal. "A book isn't about changing the past. It's about sharing your experiences. Maybe he wants his story to live on after he's gone. Would that be so bad?"

Kendall stared off down the road to their left. "I guess not." Changing the subject, he said, "The North Beach and the submarine tower are down there. There's also some longer trails and a good spot for fishing, but it goes away from the main village, so we're going to skip it today."

They made a hard right, sending Liza into Kendall's side. He didn't budge, and she struggled to keep any space between them. When they straightened out, she righted herself, but the sizzle from the body contact still radiated through her system.

Sparing a glance his way, she expected to see anger in his features. Instead, he looked defeated.

"You know this is Ray's choice, right?" she said, feeling the inexplicable need to reassure Kendall that this book wasn't a mistake. "If anything comes out that would put him in a negative light, I don't have to include it."

"Wouldn't that be unethical or something?"

Writing a memoir was different from writing a factual article. As far as Liza was concerned, she was entitled to creative license. She'd never include an outright falsehood, but that didn't mean details couldn't be omitted when necessary for the sake of the story.

"I'm writing a narrative about a man's life. We can include or omit anything we want."

Visibly relieved, Kendall relaxed beside her. "That's good to know."

🦋

Kendall appreciated Liza's willingness to compromise and wondered if she might go so far as to not complete the job at all. Of course, the book would be dangerous only if Ray revealed everything. They hadn't discussed in detail how honest the older man intended to be, but Kendall had gotten the impression the book would be a tell-all in every way. Which would be a damn fool thing to do.

Ray had been at the center of Kendall's life for as long as he could remember. He was the reason the James family had moved to Charleston, and why Kendall had seen his dad only on weekends throughout his childhood. Even Kendall's return to Haven Island after leaving the military had been for Ray Wallis.

When Kendall was a baby, his father, Christopher James, had worked as Ray's driver, but once they moved to the island, his duties changed. To what, the young Kendall never knew, but whatever he did kept him busy around the clock, robbing the boy of precious time with his dad. The only reason Kendall hadn't resented his father's boss was Ray's tendency to treat him like a grandson.

Whether hovering in the stands during his ball games or in a seat of honor around the table for birthdays and holidays, Ray was part of the family. It wasn't until the week before Kendall had left for basic training that Christopher had sat his son down and shared the details of his work. Basically, his father's main duty was to keep his employer alive. When the elder James died of a massive heart attack six months before his son returned from his third Middle East deployment, Kendall knew he'd inherited that duty.

If this book came to fruition, the sense of security that had taken hold in the last decade would be all but gone.

"Have we reached the end of the island?" Liza asked as he parked the cart at the edge of the path.

"Technically, no, but this is the end of the road here." After setting the emergency brake, he climbed from the vehicle. "This is Timicau Dock. It's the shortest walk to one of the best views on the island."

Liza stayed in her seat. "Is it safe?" she asked.

They'd passed the main alligator habitat, where he'd pointed out two baby gators hovering at the surface of the water, not far back.

"You're safe here," he said, nodding toward a narrow pathway between the trees. "Come on."

Kendall led the way, ducking the few low-hanging branches in his way and making sure Liza stayed clear of them. When they reached the start of the narrow dock, the trees cleared, leaving nothing but blue skies ahead.

"You can go on down first." He stepped aside for her to pass.

She gasped, eyes wide. "Oh my gosh, Kendall, this is beautiful."

"Yes, it is." This spot had been the main reason he'd put his house at the end of the lane. "Go on down and have a seat on the bench."

Before Liza could take a step, Amos trotted past them.

"He won't jump in, will he?"

For a woman who didn't like dogs, she showed a lot of interest in his. "Amos knows to stay on the dock."

She floated down the pier, glancing from side to side in wonder. At one point she nearly lost her balance, forcing Kendall to steady her on her feet. His hands circled her waist, and the contact threatened to fry his brain. Along with other parts of his anatomy.

"Thank you," Liza whispered in a breathy voice.

"No problem," he replied, tone gruff.

At least he wasn't the only one feeling sparks.

When they reached the bench at the end, she took a seat, and Kendall dropped down at the other end, leaving plenty of space between them. Amos took advantage of the opening and jumped up to lean against Liza's side.

"Traitor," Kendall muttered.

Rubbing beneath the dog's chin, she asked, "What kind of grass grows in water like this?"

"Spartina. It's typical in salt marshes along the coast." Since they'd reached a truce of sorts, he ventured back to the book subject. "I don't know much about publishing. You think this book of Ray's might make some money?"

"Why?" she asked. "Is he in financial trouble?"

Not the direction Kendall intended to go. "Not that I know of. I'm just curious. Could it make money for you?"

The concern she'd shown moments ago melted away. "Do you think I'm using Ray for my own benefit?"

There was no way she was doing this for free. "Writing is your job, isn't it? You aren't here out of the goodness of your heart."

Pink lips flattened as she turned his way. "Yes, I've received an advance to come here and write this book. But that doesn't mean I'm here to take advantage of Ray."

Kendall didn't see why she'd take offense at the question. "Ray says you hit one of those fancy lists. I guess that made you rich and famous."

Blue eyes narrowed as the truce went up in flames. "What do *you* do for a living?"

"A few things," he replied, unsure what his work had to do with her writing books.

"And how much do you make doing these mysterious things?"

Information Kendall had no intention of sharing. "Enough to get by."

Her eyes snapped with righteous indignation. "Not a question you want to answer, is it? Then why is it okay to ask me?"

He hadn't asked for a bank balance. And Kendall never intended this conversation to be about her damn income, anyway. "All I asked was if you might make some money off Ray's book. I was curious. That isn't a crime."

"No, it isn't. But what I do or do not make money off is none of your business. Ray reached out to me. I saw an opportunity, and I took it."

The air crackled as she cut her gaze back to the view. If Kendall was smart, he'd drop the subject, but if she was already ticked off, he might as well get to the point.

"Would you abandon the project if necessary?"

She threw her hands up in frustration. "We've been over this. I already told you that I'm willing to leave details out. If you're afraid the book will bring hordes of tourists to this island, I'll change the name. And if it's yourself you're worried about, I will gladly leave you out entirely."

Kendall rose off the bench. "This isn't about me."

"It isn't about me, either," she said, bolting to her feet. "I'm here for Ray, period. So unless you have something positive to contribute, keep your objections, and your assumptions, to yourself."

Amos whimpered as the pair embarked on a staring contest. When he nudged his owner's hand, Kendall backed down.

"Your tour is over. Let's go, Amos." Turning away from her, Kendall stalked down the pier with Amos running on ahead. Liza could follow him or stay on the bench to pout. He didn't give a damn either way.

❦

What the heck is his problem?

For two seconds, Liza held her ground as Kendall walked away. And then she remembered that being eaten by an alligator would be a horrific way to die. Self-preservation moved her down the pier fast enough to reach the sandy road right behind her cranky tour guide.

She couldn't help but be amazed at how he always started these arguments but acted as if she were the one who couldn't play well with others. How was Liza supposed to react when he made her sound like a literary gold digger? Was she getting paid for this job? Of course. Was she using an unwitting old man to fill her pockets?

Not in the least.

Now she was more curious than ever why Kendall so staunchly opposed this book. If Ray had committed a crime, Liza had to assume the statute of limitations had expired long ago. Unless the crime was murder, and she couldn't believe that was possible. Then again, she'd known her subject less than twenty-four hours. Not nearly enough time to know what he might or might not be capable of doing.

Liza tried not to let her imagination run wild. If she'd been brought here to tell the story of a man on the run, the book's potential could skyrocket. Though she knew better than to make assumptions, a jolt of excitement sent her heart racing. This would go far beyond hitting a list and land squarely on major motion-picture material.

"I'll have your cart ready by morning," Kendall said, startling Liza back to reality.

"Thank you," she replied, too distracted imagining the far-fetched possibilities to care about his surly tone. Of course, if she did learn something juicy, she'd have to do additional research. Releasing a book full of falsehoods would kill her career, which was already stalled.

They made the drive back in silence as she mentally edited the list of questions she'd eventually present to her subject. To Liza's surprise, they reached Ray's house in a matter of minutes, arriving from the opposite direction.

"Did we make a circle?" she asked, struggling to get her bearings. Without the typical landmarks, like stores and restaurants, Liza didn't know how she'd find her way around.

"Not exactly." Kendall didn't elaborate, and she wasn't about to beg for an explanation. He'd said her cart would come with a map. Surely she could follow a simple map.

Instead of dropping her at Ray's stairs where he'd found her that morning, he drove the cart back to her private entrance on the far side of the house, parking near the bottom step without a word. Liza glanced over to see Kendall staring straight ahead, chiseled jaw tight.

Men really were babies. With any luck, she would be free of this one after today.

Taking the high road, she said, "Thank you for the tour." As she climbed to her feet, Amos hopped out after her. "You stay with your owner, now."

The dog barked and trotted up several stairs. Liza did not want or need the four-legged company.

"Are you going to call him?" she asked Kendall.

The irritating man kept his eyes on the wall before him. "Let's go, Amos."

Again the dog barked before traveling up several more stairs.

"For heaven's sake." She marched up to shoo the dog back down. "Go on, now. You can't stay here."

The shooing did nothing. Instead, Amos ran all the way up to plant his little white butt against Liza's door.

"You cannot be serious." She leaned over the railing. "Get up here and fetch this animal."

Liza expected to see Kendall exit the cart and go after his dog. Instead, he yelled, "I'll get him when I come back."

Just like that, the golf cart disappeared beneath the house, only to reemerge from the back side and whip past the stairs, leaving Liza staring in shock.

"Wha . . . He can't think . . ." Unsure what to do next, she looked up to see the dog waiting patiently, tongue out and tail wagging. "I don't do dogs, you spoiled mutt."

The declaration had no effect on the canine.

"Unbelievable." Liza stomped to the top, determined *not* to let her unwelcome visitor come inside. But then she remembered the bit about coyotes and dogs and reluctantly changed her mind. "This is not going to become a habit."

When she'd left earlier, she'd nearly locked the door until realizing no one had given her a key. Leaving her belongings unprotected had seemed strange, but there wasn't much to be done if Liza wanted to get back inside. She'd assumed Ray's front door would be locked, so entering that way wasn't likely to be an option.

And heaven forbid she have to stay with Kendall longer than absolutely necessary.

The moment she opened the door, Amos scooted past to enter first. "Your manners aren't any better than your owner's."

Dropping her hat on the coffee table, Liza headed for the kitchen and retrieved a bottle of water from the fridge. When she turned back, Amos lingered by the couch, panting as if he'd run a marathon. "Does that tongue ever stay in your mouth?"

Dark-brown eyes blinked from an expressive face that said, "I need water, too."

"I assume there's a water bowl at your house. You should have gone there." But Liza wasn't immune to the pitiful puppy-dog eyes. Searching the cupboards, she found a large cereal bowl and filled it with water. "Here," she said, setting it on the floor at the edge of the kitchen. "Try not to make a mess."

As she'd assumed, the beast sent water sloshing over the sides as he slurped away. Liza grabbed a towel off the sink, covered the mess, and grabbed her laptop on the way to the couch. Maybe if she ignored Amos, he'd get the hint and not try this stunt again. She still couldn't believe Kendall had left him like that.

"Find someplace to nap, buddy. I have work to do." Seconds after she opened the computer, the dog joined her on the couch, curling against her thigh with his head on his paws. "Not exactly what I meant."

Minutes later, after Liza caught up on emails, she pulled up the file that included her plan of attack for writing the book and made slight adjustments based on the assumption there might be some criminal activity in Ray's past.

To her surprise, she didn't mind the soft snores coming from the fur ball beside her.

Chapter 6

Liza jerked awake to the sound of a ringing phone. Before she could figure out where she was, something wet swiped across her mouth.

"Ew," she muttered, wiping her face as she sat up. "That's disgusting."

The affable pooch smiled from his position between the couch and the table. At least he was on the floor.

The phone continued to ring until she located the glowing handset in a base on the counter. She hadn't noticed it before.

"Hello?" she said with the receiver to her ear.

"It's time for supper, my dear," Ray informed her. "Come on down before it gets cold."

"Oh. Um . . ." Running a hand through her tangled curls, she checked the clock above the fridge. Several hours had passed since she'd sat down to work. Work that had somehow turned into a nap. "I'll be down in a few minutes."

"We'll be ready." The line clicked dead as Liza wondered who *we* were. Maybe Kendall had returned to pick up his errant pet. She wasn't looking forward to sharing another meal with the man, but Ray had every right to invite whomever he wanted to lunch.

With luck, Kendall wouldn't stay long.

Rushing into the bathroom, Liza tidied her appearance and brushed her teeth. Her dress was wrinkled, but she didn't think her host would mind. Ready to get this project started, she snagged the laptop from the couch and exited the apartment on Ray's side of the house. Amos, of course, trotted out first and led the way.

The traitorous thought that she'd miss the company when Amos left was quickly replaced by the reminder that she was not a dog person. No matter how insistent this particular dog might be of the contrary.

While descending the stairs into Ray's living room, Liza spotted a diminutive Asian woman filling bowls at the kitchen counter. The moment Liza's nose picked up the scent, her mouth watered.

"That smells wonderful," she said as she reached the kitchen.

The shorter woman turned with a smile. "The best wonton soup this side of Shanghai." Wiping her hands on a towel, she added, "You must be the writer."

"Yes, ma'am." Liza extended a hand. "Liza Teller. Are you this Francine I've heard about?"

Dark eyes narrowed. "Depends on what you've heard."

Crap. Liza could not alienate another of Ray's friends. "Only that you took Ray to an appointment this morning, and that your house is the most unique one on the island."

A blush dappled the woman's alabaster cheeks. "Ah, then that's me. Who have you been talking to?"

"Kendall James. He's been my escort of sorts since I got here." Liza tried to keep the annoyance from her voice. "While you and Ray were out, he showed me around." Amos barked at the mention of his master, as if reminding the women that he was listening. "This guy refused to go home with his owner, so I've been watching him."

Or maybe Amos was watching her. Liza couldn't be sure at this point.

The tea towel hit the counter. "Amos left Kendall's side?"

Liza looked down at the smiling dog. "He did. Is that unusual?"

Francine crossed her arms. "Well, I'll be. I've never seen one without the other. You must have made a good first impression."

On the dog, maybe. "If I did, I have no idea how. I don't know much about dogs."

"Are you a cat person?"

"Afraid not. I didn't grow up with pets of any kind." She didn't count the suicidal goldfish she'd won at a carnival once. The poor thing had leaped out of the bowl the first night she'd had him, prompting a toilet-flushing funeral the next morning.

"None?" Francine asked. "Are you allergic?"

"Not that I know of." She hadn't sneezed once during her forced proximity with the pit bull.

"Huh. Strange."

Liza didn't think so, but before she could reply, Ray entered the kitchen.

"Hello, my dear. Did you have a good tour?"

"I did," she replied, seeing no need to discuss the differences of opinion between Kendall and her. "Did your trip to the city go well?"

Francine and Ray exchanged a look that said much more than the "It was fine" response he gave. "Should we eat?"

"I've got it all dished up." The cook carried two bowls to the table and returned to the kitchen for the third. "This recipe was passed down from my great-grandmother," she said to Liza. "You won't find any better."

Once they were all seated, with Amos lounging not far from Liza's chair, she took her first spoonful and had to agree with Francine. "This tastes even better than it smells. Wow."

Ray pointed to his bowl. "I've had close to this in Chinatown, but Franny edges them all out."

Happy to discuss familiar territory, Liza asked, "How long has it been since you were in New York?"

"Three decades this year."

Why would a New Yorker not return for three decades? That and a million more questions filled her brain, but she needed to pace herself. They hadn't even established how they were going to make this project happen.

"Can we talk about the book a bit?" she asked, uncertain if he would want to discuss the topic with Francine present.

Ray lowered his spoon and dabbed his chin with a napkin. "Of course. That's why you're here."

"Since I've never written a memoir before, I'm not sure how this works. As a plotter, I need a plan to follow, so I've come up with a basic outline and wanted to run it by you."

"A plotter?" Francine asked. "So you aren't one of those fly-by-the-seat-of-her-pants sort of writers?"

The thought made Liza shudder. "I know others who work that way, but I can't do it. My brain rebels at the thought."

"Creative minds are so different. I rarely know what will come out when I apply a brush to a blank canvas."

"You're a painter?"

"A painter?" Ray cut in. "She's an artistic genius. Have you not heard of Francine Adams?"

Of course she'd heard of her. "*You're* Francine Adams? I saw your exhibit at MOMA last year. It was amazing."

"Well," she said, "I'm glad someone went."

"Are you kidding? The room was packed." Liza couldn't believe she was having lunch with *the* Francine Adams. "Your work is breathtaking. I thought the pamphlets said you were a New York artist."

"Thank you for the compliments. As for the New York part, I have an apartment in Manhattan, but I live here on the island most of the year. As you probably noticed during your tour, Haven Island is a magical place full of inspiration. Hopefully, you'll find that true for yourself as well."

Recalling several works in the exhibit, Liza recognized some of the views she'd seen this morning. *Magical* was the perfect word for both what Ms. Adams created on canvas and the vistas available on the island.

"I hope so. I could use some inspiration these days."

"Aren't I your inspiration?" Ray said with a wink. "Or did you forget I was here?"

"No, of course you are. I didn't mean—"

He waved her words away. "I'm only teasing. I'm no fancy artist, but I think my story will interest you all the same."

"I'm sure it will. And don't hesitate to share your own ideas about how to tell it."

"You're the expert, my dear. I'm happy to follow your lead."

If only everyone on this island were so cooperative. "I appreciate that, but this is going to be a collaboration all the way." Lifting her spoon once more, Liza added, "If we touch on any subjects you'd prefer to keep private, say the word and it's off the record."

"Nothing will be off the record. It's time to tell the whole ugly truth."

A response that lent credence to her suspicions of a nefarious past.

"Duly noted," she said. "The whole truth it will be."

While the writer part of her brain grew excited at the potential this story could have, another part sent up a prayer that the last chapter would not be this sweet old man going to jail.

🦋

"I never thought I'd see the day when Kendall James was scared of a woman."

Larimore Baker never passed up the chance to bust his best friend's balls.

"I'm not afraid of Liza Teller," he defended. "I just don't feel like arguing with her again. I had enough of that this morning."

Hazel eyes twinkled from Larimore's dark face, his southern accent carrying a hint of his mother's Haitian heritage. "What do you have to argue about with a virtual stranger?"

Unwilling to reveal the secrets that had shaped most of his life, Kendall finished washing his hands and grabbed a towel off the counter next to the sink. "We don't see eye to eye on this book thing. All I'm asking is that you drive her cart over, go inside and get Amos, and then I'll drive us back here."

Larimore and Kendall lived close enough to walk between their homes, and today, Larimore had arrived on foot to deliver the bottle of whiskey he owed Kendall. They'd been wagering on football games since they were teens, though back then, the winnings had been nonalcoholic.

"I'll ride over there, no problem, but why should *I* have to retrieve *your* dog? Man up, son. Don't let the writer lady intimidate you."

"You're an ass." Kendall tossed the towel aside and marched toward the door. "I'll remember this the next time you want an excuse to get out of book club."

Larimore followed him onto the porch. "You'd avoid those meetings, too, if you had to hear Bitty Tillerson wax poetic about her bad-boy fantasy when we were supposed to be talking about *The Godfather*."

"You should turn on your best Capone impression and really get her going."

"She's old enough to be my grandmother."

Kendall hopped into his own cart as Larimore climbed into Liza's. "Grannies need love, too."

With a disgusted look, Larimore shook his head. "That's sick, man. Real sick."

Switching his cart into reverse, Kendall ignored the comment and backed out from under the house. By the time he reached the road, Larimore was behind him, and they made the quick trek to Ray's in a matter of minutes. Kendall waited for his friend on the stairs, and then they climbed to the top together.

"What's she like, anyway?"

Kendall didn't know how to answer. His first thought was that she was beautiful and smart, but then words like *stubborn, argumentative,* and *arousing* came to mind. He blocked the last one out immediately.

"You'll see for yourself."

At the top of the stairs, he gave three quick knocks on the door. Seconds later, Francine greeted them. "Hello, boys." Over her shoulder, she yelled, "Kendall and Larimore are here."

"Bring them in," Ray called.

"You heard him." Francine stepped back to let them enter. "There's wonton soup on the stove. Anyone want a bowl?"

"Heck yeah." Larimore marched off toward the kitchen.

Francine looked to Kendall. "How about you?"

"We aren't staying." From the doorway, he yelled, "Come on, Amos. Let's go."

Kendall followed Francine into the kitchen as Amos trotted around the corner. Liza followed him, offering a friendly smile. "I took him out a little while ago and made sure I stayed with him," she said.

Kendall nodded, surprised she didn't look less happy to see him. "Appreciate that. He won't be bothering you anymore."

She cocked her head as her eyes dropped to the dog. "I don't mind. He's a good dog."

"Yesterday you called him a beast and refused to get in the cart with him."

"I didn't know him then," Liza defended. "He's actually really sweet."

Kendall could have told her that, but he doubted she'd have listened. "Get your soup to go, Larimore."

"Who is Larimore?" she asked, spinning toward the kitchen.

"A buddy of mine drove your cart over. It's parked under your stairs. You need to leave it plugged in when you aren't using it."

A look of concern crossed her features. "Aren't you going to show me how to use it?"

She couldn't be serious. "You watched me drive a cart all day. They all work the same."

"Right. Of course." She backed away. "I'll figure it out."

"Figure what out?" Larimore asked, soup in hand.

"The cart," Kendall replied. "You ready?"

"You really need to chill out." Larimore turned to the newcomer and extended a hand in greeting. "Since Kendall doesn't have any manners, I'll introduce myself. Larimore Baker, Charleston native and resident real estate expert, at your service."

A faint blush crept up her cheeks as she accepted his hand. "Nice to meet you, Larimore. I'm Liza, and I'm well acquainted with your friend's lack of manners."

They acted as if he wasn't standing right there.

"My manners are fine. Can we go now?"

"What manners?" Larimore said.

"I was thinking the same thing," Liza muttered, a smile teasing her lips. "He wasn't very friendly when he picked me up yesterday." She leaned close to whisper. "And then he nearly threw me out of the cart on the way here."

Kendall rolled his eyes. He'd been expecting to pick up a man. Finding her perched on that bench had thrown him off.

"Doesn't surprise me." Larimore shook his head. "He gets flustered around pretty women. I know he looks like a tough guy, but inside he's nothing but a cream puff." Liza snorted as he continued. "Allow me to give you a proper greeting." Whipping a card from his back pocket, he said, "Welcome to our humble island, Ms. Teller. We're happy to have you. If you need anything while you're here—a friendlier guide, perhaps—I am at your disposal."

The idiot had always been a shameless flirt, but something about the way Liza's blush deepened at the offer set Kendall's teeth on edge.

"She doesn't need another tour guide; she has me."

Where the hell did that statement come from?

Two sets of eyes turned Kendall's way. While Liza's brows arched, Larimore grinned.

"I see." The Caribbean charmer turned his attention to the blinking woman as the card disappeared back into his pocket. "It was nice to meet you, Ms. Teller. I'm sure we'll see each other around."

Liza nodded, looking as if she'd lost track of the conversation.

Larimore exited the house, whispering as he did so. "This is going to be fun to watch."

Kendall ignored him. "If you have trouble with the cart, let me know, but it should be fine from now on."

"Um, okay. Thank you."

They stared at each other in silence until Amos whimpered, drawing Liza's attention. Bending down to scratch behind his ears, she said, "Thanks for keeping me company, big guy. You're a good nap buddy."

Images of napping with Liza, or rather keeping her from napping, filled Kendall's mind and heated his body. Beating a hasty retreat, he stepped outside and held the door open.

"Come on, Amos. We need to go."

The dog followed the order, and Kendall let the screen door slam behind him. When he reached the cart to find Larimore grinning from the front seat, he mumbled, "Shut up."

"I didn't say a word."

"You didn't have to."

"This is a good thing. You've been out of the game far too long."

Kendall dropped into his seat and turned the key. "Drop it."

Larimore whistled. "Come on, buddy. Admitting it is the first step."

Gripping the wheel, Kendall growled, "Drop it or walk."

"Consider it dropped," Larimore said, hands raised in surrender.

"Thank you."

As the cart rolled into motion, his friend added one last dig. "But for what it's worth, I think she likes you, too."

Amos barked his agreement, and Kendall ignored them both.

Chapter 7

As agreed upon the night before, Liza arrived promptly at eight the next morning for her first interview with Ray. Falling asleep had taken longer than she'd liked, as the odd encounter with Kendall had replayed through her mind. A casual observer might have interpreted his reaction to Mr. Baker's offer as one of jealousy. But Liza was not a casual observer.

Kendall had made his opinion of her quite clear. She was a vulture swooping into an old man's life to use him for her own gain. Despite the fact that Ray had solicited Liza, not the other way around, she couldn't help but wonder if there wasn't a hint of truth in the accusation.

If the book did well, she *would* benefit.

Until her run-ins with Kendall and his cryptic comments about protecting Ray, she'd seen this project as nothing more than a job that would hold her over until her first royalty payment arrived. Despite her first novel taking off, Liza had barely earned out her modest advance three months before. Due to the antiquated way that publishers paid their authors only twice a year, there would be no more income for several months.

That made the fifty-thousand-dollar advance Ray offered impossible to resist, but she hadn't expected anything beyond that initial payment. After all, what were the odds that the memoir of an obscure old man would draw readers?

But maybe Ray wasn't so obscure? A simple online search for his name resulted in a plethora of men named Ray Wallis but nothing on the man who'd hired her. In fact, he didn't exist online at all. Strange in this day and age, but then he *was* in his nineties. She doubted he participated in social media.

"Sorry I'm late," Ray said, shuffling into the kitchen in purple trousers and a bright-blue polo shirt. Another fedora covered his head. The day before, the hat had been a green plaid that clashed with his mustard-yellow sport jacket. Today, he wore one in solid pink.

He looked like a character from a kids' television program.

"I've only been here for a few minutes. No worries."

Crossing to the counter, he pulled a mug from a hook beneath the bottom shelf. "Did you get some coffee?"

Liza had made her own upstairs. "I'm good, thank you. Are you feeling better this morning?"

Ray had turned in early the night before with a headache.

"Much." He took the chair across from her. "So should we start at the beginning?"

"Seems like the proper place." Liza had set up her laptop before Ray arrived, but she reached into her bag for the small recorder she'd brought with her. "Do you mind?" she asked, holding it up. "This way I can have the conversations to listen to later in case I miss something now."

Ray hesitated, visibly pondering the question. After several uncomfortable seconds, he nodded. "I guess it doesn't matter at this point."

Not the answer she expected. "Are you sure?"

"It'll be for the best."

"That's what I thought. Just to be sure I don't miss anything." Ray smiled but held silent, so Liza pressed "Record" and began the interview. First were a series of basic questions about his origins. "When and where were you born?"

"March 4, 1925, in Yonkers, New York."

"And your parents were?"

"Myrtle and Abraham."

"Were they originally from New York?"

"No, Poland."

Liza glanced over her monitor. "My family is also from Poland. At least on my dad's side. Something else we have in common."

"How much do you know about your ancestors?" he asked before sipping his coffee.

She searched her memory banks for the few facts her grandmother had shared. "My great-grandparents came over from Warsaw after World War I. He was a professor and had married one of his students at the university. I'm not sure if that sort of thing was as scandalous back then as it would be now."

"It was."

She met light-blue eyes. "Do you think?"

"I know. What else?"

"They had my grandfather shortly after landing in America, another son a few years later, and eventually two daughters. All but the youngest daughter are gone now, but I wish I could have met them."

Ray's voice grew wistful. "I'm sure they all would have loved you."

Liza wasn't so sure. "From what I understand, they were a family of mathematicians and accountants. I don't know how proud they would be to have a writer in the family."

"Nonsense," he said with certainty. "You're family. They would have adored you."

"I like to think so." Realizing she was supposed to be *asking* questions, not answering them, Liza returned her fingers to the keyboard. "Back to you. Did you have siblings?"

"Three."

"Older or younger?"

"Younger."

"Are they still living?" Siblings would make wonderful resources to fill in details that Ray might not remember.

"Sadly, no."

Her shoulders fell. "That's a shame."

"Yes, it is. You mentioned your father's side of the family. What about your mother's?"

"Mom was a proud O'Dowd," Liza replied, always happy to talk about her mom. "Her parents lived in Boston, and we used to visit them every summer when I was a little girl. Those carefree weeks make up some of my favorite memories." Sadness tightened her chest, so she asked the next question. "The night I arrived, you said you're from the Bronx. Did you grow up there?"

"I did."

"What was that like?"

"Not so bad in the beginning, but then, as you know, the Depression made life more difficult."

During her time as a reporter, Liza had done a series of articles on life in New York City during the 1930s. There'd been days that she'd cried while typing. Imagining a young Ray living in those conditions made her heart hurt.

"Were you a good student?"

"I scraped by."

Liza caught the glint in his eye. "Is that a no?"

"Let's just say I was smart but unfocused and easily distracted."

"You sound like my father," she replied while typing the answer. "Grandma Teller said Dad was too smart for his own good. The lack of challenge meant regular visits to the principal's office—for both of them."

"Then yes, I'm very much like your father. Or rather, he's like me. I did come first, after all."

"Fair enough." She scrolled down to the next question. "College?"

Ray sighed. "Not until after the war. I enlisted at eighteen and fought the last two years until the end."

"Which branch?"

"Navy. I was in the Pacific."

She'd done less research on the '40s, so curiosity got the better of her. "What was that like?"

"Hot. Boring most days." He lifted the coffee mug. "There are enough movies and books about the not-boring days that I think we can leave the details out of this period."

Liza wanted to push but respected Ray's reluctance to talk about the experience. Many soldiers preferred not to discuss their time in battle, and she didn't blame them.

"Fair enough. Did you go to college right after coming home?"

"I did. Fordham University."

"Really? That's where my parents met."

Flashing a true smile for the first time since they'd sat down, he said, "I'm guessing they went a little later than I did."

She laughed. "Just a bit."

"Did you follow in their footsteps?"

"No. My mom taught at Rochester University, so I went there."

"That's too bad." Flattening his hands on the table, Ray said, "You know what we need?"

Surprised by the question, she said, "I don't know. What?"

"A brisk walk on the beach."

"But we're—"

Ray pushed her laptop closed. "We have plenty of time for questions later. Today, we put our toes in the sand."

A walk along the ocean did sound nice. "Okay, then." Liza switched off the recorder. "Let's go to the beach."

Kendall hated to have his routine thrown off, but a busted water pipe on their tiny island amounted to an emergency not unlike a raging fire. Thankfully, the renters at lot forty-seven were early risers and had discovered the problem right away.

He and his team managed to stop the leak within minutes of the call coming in, but the repairs had taken longer, which was why Kendall was taking his morning run more than two hours later than usual. The moment Amos took off barking down the sand, Kendall spotted Ray and Liza walking toward him and wished he'd skipped the daily exercise altogether.

"Good morning," Ray said, as Liza bent to accept the dog's excited greeting.

"What are you two doing out here?" he asked, shifting from side to side to keep moving.

The older man frowned. "Enjoying a morning walk on the beach. Do we need your permission to do that?"

Someone was cranky today. "No, sir."

"How long are you going to pout like this?"

Ray had a temper but rarely aimed it in Kendall's direction. "Who's pouting?"

"You've been a bear since I told you about this book, and your attitude has only gotten worse since Liza arrived. Enough is enough." The writer straightened from petting Amos and found herself being thrust forward by Ray. "Do you see this woman? She's important to me. And that means she's important to you. Understand?"

The discomfort in her face triggered Kendall's protective side. "If she's so important to you, stop shoving her around."

"It's okay—"

"It isn't okay." Kendall slammed his hands onto his hips. "Ray, you know my issues with this book, and they have nothing to do with Liza."

"You're just like your father. Stubborn to a fault." The older man turned to the woman beside him. "I'm sorry I pushed you like that. Did I hurt you?"

"No, of course not."

Ray nodded before continuing the lecture. "I'm doing this book, Kendall. It's time." The anger dropped from his voice. "It's past time. Trust me. I know what I'm doing."

Kendall couldn't let the fear go. "What if you're wrong?"

Instead of answering, Ray began to crumble to the ground. Liza reached out, catching him under one arm while Kendall caught him under the other.

"Ray," he snapped. "Talk to me, Ray."

The frail man raised his head enough to say, "Take me home."

Without hesitation, Kendall scooped him into his arms. "Where's the cart?"

"We didn't bring one," Liza replied.

"What?" They were a good half mile from Ray's house. He never should have walked that far.

As if reading Kendall's mind, she said, "I offered to drive, but he said the walk would do him good."

"And *I'm* the stubborn one." Cursing under his breath, Kendall charged down the beach, with Liza and Amos following.

"Should I go for help?" she asked. "Or call that emergency number in my phone?"

"That number calls me. Grab my phone," he ordered. "It's in my hip pocket."

"But I have mine."

"The number we need isn't in yours."

"Oh. Right." She reached for the phone. "Who am I calling?"

"Aadi Patel. Tell him to meet us at Ray's house."

"I don't need him," Ray mumbled.

Kendall ignored his cargo. "After Aadi, call Francine. I want to know what the doctor said yesterday."

The words were garbled, but Kendall made out enough to know Ray considered that none of his business.

"Too damn bad, old man. I'm making it my business."

❦

Flashes of Grandma Teller lying pale and lifeless in a hospital bed filled Liza's mind. Due to not growing up around her grandparents, she had little experience watching loved ones drift into old age. Her mother hadn't lived to see fifty, and though Liza's maternal grandparents were still alive, she didn't see them often enough to know anything about their health.

When this job was finished, she would correct that.

"How is he?" Liza asked as Kendall joined her in the kitchen. The Aadi person had met them in Ray's driveway and snapped out orders for the frail man to be carried straight to his room.

A strong hand swept through thick dark hair, leaving the damp strands standing on end. "I don't know. He was mumbling, so he's conscious."

Unsure what to do as he paced, she asked, "Do you want coffee?"

Kendall shook his head, eyes down as he prowled the room. The black T-shirt that appeared to have lost its sleeves long ago, clung to his sweaty torso, accentuating the muscles beneath.

"Was he okay last night?" he asked.

Liza hadn't spent enough time with Ray to recognize unusual behavior. The two nights since she'd arrived, he'd excused himself by eight—once claiming fatigue and the next night a headache.

"He seems to run out of energy early, but I assume that's normal for a person his age."

"It isn't. Not for Ray."

Her concern deepened. "He said he had a cold before I got here. Could that be it?"

Brown eyes met hers. "That was a lie. And now I wish I'd called him on it."

"Why would he lie?" If she was going to tell Ray's story, she needed to be able to trust him. It wasn't good that they'd started out with a falsehood. Even a minor one.

"Men don't admit weakness easily."

A disloyal, if accurate, statement about his gender. "Really? I'd never have guessed."

Kendall shot her a look that said he didn't appreciate her sarcasm. "When did Francine say she'd be here?"

"She didn't. I had to leave a message."

The pacing intensified. "There's something he isn't telling me."

Wanting to reassure him, she offered a positive thought. "If he saw the doctor yesterday, it can't be anything too serious, or surely he wouldn't have been sent home."

Liza was nothing if not an eternal optimist.

"You don't know what you're talking about."

"Hey." She hadn't done anything wrong here. "I'm worried about him, too, but it doesn't do any good to think the worst."

"Worrying about losing your paycheck isn't the same."

She tensed at the cut of his words. "That's mean and nasty and the last time you're going to insult me. I may not know him well, but Ray Wallis is a nice man who opened his home to me, and I care about what happens to him. Not because he can make me money, but because I'm not a *horrible person*."

They stared at each other in silence as Liza waited for an apology. Instead, another voice broke the silence.

"Let me know where Ray is, and you two can go back to ripping each other apart."

"Aadi is with him in his room," Kendall said, eyes shifting to peer out the window over the sink. "We're finished here."

Chest tight, Liza grabbed her sweater from the chair where she'd tossed it. "Yes, we are. I'll be in my room," she said to Francine. "Please let me know when there's news."

"I will."

By the time she made it halfway up the stairs, she realized Amos was trotting up beside her. Happy to have any kind of friend in that moment, she murmured, "Good boy."

Chapter 8

"What is wrong with you?" Francine asked, leveling him with a stern glare.

"Ray crumbled in front of me," Kendall said, defending himself, and knowing he'd crossed a line but too stubborn to admit it. "That makes me cranky."

"What happened on that beach wasn't Liza's fault, and according to Ray, you've been mean to her since she got here. I've never known you to hate anyone on sight, so what's going on?"

Francine didn't know the details of Ray's past, and Kendall wasn't in a position to enlighten her. But she was right. None of what bothered Kendall was Liza's fault. Which meant there was no excuse for his behavior the last few days.

"Ever since Ray decided to do this stupid book, things have changed. Doesn't he seem different to you?"

Francine's expression softened. "Honey, the man can't live forever. Let him do this his way."

Kendall didn't like that response. "Do *what* his way? Is he dying?"

"We're all dying, but Ray is closer to the end than the rest of us." She shared a sad smile. "He's ninety-three years old, Kendall, and he isn't the type to sit back and watch the clock run out. You know that as well as anyone. For his sake, help him see this through."

Like a wave hitting the sand, reality washed over him, stealing the breath from Kendall's chest. He dropped into a chair at the table. "I can't imagine him not being here."

"Neither can I." Francine sighed as she settled in the chair opposite. "Sharing his story with Liza is what he wants to do. Be a part of that, Kendall. You'll regret it if you keep fighting him."

There were other ways to spend your waning years than doing the one thing that could cut those years short. "Why is this book so important to him?"

Francine shrugged. "I don't know, but does it matter? Maybe he just wants to live on. Without a family of his own, this is the only way he'll be remembered."

Kendall stared at the glass dish in the center of the table. "He has family," he stated. "And he'll be remembered."

Her small hand rested on his. "You and I know that, but we aren't blood, darling. That means something to a man."

Did it mean something to Kendall? At thirty-four, he'd never come close to having a wife and children. His father's dedication to Ray, and insistence on living on Haven Island, had created a deep resentment in his mom, infecting their family with a bitterness that permeated every memory Kendall had. That resentment was a major reason he never sought a wife of his own.

Because, like his father, Kendall's place was on the island, and he would never ask or expect a woman to give up everything she knew to live there with him. Even if he found a woman willing to make the sacrifice, the resentment would come eventually, and history would repeat itself.

After his father had died, Jacqueline James had moved back to New York City. Kendall missed her, but he respected her choice. She'd spent more than twenty years away from her home and family, and she deserved to be happy.

As Kendall contemplated both his past and future, Aadi walked into the kitchen.

"How is he?" Francine asked, rising from her chair.

"He's okay," the retired doctor replied. "Skipped a couple of pills this morning, so I've suggested one of those day-of-the-week dispensers, but otherwise, a little rest and he should be much better."

"Can I see him?" Kendall asked.

"He dozed off as I was leaving. I'd let him sleep for an hour or so."

"Thank you, Aadi." Francine walked him to the door. "We're lucky you were here." The two whispered something Kendall couldn't make out before the door clicked shut and Francine turned his way. "Liza needs to know that Ray is all right, and I believe you owe her an apology." She pointed toward the stairs. "Up you go."

"I'm going," Kendall said, following the order. There was a chance Liza wouldn't open her door, at least not for him, but he was man enough to give it a shot.

If nothing else, maybe she'd give him his dog back.

❦

"I *really* don't know what you see in him," Liza said, giving Amos his third slice of ham. "He's completely irrational, rude, *and* insulting. Did you hear how mean he was to me? As if I'd be worried about a defenseless old man *only* because he paid me money." She rolled a piece of lunch meat for herself. "He makes me sound like a monster for accepting a job offer. An offer that came to me, I might add. I did not go looking for it."

Truth be told, she hadn't done her due diligence before taking on this project. Desperation had been her motivation, and that had led to assumptions she never should have made. Interview the man, put the details on paper, and hopefully get a real book idea out of the process. Liza hadn't considered the human factor at all.

This was the downfall of living like a hermit. She'd forgotten how complicated people could be. Ironic, since human complications had pushed her into hermit mode in the first place. In her previous life as a reporter, the real reason she'd preferred historical articles was that the individuals involved were typically deceased, which made them less likely to take offense at a perceived slight or her omitting them altogether.

Three years ago, she'd written what she'd felt had been a well-researched article on the advancement of women in the workforce over the last fifty years. The result had been hurtful personal attacks from every direction. Women who'd chosen not to work had been offended, as if she'd implied that they hadn't been part of the fight for women's rights. Working women had insisted they still faced more obstacles than she'd included in the article, which meant she'd belittled their continuing battle.

To avoid offending anyone, from then on, Liza had limited her work to topics that included little to no human involvement. As expected, she'd run out of viable subjects in a matter of months. Hence, a life of fiction writing. Thankfully, she'd fallen in love with the form almost immediately.

"I'm really not a bad person, Amos. I wish I could convince people of that."

How to do so was the question. Regardless of approaching all endeavors with the best of intentions, she was misunderstood time and again. Unless the whole world had somehow conspired to give her a hard time, Liza had to be the problem. A depressing thought.

"Maybe getting a dog is the answer." She stared into Amos's smiling face. "You seem to like me no matter what I say. Which probably explains your tolerance for your owner."

A knock sounded at the door, and Liza hopped up, expecting news from Francine. Instead, she found Kendall. Still annoyed, she didn't invite him in.

"How is Ray?"

"Aadi says he missed a medication this morning, but he should be okay with a little rest."

She let out a breath. "Thank goodness. Thank you for letting me know." When he didn't immediately walk away, she crossed her arms. "Is there something else?"

An apology, perhaps? A little groveling for being a jerk.

Kendall rubbed the back of his neck. "I owe you an apology."

Will wonders never cease.

"I'm listening," she said, not ready to trust him yet.

He rubbed his whisker-covered jaw. "Can I come in?"

Willing to hear him out, she stepped back. "Okay."

Amos's entire body wagged with excitement at the new arrival. "Hey, boy," Kendall said, bending to offer a scratch behind the ear.

After closing the door, she crossed to the counter and leaned against it, waiting for his apology with well-earned skepticism.

"I've been an ass the last couple days."

Good start. "I hadn't noticed."

Dark brows furrowed. "You don't have to be sarcastic."

"Sarcasm is the best I can do right now. How would you feel if I suggested you only care about people who can fatten your bank account?"

The grimace softened. "That was uncalled for. Sorry."

Not the most effusive apology, but considering the source, she accepted. "Thank you. But how do I know you won't turn back into a jerk in an hour?"

Kendall relaxed, leaning his bulk against the wall beside the door. "Francine set me straight on some things. I've decided to get on board with the book idea."

Suspicion tightened her shoulders. "That's an abrupt change." Did this mean there really wasn't some nefarious crime in Ray's past? "What happened to protecting Ray from what a book would reveal?"

Holding her gaze, he considered his answer. "You said that details could be left out. Is that still true?"

"Yes, but what if Ray doesn't want to leave them out?"

"Who gets final say?"

Excellent question. Liza hadn't insisted that the contract give her full control, mostly because the story she'd be writing didn't belong to her. She'd also never assumed that Ray Wallis might possess some deep dark secret.

"This is Ray's story, so it's up to him."

Kendall closed the space between them, stopping much too close for Liza's comfort. His heat surrounded her as his deep baritone dropped to a whisper. "Just promise me you'll consider the consequences once you know everything."

Eyes dropping to his full lips, she leaned in. "What kind of consequences?"

He shook his head. "Just promise."

The journalist in her wanted to argue that anything on the record was fair game, but the genuine concern in his brown eyes had her rethinking that position. "I promise."

Relief softened his features, and the half grin did funny things to her brain. "Thank you," he said. "I appreciate that."

They lingered, a mere foot apart, and Liza noticed the hint of a dimple lurking beneath the dark stubble on his left cheek. "You should smile more," she said. "You don't look like such a grumpy bear when you smile."

"A bear?" he repeated, brows arched.

"Yeah. I mean," she added, leaning back, "you're still the size of a bear, but flashing that dimple makes you less scary."

Leaning a hand on the counter, he invaded her space. "You've been afraid of me?"

She didn't say that. "I'm not afraid of anything. I'm just suggesting that a smile now and then can go a long way."

"With you?" he asked.

Liza wasn't sure what he meant. "What with me?"

"Smiling goes a long way with you?"

When had she lost control of this conversation? "Are you *flirting* with me?"

Still grinning, he leaned his hip on the counter edge. "You're the one saying nice things about my smile."

Bristling, she put several more feet between them. "I was making an observation. Not offering compliments."

"Okay, then." Kendall rose to his full height. "Ray should be up for talking in a couple of hours. While I'm here, do you want me to show you how the cart works?"

Liza did want to know how to use the thing. A quick walk around it the night before hadn't yielded much information. She'd figured out how to turn it on—since turning a key seemed obvious enough—but not how to put it in gear. If only she'd paid better attention the day of the tour.

"I would, yes."

"Okay, then." He strolled to the door that led outside. "Come on, Amos."

The dog hopped into action, and once beast and owner reached the small porch, Kendall turned her way. "Are you coming?"

"I need some shoes, and then I'll be down."

"All right."

The door closed, and Liza remained frozen near the counter. Cranky Kendall had been exhausting and annoying, but friendly Kendall might be much more of a threat. That dimple was a weapon all by itself, and sadly, she couldn't claim immunity to its charms.

Having Kendall on her side would make life easier over the next few weeks, Liza reminded herself. This was a good thing. But from the way her body hummed in response to one flash of a grin, it was maybe *too* much of a good thing.

❦

"Make sure both cords are plugged in or the battery won't charge." Kendall pointed to the outlet under the driver's side of the seat. "When you want to use the cart, unplug everything and wrap the cords around the battery in the back. Any questions?"

Liza had paid close attention throughout his instructions, always keeping a safe distance between them. He hadn't intended to tease her upstairs, but she'd started it. There was no need to act as if he might attack her at any minute.

"What do I do if it rains?" she asked.

"You get wet." Seemed like that should be an obvious one. "Anything else?"

"Is this thing fast enough to outrun an alligator?"

"Maybe," he joked.

As expected, blue eyes went wide. "What do you mean, maybe? I need this job, but that doesn't mean I'm willing to die for it."

Interesting statement. "You *need* this job?"

A hand slid through her blonde curls as the wind whipped the long dress around her legs. "Yes, I do," she confessed. "Contrary to what you and everyone else seems to think, writing one bestseller does not make you rich. Or even moderately comfortable."

So that's why she'd bristled when he brought up money.

"Wouldn't it help to write another one?"

"Now why didn't I think of that?"

Okay. So he'd asked a stupid question. "Too bad you can't make a living off sarcasm."

She smiled. "If that were possible, I'd have a Manhattan penthouse."

Kendall didn't think so. "You don't strike me as the penthouse type."

Liza looked off in the distance as if considering his analysis. "You might be right," she said, turning back his way. "I'd rather have a historic brownstone on a quiet neighborhood street. Though I might go stir-crazy in something that big all by myself."

"You could take home an alligator, so you wouldn't be alone."

Laughter danced on the breeze. "First flirting and now a real joke. Where's the cranky caveman who tried to hurl me from a moving cart?"

"That wasn't my fault. *You* let go of the bar."

"*You* should have slowed down for the turn."

"If you hadn't worn such a short dress, I wouldn't have been distracted." Liza blushed as Kendall cursed his stupid mouth. "If we're good, I'll head home to shower." He was still in his running clothes and likely stank.

"We're good," she said. "Thanks for the compliment."

"The what?"

One corner of her pink lips curled up. "The dress comment. That *was* a compliment, wasn't it?"

Kendall's body tightened at the gleam in her blue eyes. "Yeah, it was. Let me know if you have any problems with the cart."

Liza saluted. "Will do."

Backing into the sunlight, he snapped for Amos to follow him. "See you around, then."

"See you around."

Trudging through the sand to his cart at the front of the house, Kendall's thoughts wandered into dangerous territory. He wouldn't have minded sparring with Liza a little longer. She challenged him one minute, shoulders back and spine straight, only to soften at the slightest compliment. The combination of strong and soft pulled at Kendall more than a mere physical attraction.

To his surprise, he was starting to genuinely like the challenging writer with the pretty smile and quick wit, which is where the dangerous part came in. Like she'd said, Liza was a brownstone-in-the-city kind of girl. Not a woman who would be happy living on Haven Island. If her working relationship with Ray wasn't reason enough, this fact alone would keep Liza Teller squarely in the off-limits category.

Chapter 9

The week went by in a blur.

They'd worked out a solid routine for both Ray's pill-taking and his interviews with Liza. He'd insisted she enjoy the island for at least a few hours each day, and every evening he invited another neighbor to dinner. After the first few days, Liza noticed a pattern. One she wouldn't have expected when she'd stepped off the ferry more than a week before.

Everyone on Haven Island was rich.

Ray's home had been evidence enough that he was well-off, plus the generous advance, of course. And then there had been Francine, the world-renowned artist. The day of Ray's episode, she'd met Aadi, the retired doctor who happened to be a groundbreaking heart surgeon from Atlanta. He'd bought a vacation home on the island nearly a decade ago and had been living as a retiree on Haven for just under three years.

After that, she'd met the Boston lawyer—a man named Jacob Michaels who'd come on a little stronger than Liza liked—then the Wall Street trader, the professional baseball player who'd grown up in the Lowcountry, and a woman who owned a city block in downtown Charleston.

All of them appeared to have more money than the Pope and considered Haven an island paradise where they could leave the world behind once they stepped off the ferry. Or off their own yachts, in at least two cases.

Liza felt obscenely out of place with each new acquaintance. Not that anyone had acted as if she were beneath them. On the contrary. If she hadn't grown suspicious and typed a few names into a search engine, she never would have guessed these island residents weren't ordinary people.

In truth, nothing on Haven was ordinary.

Not the quiet beaches, the graceful birds, or the startlingly large alligator she'd spotted sunning himself on a floating dock during one of her afternoon jaunts around the island. She'd stopped long enough to get a picture—because Vanessa was never going to believe the story without visual proof—from the safety of her running golf cart.

When she'd conveyed the story to Ray, he'd replied with a simple, "That's just Bruce. He's harmless."

The natives may have fooled themselves into believing that this creature was harmless, but Liza wasn't falling for it.

As far as she knew, Kendall was the only resident who wasn't wealthy, which made Liza wish he'd come around more often so she wouldn't feel so much like a peasant among nobility. When they'd parted the day of Ray's fainting spell, she'd felt lighter than she had in a long time. Liza couldn't remember the last time a man had flirted with her, let alone one as attractive as Kendall James.

Not that she would partake in anything more than a friendly flirtation with a man whose moods swung from sweet to surly with the regularity of a metronome, but still. There was no reason she couldn't enjoy a man's company while she was here.

Unfortunately, she hadn't seen Kendall since that day. Not even on her frequent outings driving herself around the island and taking dozens of photos. Liza told herself she missed Amos, and that was why she looked for the pair down every narrow lane.

"We have a new adventure for tonight," Ray said as Liza watched a heron glide along the glowing horizon line. They'd been working two hours in the morning and two hours after lunch before her subject followed doctor's orders and retired for a daily nap. Late afternoon, they'd have supper, and then talk on Ray's deck until just after sunset.

"Shouldn't you be going to bed?" she asked. Ray rarely stayed up more than a half hour after the sun went down.

He rose from the rocker with surprising agility. "Tonight, we're going to the movies."

"The movies?"

"Yes. Bradley's Bargain Cinema kicks off the season with a viewing of *Casablanca*." He rubbed his hands together. "One of my favorites."

Liza loved the film as well, but since when did the island have a cinema? "I thought there were only homes here."

"You don't need a big old movie house to have a cinema."

Actually, you did. "I don't understand."

Ray patted her hand. "No worries. I'll take care of everything. Just grab a sweater while I get the wine."

She'd nursed enough glasses of wine since arriving to feel bad about wasting it. "If you don't mind, I'd prefer water."

"Of course I don't mind, but are you sure?"

Feeling like a heel, she confessed the truth. "I don't actually like wine."

"Liza! Why didn't you tell me that before?"

Excellent question. "I didn't want to offend you."

He shook his head. "Child, you couldn't offend me if you tried. Now I feel bad for making you drink it all this time."

"You didn't make me do anything." Liza waited for him to pass by her chair before rising to her feet. "I'll grab my sweater from upstairs."

"Hurry back. We want to get good seats."

Where in the world were these people hiding a movie theater? Liza dashed up the stairs to grab her heavier sweater off the bed. Despite the island warming up nicely during the day, the evenings turned cool with the wind coming off the water. Hustling back down, she reached Ray as he packed a bottle of wine, as well as a large bottle of water, into a tall lunch-bag-looking sack.

"Let me carry that," she said, taking the bright-green bag and zipping it closed. "Am I driving?"

Before Ray could answer, she heard a horn outside.

"No need," he said. "Our ride is here."

Disappointment dimmed her enthusiasm. She *really* enjoyed driving the golf cart. So much so that she wished owning one in the city wouldn't be completely impractical.

"I grabbed a little cash to pay for the movie," she said, opening the door for Ray. "Is ten dollars enough?"

"You don't need money for this."

When they said bargain, they meant it.

Ray all but tap-danced out the door, and Liza enjoyed watching his display of happy excitement. After discussing the details about Ray's childhood, they'd moved on to his high school days. The more stories Ray had shared, the more animated he'd become. It was as if moving on from the Depression years had lightened his mood.

"Do you remember the first time you saw *Casablanca*?" she asked, staying close as he progressed down the stairs.

"A man doesn't forget the night he meets the girl of his dreams."

The comment didn't match what she already knew. "I thought you met your wife after the war."

"Ah," he said, "that was the love of my life, but Ingrid was the girl of my dreams."

Liza couldn't help but laugh. "I see. I'm sure if she'd ever met you, she'd have felt the same way."

"Of course she would. I was a catch." He punctuated the response with a wink, and Liza couldn't help but laugh again.

"What's so funny?" Kendall asked.

85

Startled, she looked up to see her former tour guide dressed in dark jeans and a gray button-down shirt. His hair had been brushed but was still wet, she assumed from a shower, and the always-present stubble along his chiseled jawline had been shaved away.

"Wow," Liza said. "You clean up well."

"Thanks?" Brown eyes trailed down her frame before returning to her face. "You're wearing jeans."

Liza hadn't planned on leaving the house and now feared the faded denim might not be appropriate. "Should I change?"

"No, ma'am." He grinned, flashing the deadly dimple. "The jeans work."

Butterflies burst to life in Liza's stomach, and she could feel the blush crawling up her cheeks. "Thank you."

By the time they finished the exchange, Ray had climbed into the back seat of the cart to settle in next to Amos.

"I can sit back there," she said.

He waved the words away. "I'm good. You young people can sit up front."

Twenty minutes ago, Liza thought she'd be spending the evening working through her notes and seeing where she needed to fill in the blanks tomorrow. Now she felt as if she'd been fixed up on a date.

With no alternative, she scooted onto the seat beside Kendall and learned he didn't just look good—he smelled good, too. Earthy with a hint of lavender. She told herself not to lean in, and instead, held tight to the chrome bar and tried not to think about the creatures lurking in the darkness.

"Here we go," Kendall said, flipping a switch beside the ignition key. The sun hadn't completely set but was well on its way.

"You have headlights," she said with amazement. "Does my cart have those?"

"All the carts have them. Did I forgot to point them out?"

He must have, because she would have remembered that. On the days she explored the island, Liza had been careful to return well before the sun went down for fear she would get caught out in the dark and be unable to find her way back.

"Yes, you did."

"Sorry about that. Now you know."

True. And if she'd been the least bit curious and tried the same button she most likely had on her cart, she'd have found out for herself. Kendall put the cart in motion, and they made a left out of Ray's drive. As expected, the night air was cool, and Liza hugged the sweater tightly across her chest.

"Where are we going?" she asked, raising her voice over the wind and the motor.

"To the movies," Kendall answered, as if they were headed to the local theater to load up on popcorn and check out the latest blockbuster.

"I got that part, but where?"

"Didn't you tell her?" Kendall asked, looking at Ray in the wide rearview mirror.

"Of course I did. Bradley's Bargain Cinema."

"But there's no cinema on this island," she argued.

"Sure there is." Kendall glanced her way, but Liza couldn't make out his expression. "Bradley's Bargain Cinema."

Fine. If they didn't want to tell her, she'd hold her tongue and see where they ended up.

🦋

Bradley's Bargain Cinema was really Doreen's house. Or rather, Doreen's gazebo. The huge screened-in structure measured twenty-by-twenty feet, and Doreen's husband, Bradley, had added a screen and projector four years prior. The balding man with the big personality loved movies— having made his fortune with a chain of convenience stores only *after* spending fifteen years as a bit player in Hollywood—and when the social committee had sent out requests for new ideas, Bradley had established his mini–movie theater.

Ever since, the residents, along with the occasional tourist, had been enjoying movie nights throughout the warmer months. Kendall didn't always attend, but when Ray asked if he'd once again play chauffeur, he'd agreed. If he were honest, he'd admit that tonight was really about seeing Liza. Despite his not seeing her for a week, she'd been on his mind nearly every day.

Either he'd encounter someone who would mention her, or his mind would simply float back to their past encounters. The soft curls twirling around her face when he'd found her at the pier. The desire in her eyes when she'd found him shirtless in the kitchen. The sparks flying, whether from anger or mutual attraction, every time they were together.

He could keep telling himself that the best course of action was to avoid the resident writer *or* stop being an idiot and admit that all he really wanted was to spend more time with her.

Watching Ray introduce her around, Kendall admired how easily she blended with the locals. This wasn't an easy group to step into, but she smiled and nodded, and everyone seemed to like her. Still, he caught the tension in her face when she thought no one was looking.

"When are you going to make a move?" asked Larimore as he handed Kendall a beer. "She won't be here forever, you know."

"All the more reason to leave her alone." Kendall considered his parents' relationship a cautionary tale. One he had no plans to repeat.

"Come on, man. I haven't seen you look at a woman that way since before you joined up." Larimore pressed his back to the post that Kendall leaned against. "Take a chance. What do you have to lose?"

More than he was willing to admit. If Liza had been a passing tourist, in for a weekend and gone days later, Kendall might have acted on the attraction. But she wasn't just a tourist, and he'd already spent enough time with her to know she wasn't a woman he could tangle with in the sheets and forget about come Monday.

"We're nothing alike."

"In your case, that's a good thing."

Kendall ignored the quip. "She doesn't like me."

Liza glanced his way for the third time in the last five minutes.

"I beg to differ," Larimore drawled. "Go on. People will start taking their seats soon, and I've noticed Jacob watching her a little too closely. Are you going to let that fancy lawyer move in on your territory?"

Scanning the room, Kendall spotted Jacob making his way toward Liza, and the look in his eyes said he intended to make the move Kendall had ruled against. "Hell no," he muttered, setting his feet into motion. In three strides, he reached Liza's side and slid an arm around her waist just as the lawyer arrived. "How's it going, Boston?"

The northerner hated the nickname, which was why Kendall continued to use it.

"It's going well, James," Jacob replied through a clenched jaw. "Nice to see you again, Liza."

Instead of pulling away, Liza leaned into Kendall's body. Not the reaction he expected. "You, too, Jacob. Did you have a good trip to Seattle?"

"Yes, I did. How are things going with the book?"

"Moving right along."

An awkward silence settled around them before Bradley yelled, "Lights out in two minutes. Everyone take your seats!"

"Guess we'd better grab our chairs. See you later, Boston."

Michaels fumed as Kendall navigated Liza toward their seats with a gentle hand on the small of her back. He'd expected her to pull away the moment they'd put some distance between the lawyer and themselves, but instead, she leaned closer and whispered, "Thank you." Liza settled into the chair beside Ray and Kendall took the one beside her. "I'm sure he's a nice man," she whispered, "but something about Jacob Michaels makes me uncomfortable."

Smart woman.

"He didn't seem to like you calling him Boston," she observed.

Kendall caught the lawyer's eye as he leaned close to reply, "He doesn't."

Lips pinched as if he'd eaten something rotten, Jacob Michaels sauntered out of Kendall's line of sight, presumably to bother someone else. Too bad all the women in attendance knew his tactics and how to avoid them.

"Have you seen this movie before?" Liza asked. She crossed her legs and bounced her Ked-covered foot close to his knee.

"Yeah, but only because they kick off the season with the same film every year." Black-and-white love stories were not his thing. "I was hoping they'd change things up this time. Toss in a *Die Hard*, or maybe a Bond flick."

Liza surveyed the crowd gathering around them. "Wouldn't the language in *Die Hard* be a bit racy for this bunch?"

Little did she know. "You'd be surprised how some of these folks talk. Don't let the leather loafers and fancy jewelry fool you. Most of these people started out as low on the food chain as anyone."

"Regardless of where they started," she said, voice low, "they all have more money than I'll ever see in a lifetime."

That didn't have to be true. If she could write one successful book, she could write others. They had to add up at some point.

"Who knows? You might write the next wizard-kid or psycho-killer book that takes off. You'll be a household name in thirty-seven countries and have to buy a house here just to get some privacy."

She burst out laughing. "And Ray says *I* have a vivid imagination."

Kendall liked her laugh and the easy way she relaxed beside him. Until tonight, they'd either been fighting or flirting, dancing around an unexpected physical attraction. But even when he'd been a brute or pouted like a toddler about something she had no control over, Liza had forgiven him.

So though he had no intention of making a move, as Larimore had put it, Kendall didn't see any reason they couldn't progress from truce to friends.

"It could happen."

"Not likely, but I appreciate the enthusiasm." Leaning forward, she rubbed a hand down her shin. "So what's your story? You're the only normal person here, which I appreciate, but how did you end up living amid all this wealth?"

By *normal* he assumed she meant broke. Or at least less well-off. Kendall considered being offended. Then he considered setting her straight. Instead, he replied, "A fluke, I guess. Like you, I inherited some property."

Liza sat back. "I just realized, when we did the tour, you didn't show me where *you* live."

"I did, actually." Or he would have if they hadn't gotten into that fight. "Remember the last place we visited?"

"The one with the gorgeous view? Of course I do."

That she didn't say "The place where we argued?" seemed like a good sign. "My house is next to that pier, at the end of the lane."

"Oh. Wow." She faced forward before looking his way again. "That must be amazing."

Testing the waters, he said, "I could show you sometime." Friends visited each other, right?

Pink lips turned up in a smile. "I'd like that."

Eyes locked, they sat in silence for several seconds before the lights dimmed.

"Time for the show!" Bradley yelled from the back, as he always did.

Kendall draped his arm over the back of Liza's chair, catching a curl between his fingers as the screen lit up. Sitting in the darkened gazebo with her scent surrounding him, he decided that maybe black-and-white love stories weren't so bad, after all.

Chapter 10

The audience applauded the moment Bogart gave his famous final line, and the lights came up seconds later. Somehow, the giant gazebo looked even larger than it had when she'd first walked in. Like a beautiful gift box with a pointed top, the structure sat nestled beneath the trees with an amazing view of the sunset.

The colors lining the horizon when they'd arrived had been breathtaking. As pinks and purples faded into fiery gold, Liza could only stare in wonder, knowing for certain that she'd never seen a more tranquil place than Haven Island.

Before the film started, Ray had introduced her to the few residents she hadn't met yet, and as Liza had walked around the enclosure, doing her best not to let her discomfort show on her face, an awareness sizzled along the back of her neck. With each sizzle, she'd caught Kendall watching her. On the third instance, she'd acknowledged him with a wave, hoping he'd join them and insist on pulling her away for some reason or another. Just so she could relax her cheeks and not feel like the newcomer in the hot seat.

Liza enjoyed meeting Ray's friends, but as an introvert, the energy of so many people, all buzzing and catching up, threatened to overwhelm her senses. By the time the movie ended, she'd been leaning so far into Kendall that she'd nearly fallen asleep on his shoulder. A position she corrected the moment the lights came up.

"That movie never gets old," Ray mumbled before turning to Liza. "I need to chat with Francine. Have Kendall show you the beach. You haven't seen it at night yet."

Refusing to leave her apartment after dark did have its drawbacks.

"I can walk out on my own," she said, all too aware of how comfortable she was getting around the big man on her left. Being friendly was one thing. A moonlit stroll on the beach was another.

As usual, Kendall ignored her comment. "I'll take you."

Amos, who'd been sleeping beneath his owner's chair, leaped into action the moment Kendall rose to his feet. Like a pro, the dog weaved his way through the crowd and reached the screen door closest to the water before they did.

Kendall pushed the door open and said, "After you."

"Look at that," she teased. "You do have manners."

"I only whip them out on special occasions."

Amos strolled off ahead of them, and the farther they walked from the gazebo, the quieter the night grew. Liza stopped at the edge of the sand. "Is it okay to take off my shoes?"

"Sure." He extended a hand.

She accepted his assistance and bent to remove her sneakers. Her palm still tingled even after she let go. "Thank you." Dropping the shoes to the ground, Liza hugged her sweater tightly and turned her face to the stars. "I've never seen a sky like this. I can't imagine getting to see it all the time."

He followed her lead and looked up. "We're lucky that way." They walked out onto the sand. "You put on a good act while Ray was taking you around, but I get the impression you don't like crowds."

Liza hadn't pegged him as the observant kind. "I'm an introvert, so it isn't necessarily the number of people, but the energy they give off. It wears me out."

"Then how do you handle living in New York City? Isn't that energy overload?"

Her mother had said the same thing when Liza begged to attend a college in the city. Mary O'Dowd had been certain her daughter would hate the noise and large crowds. Liza had wanted the chance to try it, but she had been overruled.

"My little corner of the Bronx isn't so bad." Rarely leaving her apartment also helped. "I couldn't make regular visits to Times Square, but a walk to the store is fine. Do you remember the city at all?"

"Not much, but Mom moved back up there about nine years ago, so I've made the trip a few times." He paused to pick up a stick and hurl it over Amos's head. The dog ran full out to catch it in midflight.

"A few times doesn't seem like much over nine years." The moon shone brightly enough for Liza to spot a large shell in her path. She bent to retrieve it, turning it over in her hand and remembering the time she and Mom had collected seashells on a Nantucket beach. What she'd give to walk beside her again. "Don't you miss her?"

The sigh let her know she'd broached a delicate subject. "We talk once a week. She understands why I stay here."

"And why is that?" Liza would live anywhere if it meant having her mom back.

Kendall knocked her off-balance with a bump of his shoulder. "You writing a book or something?"

Her laughter scared a bird into flight. "I could be. Is your life story as interesting as Ray's?"

"Not even close."

They stopped at the water's edge, facing the most powerful force on earth, yet Liza felt nothing but peace. Waves sent cold droplets dancing over her toes as she dug them into the sand. Closing her eyes, she took a deep breath, filling her lungs with exhaust-free air for possibly the first time in her life.

"Good, isn't it?" Kendall murmured.

"The best." Eyes still closed, she sighed. "If we found a way to bottle this, we could buy and sell half the people in that gazebo."

Kendall brushed a curl from her cheek. "This doesn't belong in a bottle."

She turned to find him standing close, watching her. "No, it doesn't."

He cupped her cheek with one strong hand, his thumb gliding over her skin. "Moonlight looks good on you."

Pressing a hand over his, she turned her face away as he leaned in. "We should get back," Liza whispered. "Ray is probably getting tired."

Cool air replaced the heat of his touch. "You're right. We should go."

Liza didn't have a clue what she wanted. Her body said *stay*, while her brain screamed *run*. She'd never had a meaningless fling and knew herself well enough to realize how much she was growing to like this complicated man. Too much to fall into his bed and walk away unscathed.

In the name of self-preservation, Liza turned to walk back up the beach, the moon illuminating the way. Awareness raised goose bumps on her skin as Kendall walked behind her. She bent to retrieve her shoes, not sure whether he was angry or disappointed, but hoped this wouldn't replace their budding friendship with awkward discomfort.

Kendall was the only islander she could completely relax with. The rest of her visit would be lonely if that went away.

Amos caught up to them just as Liza reached the screen door of the gazebo. Tongue hanging out and tail swinging side to side, he trotted on through to a water bowl in the corner. She searched the gathering for Ray but didn't see him.

Approaching the first familiar face she saw, Liza said, "Excuse me, Doreen, do you know where Ray is?"

"Home," the woman replied. "Francine gave him a ride. He said to tell you and Kendall not to hurry." Green eyes shifted to Kendall behind her. "Did you enjoy the beach?"

"The beach is lovely," Liza replied. "You have a beautiful place here. Thank you for making room for one more."

"You're always welcome, darling," she said with sincerity. "Anytime."

Leaning around Liza, Kendall dropped a quick kiss on Doreen's cheek. "Another great kickoff. Tell Bradley to call me about that creaking step."

Doreen patted his cheek. "I'll do that. You kids have a nice night."

"He's just taking me home," Liza explained, preferring to cut off any rumors about her and Kendall before they could start. She now realized Ray had sent them outside on purpose. Time to have a little chat about any matchmaking ideas he might have.

Shoes still in her hand, Liza navigated the remaining crowd to reach the exit to the parking area. She was already sitting in the cart when the driver and his dog joined her.

Without a word, man and beast took their respective places, and within seconds, the cart cut through the trees toward the main road. A vibration hummed through Liza's body that had nothing to do with the vehicle beneath her. Every nerve ending seemed to fire at once, sending her heart racing and making the hair on her arms stand on end.

As if sensing her distress, Amos rested his big head on her shoulder. Instead of pushing him away, she leaned in, pressing her ear to his. Like magic, as the dog's even breathing soothed her, her body settled.

The journey didn't take long, and before she knew it, Kendall had delivered Liza to her private stairway. With the motor running, he waited in silence for her to step out. Instead, she turned to face him.

"Thank you."

"No problem."

Liza knew he misunderstood. "I mean for earlier."

Kendall leaned his elbows on the wheel. "What about earlier?"

"Thank you for not pushing me on the beach."

His jaw clenched. "I'm not that type of guy."

She was botching this terribly. "I don't think you are. I mean, I know you aren't. I just . . ."

He shook his head, turning to meet her gaze. "I shouldn't have—"

"I like you, Kendall," she cut in. "I really do."

Though she hadn't planned the words, Liza knew them to be true. He'd been rude, taciturn, and even insulting at times. But he'd also been considerate, generous, and as devoted to Amos as he was to Ray. On more than one occasion, he'd even been protective of her.

"I'm hoping we can be friends. Just friends."

Her escort flashed a heart-melting grin. "You like me, huh?"

Of course that's the part he'd focus on. "I knew I'd regret admitting that," she replied, unable to suppress her own smile. "I'm afraid I'm too practical for this sort of thing."

"What sort of thing?"

The jerk was going to make her say it. "A casual, short-term fling."

Kendall sighed before meeting her gaze. "I don't want to have a fling with you, either."

Humiliation washed over her. "I'm sorry. I misunderstood."

"No," he said, mumbling a curse. "I mean, I like you, too, Liza. But I get it. I live here. You live there. Being friends is smarter. Less fun, but smarter."

The flood of embarrassment ebbed, but her cheeks remained warm from his admission. An admission that confirmed her earlier suspicion. If Kendall wouldn't leave this island for his own mother, nothing would make him go.

The lesson of her parents' marriage danced through Liza's mind. If only her father had loved them enough to sacrifice. To compromise. To put them first.

Liza climbed from the cart, still carrying her shoes. "Friends, then."

Kendall nodded. "Friends."

Leaning in, she kissed the top of Amos's head. "Good night, buddy. Thanks for being my date."

Kendall laughed, and some of the tension slipped away.

"Thank you, too, for being our chauffeur," she added, and from the bottom step, she said, "Good night, Kendall."

"Good night, Liza."

Clutching the Keds to her chest, she watched the cart fade in the moonlight, leaving her both conflicted and relieved. They'd established two things this evening—a mutual interest and an unwillingness to put either of their hearts on the line. She hadn't expected him to agree with her about why they shouldn't get involved, but his doing so had sparked an interesting question: What if she were the one to sacrifice? Staring up at the moon, she considered her options, remembering the feel of Kendall's hand against her cheek. "Could I live here?" she murmured, but an answer didn't come.

She still didn't have the relationship she'd hoped for with her father. Despite his absence from her life, Liza yearned for the father-daughter connection she'd missed out on. That yearning is what had driven her back to the city after Mom's death.

If she moved away now, what little progress they'd made would be gone.

Shaking her head, Liza came to her senses. She'd known Kendall James for one week. An unexpected bout of lust was no reason to consider altering her life entirely.

"Get a grip, Teller. He's practically a stranger."

But Kendall didn't feel like a stranger. A thought Liza ignored as she climbed the stairs to her apartment.

🦋

Kendall was still thinking about Liza as he plugged in his cart for the night. His instincts had been correct, but at least his loss of control on the beach hadn't destroyed the progress they'd made. That was something.

Taking the steps two at a time, he bounded up to his front porch until a deep baritone cracked the night silence, nearly sending him hurling back to the bottom.

"You're in a good mood," Larimore said, chuckling when Kendall grabbed his chest.

"What the hell is wrong with you?"

"Nothing." A cell-phone screen lit up as he said, "The movie ended a while ago. I thought you'd be home by now."

"I didn't realize I had a curfew." Opening the door for Amos, Kendall added, "Is there a reason you're lurking on my porch on a Friday night?"

Larimore rose from the rocker. "I've got a buyer for the North Point house, but they want to move quick. I need an answer by morning."

North Point had been his father's home, and Kendall's as well, when he'd stayed on the island during his childhood. After the service, he couldn't bear living in the house without his dad, so he'd built his own and rented out the other. Only recently had he considered selling.

"I haven't even agreed to put it on the market."

"Come on, Kendall. It's time. Prices are at an all-time high, and you haven't walked into the house in years."

Nothing he didn't already know. "Who's the buyer?"

"An older couple from Florida. The man likes to tinker in his work-shop and invented a gadget that made him rich. They visited as tourists a few years ago and fell in love with the island. Now they're looking to retire here."

Maybe Larimore was right. It was time.

Stepping inside, he said, "Come on, then. Show me the offer."

Kendall turned on the kitchen light as his friend took a seat at the table. By the time he took his own seat, the documents were spread out for his perusal. Spotting the seven-figure amount, he whistled. "That's a pretty penny."

"I told you prices were good."

Tapping the table, Kendall considered the implications. "So you'd make a pretty penny here, too."

Larimore rested an ankle on his knee and tilted back on two legs. "Commissions are a wonderful thing, but don't consider me in your decision."

Shoving emotion out of the equation, Kendall reviewed the papers. "What's the rent pulling in a year?"

"One-fifth of that offer."

Damn. Kendall didn't necessarily need the money, but he wasn't a fool, either. Pushing the document Larimore's way, he said, "Let 'em have it."

A dark brow arched high. "You sure?"

He was. "I want to pull a few things before the sale, but they can have the rest."

Two chair legs hit the floor. "You want to sell it furnished?"

"Why not? I don't have room for everything here." There was little of sentimental value in the house, as his father had never been one for material things. Before he could turn the place into a rental, Kendall had needed to buy furniture for most of the rooms.

Larimore leaned his elbows on the table. "You might be able to spread stuff around your other rentals."

True. A few places could probably use the fresh pieces.

"Okay, then. I'll figure out what I can keep, and the rest goes with the house." Kendall shoved back from the table. "Mom might want something, too."

The two men walked to the door. "She never liked this place much, did she?"

The house hadn't been the problem. Mom had never liked the island the house was on. "No, but we did spend some time there together as a family." Not much, but Kendall had a few good memories to look back on. "I'll see if she wants anything."

"Sounds good." Larimore extended a hand. "Congratulations, hoss. You're a wealthier man than you were a few minutes ago. Or will be soon."

The comment brought to mind Liza's assumption from earlier. Would she be pissed that he hadn't confessed the truth? Technically, she hadn't *asked* if he had money—just assumed that he didn't. Kendall had answered her question honestly.

Besides, the size of his bank account didn't change who he was. She'd said she liked him and that they should be friends. That wasn't likely to change because he had a few million in the bank.

Chapter 11

"You did *not* skinny-dip at Orchard Beach!"

Not that Liza should be surprised by anything at this point. Each of Ray's stories was more scandalous than the one before. The teenage Ray had been more than a little adventurous. From smoking and drinking to streaking and now skinny-dipping. Such a wild child.

"Oh yes, we did. Malcolm was the ringleader on that one, but we didn't take much convincing. Three of us were leaving for basic training the next day. Benny had a few more months before his eighteenth birthday, so he had to wait. Jed had swiped a couple of bottles from his dad's wine stash, and we were feeling pretty good by the time we stripped down to our skivvies." Ray's eyes dropped to the table. "We all figured that night might be the last time we'd ever see each other. At least, I did."

Liza's heart broke for the innocent boys being thrust into a situation they were in no way ready to handle. "You still volunteered? Even knowing you might not make it home?"

Narrow shoulders shrugged. "There wasn't much choice. I mean, we weren't all drafted like those boys during Vietnam, but signing up was a given. Unless you were like Jimmy with his bad ear. They wouldn't take him. Getting on with a life that was likely to be interrupted anyway didn't make much sense, so we volunteered and did our duty."

"Did anyone else make it back?" she asked, hoping the answer was all of them.

"Malcolm did, but he'd stepped on a land mine in France and lost a leg. I saw him a couple of months after I got home." Ray shook his head. "He wasn't the same."

Something told her Ray wasn't, either.

"The others?"

"Benny's plane went down somewhere in the North Atlantic. Jed died in a firefight in Germany." Leaning back, he crossed his arms. "At least they died for something, though. Seems like ever since then, we've been getting into wars we have no business being a part of. Too many boys and girls lost, and for what?"

Liza had asked the same question in a piece she'd written five years ago. "Based on the research I've done," she said, "it almost always boils down to money. They never admit as much, of course, but greed is often an underlying factor. Greed and some wayward ideal about making the world look just like us."

They'd gone from a fun story about skinny-dipping to the bleak realities of war. Talk about a depressing transition. Though she supposed they couldn't linger in the happy years of youth forever.

"How much would you like to share about your time in the service?" she asked. Part of her wanted to know everything, while the rest of her preferred to spare him the trial of reliving the whole ordeal.

Ray flattened his hands on the table. "I'm going to leave that up to you." Reaching for the chair to his right, he retrieved a tattered gray journal and set it on the table. "You're welcome to take this home with you, but I'd like to hold on to it until you leave. I haven't read the entries in nearly seven decades, but I knew they might come in handy someday." With a halfhearted smile, he added, "Looks like I was right."

Liza ran a fingertip over the faded cover. "I'll take good care of this," she whispered, honored to be entrusted with such a treasure. "And if I include anything you'd rather I didn't, say the word and I'll edit those parts out."

"Like I said before. I trust you." Rising from his seat, he retrieved the journal. "Now it's time for this old man to rest his bones." Bracing himself on the back of the chair, he grew somber. "Don't judge me too harshly when you read the journal. The world was a different place back then, and I was just a boy."

She'd never wanted to hug anyone quite so much as she did Ray in that moment. "My job is to tell the story of your life, not to pass judgment on it. Besides, we've all done things we aren't proud of."

"Yes," he agreed. "But some of us more than others."

Looking more exhausted than he had in days, he disappeared into his bedroom and shut the door. The poor man. Liza could only imagine what he'd endured. What all of them had. So many young lives cut short before they'd even gotten a chance to grow up. She stopped the recorder and dropped it into her bag as her thoughts drifted to Benny. She imagined a boy of seventeen watching his friends drive off to war, knowing he'd be joining them in a few months.

Seventeen-year-olds were supposed to dream of prom and college, not land mines and flying bullets.

"War sucks," she said aloud.

"I'll second that." Kendall closed the front door behind him as Amos sprinted toward Liza.

She hadn't seen Kendall since movie night and had started to wonder if he'd changed his mind about them being friends until he'd called the night before asking if she still wanted to see his house. Bracing for impact, Liza caught the dog in her lap, barely avoiding a giant open-mouthed kiss.

"You're way too big for this, buddy." She scratched behind his ears before shoving him off.

"How far have you guys gotten in this book thing?" Kendall asked, seemingly trying to sound casual, but Liza picked up the interest in his voice. So much for him giving up the fight.

"Today we talked about Ray's time in the war. Or more accurately, the time before the war. He told me about his high school friends who never came home." Indignation rose on their behalf. "They were only boys, Kendall, barely out of high school."

He filled the chair Ray had vacated. "So was I."

"You were in the service?"

"Six years," he replied matter-of-factly. "Three tours—two in Afghanistan and another in Iraq." After three taps on the table, he said, "Have you discussed how much of his life he wants included in this book?"

They were back to this again. "I believe he's leaving that up to me."

"So you can still leave things out?"

Every time Kendall started down this path, Liza grew more curious about Ray's past. What could possibly be so explosive that this man wanted to keep it out of print? The only reason she didn't push back now was their hard-won truce, and because she truly believed Kendall's efforts came from a place of concern for Ray.

"Once I get home and can review all of the information he ends up sharing, I'll decide what goes in and what can be left out. After all, nine-plus decades is a lot for one book."

He nodded his head in agreement. "Sounds like a plan. You still want to come see the house?"

After the depressing topic of young men going off to war, Liza needed a mental break. "I do. Just let me run my things upstairs, and I'll be ready."

Kendall rose at the same time she did. "I'll pick you up on your side, then." With a tap of his leg, he said, "Let's go, Amos."

The pair exited the house, and Liza sprinted up the stairs, not wanting to keep them waiting. Or at least she told herself that's why she was hurrying. Not because she was excited to spend some time with Kendall. She didn't brush her hair or pinch her cheeks for any particular reason, either.

"He's shown me around before," she informed her reflection. "This is nothing new."

But it was. Liza knew to the tips of her toes that this was definitely something new.

♥

"This is your house?" Liza said, staring up at the blue two-story home with wraparound porches surrounding both floors.

Kendall unhooked the empty box he'd strapped to the back of the cart, ignoring the hitch in his gut at what he was about to do. "Not for much longer."

"Wait. What?" She caught up to him halfway up the stairs. "You said you live over by the pier at the other end of the island."

Someone was learning her way around. Kendall pushed the front door open. "That *is* where I live. This is the house my dad built when we first moved here." Blocking the doorway with his foot, he said, "Stay out here, Amos."

The dog whined as Liza followed Kendall inside. "You're selling your family home?"

He'd never considered the place a *family* home. Though Dad had built the house in hopes of making his wife happy, Mom had never taken to the remoteness of the island. In fact, other than a few summers when Kendall was small, she'd never lived in the house with them, choosing instead to remain in Charleston.

This meant his parents had lived separate lives, yet his mother had never asked for a divorce or refused Kendall the opportunity to spend time with his father. From a young age, he often felt as if he were choosing one over the other, which created a deep sense of guilt no matter where he stayed. In middle school, some of his classmates had divorced parents whom they saw during scheduled visitations. The kids were told where they were going and when.

106

That led Kendall to wish his parents *would* divorce, so that he'd no longer have to choose. But they never did, and at some point in his teens, he'd decided that if he was going to feel bad no matter what, he might as well feel bad in the place he fit the most.

On Haven with his father. In this home.

"It's just a house," he replied, carrying the box to the counter and opening the blinds. "I haven't lived here in more than a decade. It's been a rental property since Dad died of a heart attack nine years ago."

"Mom's been gone eight years as of this past March. Pneumonia complicated by asthma." Liza's voice cracked with emotion, and she cleared her throat. Peering out the window over the sink, she said, "This view is amazing. Are you sure you want to part with this place?"

Kendall understood the quick change of topic. He didn't like to talk about his dad's death, either. As for her question, he'd spent the last few days convincing himself that he was fine with the sale. And he almost was.

"The deal is in motion now." Scanning for items to keep, he spotted a piece of light-green sea glass on a table beside the back door. He'd stumbled across the rare treasure the first time his father had taken him fishing on the north side of the island.

"It's a lovely place," she said, strolling through the living room. "This is an odd piece, though." Liza picked up a small jar of sand. "Why keep sand in a jar when you can walk outside and collect as much as you want?"

Surprised his father had kept the souvenir, Kendall took the jar from her grasp. "I sent this back from Baghdad, so Dad could see the difference between desert and beach sand. I didn't realize he'd kept it."

"My mom kept a macaroni-covered cross I made in third grade." She dusted off the top of the jar. "Parents keep everything from their kids."

He put the jar back on the windowsill. "Like you said, there's plenty of sand outside."

Before he could move on, Liza put the jar back in his hand. "I think your dad would want you to keep it." She retrieved the box from the kitchen. "I'll carry this while you collect what you want to keep."

Kendall reached for the box. "You don't have to follow me around."

Liza held tight. "There's nothing wrong with needing a little moral support, Kendall. You gather. I'll carry."

Recognizing the stubborn set of her jaw, he gave up arguing and strolled farther into the room. He hadn't really thought about why he'd brought her with him. Kendall had intended to clean out the house before picking her up, but then he'd pulled into the drive and failed to make himself go inside. Since Larimore wasn't around to be dragged along, he'd driven to Ray's house instead.

"I took three friends with me to clean out Mom's house," Liza said, close on his heels. "I couldn't bear to do it alone. We had more than twenty years of memories to go through."

"How old were you when she died?"

"Twenty-three. I graduated college the year before, and though I'd considered moving away from Rochester, something told me to stay."

Opening the drawer on a side table, Kendall found a pocket tool kit behind some ink pens and a notepad. Images of Christmas afternoons flooded back, when he'd watch his dad assemble whatever new toy or gadget Santa had delivered.

"Was she sick for a long time?" he asked, setting the tools in the box.

"Not at all. From diagnosis to the end was less than a week." He spun to see her face, but Liza kept her eyes averted.

Death was a ruthless son of a bitch. Christopher James had survived his sudden heart attack, but only long enough for his son to make it home to say goodbye.

Catching the sound of a sniffle, he said, "I'm sorry. I shouldn't have brought you here."

She swiped a hand beneath her nose. "It's fine. Really." After clearing her throat, she said, "Tell me your favorite memory from this house. I need a story that'll make me smile."

Kendall filed through all the memories he could recall, but only one stood out.

"The summer after I turned nine, Dad made burgers on the grill while Mom peeled potatoes in the kitchen. That morning, I was told there would be a big announcement during supper, so I kept running back and forth, begging them to spill the secret." Pulling an astronomy book off the shelf, he said, "I wasn't the most patient nine-year-old."

"None of us were."

He set the book inside the box. "I was sure that they'd say we were all going to live together on the island."

"I don't understand. You *didn't* live on the island?"

Kendall had often been confused by the strange arrangement himself. "There was no school on the island—and still isn't—so my mom and I stayed in a rental in Charleston. Even after more kids moved to the island and a bus started picking them up at the ferry landing over on Isle of Palms, Mom refused to move full-time."

"That must have been tough, being away from your dad so much." Liza's voice grew softer, and Kendall remembered what she'd shared that first night on the island about not growing up with her dad.

"I came over a lot, and Dad traveled over to Charleston for my games and school activities." Surveying the rest of the bookshelf, he asked, "How often did you get to see your father?"

Liza's fingers tapped out a rhythm on the box. "Not much. A couple of weeks each summer. Thanksgiving a few times."

"No Christmases?" That was the one occasion his mother always made sure the family was together.

Except the time she'd taken Kendall with her to New York City to spend the holiday with her family. She'd insisted that his father come, and the conversation had devolved into a yelling match. That was the only Christmas Kendall had ever spent away from his father. At least until he joined the service.

Shaking her head, Liza flashed a crooked smile. "The Tellers are Jewish. I spent a couple of Chanukahs in the city, but as a Catholic-school student, I didn't understand the language or the rituals. I missed my mom so much that on the second visit, I ended up crying for hours on Christmas Eve until my dad finally agreed to drive me home." Her fingers trailed through the fringe hanging from an old lampshade. "He was furious and never took me for another Chanukah again."

Liza's father didn't sound like Dad-of-the-Year material.

"Back to your story," she said, breath hitching as she tried to look unaffected. "What was the big secret?"

Kendall slipped back to the memory. "After dinner, Mom whipped out a pair of pink socks and announced she was having a baby."

"Oh, a baby," Liza said, making that weird face women did when minihumans were discussed. "I didn't know you had a sister."

Too late, he realized this story was not going to make her smile. "I don't. Mom miscarried at six months."

One slender finger poked him in the chest. "You suck at happy stories."

"Just because there wasn't a happy ending doesn't mean it isn't a good memory. That was the happiest day we had in this house. I'd never seen Dad so proud or excited about anything, and Mom danced around singing that old 'Buffalo Gals' tune."

Liza broke into song. "Buffalo Gals won't you come out tonight, and dance by the light of the moon."

Kendall chuckled as she drew out the last word. "Not bad. You know that one?"

"Anyone who's seen *It's a Wonderful Life* knows that song."

"Oh yeah." Kendall moved on to the dining room. "I think they showed that on movie night once."

She tugged on his arm. "Are you saying you don't watch *It's a Wonderful Life* every Christmas? What kind of a monster are you?"

"Not the movie-watching kind." He took the box and set it on the table. "Your turn. What's your favorite memory with your parents?" Despite the failed holiday experiment, Kendall assumed there must have been good times at some point.

Liza plucked a dusty apple from the bowl in the center of the table. "I didn't know they still made rubber fruit."

"Pretty sure that's as old as the house."

Without answering his question, she dropped the fruit back in the bowl and strolled to the far window.

"Don't be dodging the question, Teller. You started this."

Breathing in, she pressed a hand to the warm glass. "I don't have any good memories of the three of us together. They split up when I was two, and on the rare occasions we were ever all in the same room together . . . well, let's just say, things were tense."

An experience Kendall knew all too well. "At least yours divorced. Sometimes I wish mine had taken that step."

"That's a horrible thing to say," she said, spinning around. "Your parents obviously loved each other."

"Yeah. Enough to make each other miserable. If they'd gone their separate ways, they both might have found people to make them happy."

"Did they fight a lot?" she asked, dropping her bottom onto the windowsill.

"No." The fight before the Christmas trip to New York was the only yelling match Kendall could remember. "But Mom resented having to leave her home and family to live down here, while Dad spent years trying to make her happy. He built this house. Then, when she refused to live in it, he finally bought her one over in Charleston and made sure she never wanted for anything."

"But she wanted to go home," Liza said, reading between the lines. "Did they ever talk about moving back?"

"Dad wouldn't leave the island."

"Why?" She rose off the sill and crossed her arms. "Why would he put this island before his family?"

To answer that required sharing details that weren't his to share. "He had his reasons." Kendall scanned the next shelf and opted to change the subject once again. "So what was life like in Rochester? Cold, I imagine."

"Very cold, but Mom always made things fun." He looked over in time to catch her eyes soften as her lips curled into a smile. "Like the time we drove to Nantucket Island and stayed at this ancient B&B. The water was freezing, so I kept running in and out while Mom laughed until her sides hurt." Liza wrapped her arms around herself, grinning as the memory came back. "We ate way too many crab legs, got painfully sunburned, and every night I dozed off curled against her side as she read a book."

Definitely a happier story than his.

"Sounds nice." But despite the positive memory, her expression turned sad, and Kendall decided they'd both had enough. "Let's get out of here."

Liza looked around. "But you've barely taken anything. There's a whole other floor to go."

Kendall retrieved the box before leading her back to the kitchen. "I cleaned out Dad's bedroom after he died, and checking the storage room can happen another time."

"I don't mind waiting while you finish."

"No need." Taking her hand, he pulled her toward the door. "That's enough memory lane for today."

When he dropped her hand to reach for the door handle, she said, "Wait." Liza dashed back to the dining room and returned with the rubber apple. "This is antique fruit." Full lips turned up in a mischievous grin. "You don't want to leave it behind."

Shaking his head, Kendall held out the box, and she added the dusty apple to his collection. "You're weird, Teller."

"Writers usually are."

Kendall couldn't help but laugh at her matter-of-fact reply. When he opened the door, Amos leaped off the welcome mat, more excited to see Liza than his owner. The dog stared adoringly as she bent to scratch his chin, thoroughly smitten with his new best friend.

Not that he blamed the fur ball. If Kendall wasn't careful, he'd find himself smitten as well.

Chapter 12

Holding Kendall's small box of mementos in her lap, Liza let the salt air soothe her aching heart. She knew better than to talk about her mom. Growing up, it had been the two of them against the world. More than mother and daughter, they'd been best friends who did everything together. Years passed before she stopped picking up the phone, dialing half of the phone number, and realizing the person she needed to talk to would never answer the phone again.

Closing her eyes, she let the wind cool her cheeks, and her spirits rose once more. There really was something magical about this island. A balm that soothed any and all ills.

When she opened her eyes again, they were passing through heavy shadows cast by the intertwining branches above. Kendall brought the cart to a stop in front of a large white door.

"You have a garage?" she asked, letting Kendall take the box. "Why would you need a garage when you can't have a car?"

"For one," he replied, stepping to his feet, "I do have a car. A truck, to be exact, parked over at the ferry landing on Isle of Palms. And for two, men use their garages for more than storing a car. Mine is my workshop."

At least he didn't call it a *man cave*.

Liza exited the cart and stared up at the first reasonable-looking house she'd seen. Other than being up on stilts, the charming blue cottage looked nothing like the monstrosities covering Haven Island. Just yesterday she'd spotted one four stories tall. Who needed that much house?

"It's normal," she said, feeling like Dorothy must have once she'd returned from Oz.

"What did you expect?" Taking the stairs two at a time, Kendall left the box at the top and snagged a metal bowl off the porch. Returning, he filled it using a hose hanging on the corner of the house. "It looks like any other house around here."

"Oh no, it doesn't," she said incredulously. "You could fit this cute little thing inside most of the other homes, and still have room to spare."

The water cut off, and he shot her an offended look. "Are you calling my house dinky?"

Liza struggled to keep a straight face. "Do people really use the word *dinky* anymore?"

Kendall took aim with the hose. "You can't insult a man's house and not expect to pay the price."

He wouldn't. "Kendall James, don't you dare spray me with that."

"I don't know what you're talking about," he said with a devious look in his eye. "Why would I do that?"

"Amos, come protect me from your owner!" Liza backed away from the stairs, hoping the hose couldn't reach very far. When the dog barked with excitement, she yelled, "Sic him, boy. Sic him!"

Kendall took one more step before pointing the nozzle straight up. A stream of water arched through the air, and Amos lost his ever-loving mind. Leaping off the ground, the animal attempted to catch the water in his mouth.

When the stream vanished, determined paws stomped in the newly formed puddles, and Liza couldn't help but laugh at the joyous canine.

"Get it, boy," Kendall encouraged as he shot quick bursts at the sand. "You've gotta catch it."

The mostly white dog quickly turned brown, rolling in the mud with reckless abandon.

"He's getting filthy," Liza said, breathless with laughter.

"We can fix that." Kendall grabbed the blue collar and used the hose to spray sand and muck from the dog's short fur. In no time, he was glistening white again, smiling and spent. "Come hold him while I grab a towel." Kendall tossed the hose to the ground.

Liza did as asked, failing to recognize the inherent danger of holding a wet dog until it was too late. Kendall wasn't even up the stairs when Amos gave a full-body shake, soaking her dress until it clung to her body.

"Oh my gosh. Look what you did!"

A cool breeze picked that moment to travel through the trees, raising goose bumps on her skin, and other parts that were much harder to conceal.

Clenching the sweater tightly with her free hand, Liza tugged Amos up the stairs and yelled through the screen door, "Bring me one, too, please."

When no response came, she couldn't be sure he'd heard her. With the only option being to wait, she shuffled to a rocker and dropped to the seat, failing to bob and weave quickly enough to avoid the face lick.

"If you're going to keep insisting on this licking thing, the least you could do is brush your teeth once in a while."

"Here you go." Kendall tossed a towel into her lap at the same time he wrapped another around Amos's head. "I guess he got you." The laughter in his voice said he'd known her fate the moment she took the collar.

"Yes, he did." She tried to sound stern. "Now my dress is soaked, and I have nothing else to put on."

Pulling the dog with him, Kendall settled in the rocker beside hers. "I might have something."

Liza stopped dabbing at her neck. "You have a closet full of dresses in there?"

Amos closed his eyes as Kendall towel-dried his belly. "There's that sarcasm again. No, I don't have dresses, but something tells me one of my shirts would hit pretty close to your knees."

He had a point. Though Liza stood average height, she'd been graced with long legs and a short torso. The seconds clicked by as she debated, cotton growing colder against her skin.

"If you don't mind . . ."

Finishing with the dog's hind feet, Kendall swatted the beast on the bottom and said, "You're done, buddy." Turning to Liza, he wiggled his brows. "Now let's get you out of that dress."

The giggle slipped out as heat danced up her cheeks. "Only because I'm freezing," she said, hugging the damp towel to her chest. "Do you have a dryer I can use?" She wasn't about to wear nothing but one of Kendall's shirts home to Ray's house.

"Yes, ma'am." He held out a hand, and she gave him hers. Grinning, he said, "I meant to take the towel, but this works, too."

Before Liza could pull away, Kendall swiped the towel from her grasp and tossed both strips of terry cloth over the porch rail before tugging her into the house. With Amos leading the way, of course.

๛

Contrary to how things looked, Kendall had not planned the afternoon water games, but he also wasn't above taking advantage of them.

"Where's that jacket you wore at Ray's house?" Liza called through his closed bedroom door.

A jacket wasn't going to be any fun. "I keep it in the golf cart."

Seconds passed until she said, "Can you go get it?"

Why hadn't he said he didn't know? *Idiot.*

"Sure. I'll be right back." Half a minute later, he knocked on his own door. "Open up."

Another moment of silence passed before the doorknob turned and light streamed out a three-inch opening.

"Squeeze it through."

"Liza," Kendall snapped. He'd let her pick anything she wanted from his closet. Surely she'd found an option that covered all the important parts. "You can open the door."

"Turn around," she ordered.

"Are you—"

"Turn around or I'm not opening this door."

"Fine," he mumbled. He turned to find Amos staring at him with his head cocked to the side. "Don't look at me like that."

As if embarrassed by his owner, the dog strolled over to his bed and collapsed with a paw over his face.

"I don't see you bringing any girls home, smart-ass."

"Where's the jacket?" Liza asked behind him.

Kendall extended his arm. "Here it is."

The fleece was snatched from his hand, and the door slammed shut. He'd met his share of modest women before, but this was ridiculous. As Kendall turned to tell her so, the door opened and the breath left his body. Curls wild and cheeks pink, she stood drowning in his jacket, hands shoved in the pockets, and the tails of his white dress shirt barely covering her slender thighs.

Lacy lingerie could not have been sexier.

"You found something," he said, voice cracking like a prepubescent schoolboy.

Liza looked down. "I did. The armholes in the basketball jersey revealed a little too much, so I went with this. I hope it's okay."

More than okay. Though he'd hand over half his bank account to see her in that jersey.

"Sure. Yeah. That's good." Rubbing his hands together, he struggled to focus while the blood in his body raced south. "You want to see the rest of the house?" Not that there was much to see, but they really needed to get away from his bedroom.

"I would, but can we start with the laundry room? I need to put my dress in the dryer."

"Right. That's back off the kitchen." Kendall led her through the living room. "Nothing special in here."

"Nothing special? Your television is the size of a Winnebago."

Other than his tools, the flat screen was his one splurge. "You should see how good the games look on that thing. Like being there."

"For what it must have cost, you *could* be there. In every city east of the Mississippi."

Kendall embraced his right to remain silent and continued into the kitchen. Despite the open floor plan being the current trend, he liked a separation from one room to the next. That way, a conversation could happen in the kitchen without competing with noise from the living room.

"Laundry is through there." He pointed to a door behind the small table. "Controls are pretty basic. Set the time and push the button."

Liza padded into the little room while Kendall crossed to the fridge, surveying the options. He didn't keep wine around, and assumed she wasn't likely to ask for a beer. That left water and soda.

"What can I get you to drink?" he called out, withdrawing two glasses from a top cabinet.

"Water is fine," she answered, before sticking her head into the room. "From a glass this time."

"One quick dousing from the sink sprayer. Got it."

"You aren't funny." Liza joined him in the kitchen and leaned a hip against the counter. "This is a nice kitchen, Kendall. Love these countertops." Running a hand along the surface, she said, "Marble?"

"Quartz. Same look with less maintenance." He handed her a glass of water. "Other than the guest bed and bath, you've seen it all. As you pointed out, not as big as others on the island, but I don't need much."

She turned the glass in her hands. "To be honest, I like this much better. I mean, Ray's place is beautiful, but I feel like I'm staying at a resort. Even the apartment is a little too polished, you know? Too perfect." Blue eyes darted around Kendall's kitchen. "*This* is a home."

"Thanks," he said. "But according to Larimore, you're in the minority. The bigger the better for most people."

Liza shook her head. "Maybe it's because I grew up in a modest home like this one, or I've acclimated to my teeny apartment in the city, but high ceilings and sweeping staircases are not for me."

An unusual stance, but then she'd been surprising him for days. Playing devil's advocate, he tested her resolve.

"You're saying that if someone offered you a million dollars for your apartment, you wouldn't turn around and buy a bigger place?"

She snorted into her water. "A million dollars would barely get me a hundred more square feet in New York City."

"I didn't say it had to be in the city."

Blue eyes narrowed. "So you want to know if I'd move out of the city?"

For crying out loud. "I'm not talking location. I'm talking size."

"So you want to know if size matters?"

Kendall opened his mouth, then closed it again. The smirk on her face said they weren't talking about houses anymore. "Size always matters."

Liza chewed on a fingernail. "*Hmmm* . . . I'm not sure I agree with that."

Reaching for the jacket zipper, he said, "I could prove it to you."

"Oh, no-no-no." She swatted his hand away and wagged a finger in front of his nose. "Just friends, remember?"

Regretting that agreement, he stepped back. "It was a friendly offer."

"I'm sure it was." Curling her toes into the mat in front of his sink, she said, "So what now?"

She'd already shot down his suggestion, but Kendall did have one more thing to show her.

❦

"Remember the view from the pier?" he asked, backing toward a set of glass doors.

"Of course I do."

"Here's a better version of it."

The lock clicked, and he tugged on the handle. Amos barreled through the doorway before Kendall could pull it all the way open, but Kendall remained inside. "After you."

Liza stepped out, careful where she put her bare feet. Having the previous setting to go on in no way prepared her for the view off Kendall's back porch.

"This must be what heaven looks like," she mumbled, strolling slowly across the reddish-brown planks to stop at a wide set of stairs. Towering oaks framed the breathtaking vista, drawing the eye to the endless expanse of sparkling water. "Is that the ocean?"

Kendall joined her at the railing. "Yes, ma'am. Dad used to bring me here when I was a kid to watch the sunrise. It comes up right over there." He stood close, pointing over her shoulder. "The lot was available for years, but most folks prefer a sunset view, so no one bought it."

Wind chimes clanged a low-octave tune as the cool evening air blew in with the waves. Darkness wouldn't come for hours, but Liza had learned the weather patterns of the island, and often chose this time of day to shut down the computer and watch nature's subtle shifts from Ray's now less-impressive west-facing deck.

"I could live here," she whispered. "Right here in this spot."

"You'd need to shift to the left a bit, so Amos doesn't trample you every time he goes outside."

Wrapping an arm around the post, Liza sighed. "I want to take a picture, but I know my phone could never do this justice." Damp curls pressed against the post. "Kendall, you're so lucky to live here. Do you ever get used to this?"

"You do. But after thirty years, the trick is not to take the place for granted."

Liza made a connection she'd somehow missed before. "Thirty years? You moved here the same time as Ray?"

He kept his gaze on the view. "My dad worked for Ray. We followed him down here."

Talk about loyalty. "Couldn't your dad have stayed in New York and worked for someone else?"

"No, he couldn't." Kendall let out a high-pitched whistle, startling Liza and grabbing the attention of his dog, who trotted toward the porch. "I need to feed Amos. Have a seat, and I'll check your dress once he's eating."

"Oh. Okay."

Her host disappeared inside, and Liza felt a cooling off that had nothing to do with the breeze. What kind of a job required a man to move his family so far from home? Assessing the landscape with new eyes, she wondered what the island must have looked like thirty years ago. Likely much more desolate and uninviting. She almost couldn't blame Kendall's mom for preferring a more civilized living arrangement.

And how had Ray found this place anyway? Liza had never even heard of Haven Island until Vanessa called with the book offer. The place must have been even more obscure back in the '80s.

Hugging the jacket close against the chill, Liza pondered the riddle that was Ray Wallis. No one landed in such a remote spot by accident. Whatever transgression Kendall kept hinting at must have been the impetus that drove both Ray and the James family to make such a drastic move.

Which meant that any secret that could take down Ray was likely to implicate Kendall's father as well. Shoving the curls from her eyes, Liza took one last look at the view, hoping that she was wrong. Everything was conjecture at this point, with no basis in proof or reality. Ray was a sweet old man who'd been lucky enough to find an island paradise to live out his days.

And as far as she knew, the James family just happened to be in the right place at the right time to tag along. A completely plausible explanation that her reporter brain wasn't buying in the least.

Chapter 13

Two days after the silent ride home from Kendall's house, questions continued to plague Liza. Questions that grew even more troublesome due to her growing fondness for the darling old charmer who loved nothing more than to make her smile at every opportunity.

While she was with him, Liza felt certain there were no dark secrets to discover. They'd spent the day Tuesday talking about his college years, which were filled with parties, practical jokes, and more parties. And these were not the frat-house keggers of today. Ray's generation partied in style, probably because many of them had been older than the average college student and already had seen more than their share of human tragedy.

As had become her habit, she'd spent Tuesday evening watching the sunset from the deck, but this time wondering if the sunrise from Kendall's vantage point contained the same magnificent shades of violet, magenta, and vibrant gold. In truth, Kendall had occupied her mind with troubling regularity throughout the day.

Not a smart habit, considering how the previous day had gone.

Thankfully, Wednesday morning had provided the perfect distraction when Liza received an invitation to the afternoon meeting of the Haven Island book club. Her efforts to learn which book they planned to discuss were unsuccessful, but between her lifelong devotion to reading and her current occupation, she felt confident that she could hold her own in the discussion.

A presumption that would prove more accurate than she could have guessed.

To Liza's dismay, the first thing she spotted upon entering Francine's unique home was a stack of her own books. As in, several copies of the book *she* had written.

"Why are those here?" Liza asked before the hostess could offer a greeting.

"That's the book we're discussing, of course. We couldn't have an author in our midst and not take advantage of the opportunity." Francine squeezed Liza's shoulders. "You're a wonderful writer. I couldn't put it down!"

High praise that Liza appreciated, but the only thing worse than explaining *why* she hadn't written a second book was being forced to talk about the first one.

"This is a bad idea."

"Why? Who better to discuss *Leaving Alone* than the person who wrote it?"

Anyone else! Liza wanted to cry, but instead went with the obvious. "You won't be able to have an honest discussion with me here. People who didn't like it will feel obligated to say nice things." She reached for the door behind her. "I'll come back to another meeting, when you discuss a different book. Then no one will feel awkward."

Most of all *her*.

Francine cut off Liza's escape route. "Listen. I get it. Why do you think I don't go to my own exhibits?"

Oh, thank goodness. "I'll be happy to come to the next one. I promise."

"But you have to stay."

Panic returned. "You just said you understand." Liza reached again for the door, but Francine wedged her body in front of the knob. This was ridiculous. She couldn't keep Liza here like a prisoner.

Going for reason, she said, "I'm being serious here. I can't talk about my own book." Liza twirled her fingers above her ears. "I'll get all up in my head, and nothing I say will make sense. Plus, once the book is in the reader's hands, it really isn't my story anymore. Let them share without me mucking things up."

The tiny woman held her ground. "I'm sorry, Liza, but this is a competitive group, and when I say I can deliver an author, I deliver an author." Before she could process that statement, Francine yelled, "Look who's here, everybody! The guest of honor!"

Within seconds, Liza found herself surrounded by half a dozen islanders, all talking at the same time as they dragged her into a living space surrounded by eight bare walls encompassing an ultramodern setting in stark white.

Minimalist and monochromatic, the couch looked like a rectangular block of foam with an oversize bolster pillow placed down the center. Triangular ottomans sat on each side, with simple white tables anchoring the ends. As Liza took in her surroundings, two thoughts raced through her mind—*Amos would destroy this place in seconds*, and *how does a vibrant artist like Francine not display art?*

Those two thoughts vanished when a heart-shaped face impeded her view of the room.

"When Francine said she knew the author of *Leaving Alone* and, even better, that she was right here on Haven Island, I didn't believe her." The round woman with blonde hair and a Jersey accent tugged Liza down to sit on the couch beside her. "Your book changed my life. I'd known I was adopted forever, but I never had the guts to find my birth family until I read Penelope's story. Now I have two brothers I didn't even know existed!"

Despite writing a book about a girl who set out to find her family, Liza considered the story more of a study in creating families, since Penelope never actually finds a blood relative.

"I'm glad you had the courage to do that."

"All right, Bernadette. No monopolizing the writer." An olive-skinned man in wire-rimmed glasses plopped down on Liza's opposite side. "I'm Marcelo," he said, pushing up his glasses before extending a hand. "I have to know. Is Penelope a real person?"

She'd received the same question in countless letters and emails—some even suggesting Penelope could be their own long-lost relative.

"I'm sorry, but no. She's a complete work of fiction. A figment of my imagination."

With a pleading look, Liza begged Francine to save her, but the overture went ignored. Not that she wasn't grateful for the interest the group had taken in her work or the enthusiasm with which they'd greeted her. But each of these readers had created an image of author L. R. Teller in their minds, and Liza doubted she could live up to any of them.

"Snacks are out," the hostess announced from the kitchen. "Fill your glasses and your plates before the discussion starts. You know the rules."

As quickly as they'd converged around her, the merry bunch dispersed in a mad dash to the kitchen, most reaching for the wine first. Liza hoped no one would offer her a glass.

"You're doing great," Francine whispered, handing over a plate of various finger foods. The only thing Liza recognized was the caprese skewers. "Red or white?"

"Water," she replied. Her hostess's eyes narrowed, and Liza explained, "I don't want to spill wine on this beautiful sofa." A true statement, though not the reason she'd turned down the proffered beverage. Changing the subject, she whispered, "Why don't any of these people look familiar?"

Francine's expression relaxed. "Bernadette and her husband only come for the summer, and their kids were in school until last Friday." She took a seat beside Liza and pointed to a man struggling with a stubborn cork. "The guy in the green Polo shirt about to break my bottle opener is her husband, Daniel."

Together they watched Bernadette snatch the bottle from her husband's grasp and remove the cork in one graceful move.

"Marcelo lives in Mount Pleasant," Francine said. "His local library has a book club, but he likes ours better, so we let him join. Carrie, the cute little thing in the cutoffs, lives on Goat Island and has been cleaning rental houses here for nearly ten years."

"She doesn't look old enough to have been cleaning that long." The woman in question topped off a glass of red, and Liza felt the urge to card her.

"Don't let looks fool you. She's a divorced thirty-five-year-old with four kids at home."

"She has *four* kids?" Liza hadn't even had kids yet and couldn't wear shorts that tiny.

"I know, girl. I had two, and my body never bounced back like that." Leaning closer, Francine lowered her voice even more. "The two debating in the corner are an interesting pair. Never seen eye to eye a day in their lives. If Kathy, the one on the right, said the earth is round, Tabby would declare it flat as a pancake."

As if proving Francine's words, the women glared at one another. The one Francine called Kathy sported long dark hair and stood several inches shorter than her blonde counterpart. "If they don't like each other, why do they stay friends?"

"Friends? Honey, those two are twins." Liza searched for a resemblance as the hostess continued. "Fraternal, obviously. And if you say something bad about one, you better be prepared for the other to come knocking on your door. Thick as thieves, they are. Thieves who'd rather swallow their own tongues than agree on anything, but a bonded pair all the same."

Liza's fingers itched to take notes as her writer mind kicked into gear like the Tin Man after a good oiling. All these characters belonged on the page. The single mom was an obvious lead, with a story that could go in several directions, and the twins were a gift to her ailing imagination. Liza imagined a black comedy exploring the darker side of sibling rivalry, with a murderous plot twist involving the smarmy lawyer who tried seducing them both.

"Is either of them married?" she asked.

"Tabby is divorced, but it happened long before they moved here." Francine turned her face away from the kitchen to whisper, "Legend has it hubby suggested the sisters would get along better with some distance between them. The marriage didn't last long after that."

The twins chose that moment to head Liza's way. Her shoulders tensed as she whispered, "Are they nice to other people?"

"Absolute dolls." Francine rose to her feet. "I better get your water before everyone sits down. Do you need anything else?"

A pen and a legal pad would have been nice. "No, I'm good, thanks."

Francine walked away, and Liza tried to look relaxed when the twins joined her. As if they might smell her fear and attack.

"Ms. Teller, we just wanted to tell you how much we enjoyed your book," Kathy said. "The writing drew us in from the first page."

"Thank you. I'm glad—"

Tabby cut her off. "I knew that Miles was going to come back for her. Kathy thought he was too shallow, but I knew there was more to that boy."

Kathy leaned forward to cast a narrowed eye at her sister. "I said Miles was too jaded, not too shallow. If you're going to tell the story, get it right."

"Either way, you were wrong." Tabby grinned with great satisfaction. To Liza she said, "We really did love it, and are so honored to have you with us. Thank you for sharing your talent."

The ladies rose together, Kathy echoing her sister's gratitude before mumbling something under her breath. Liza feared the shallow-versus-jaded argument would continue for a while. She could have told them that in her original draft, Miles never went back for Penelope, but that was just the sort of thing that ruined books for readers.

Once they learn tidbits like that, they begin to question all the parts they love, and before long, the magic of the story is gone. Exactly the type of thing Liza did not want to happen, which meant getting through this discussion by saying as little as possible.

The gathering made their way back to the living room as Francine handed Liza a glass of water. The meeting commenced, and in short order, any notion that the author's presence would hinder the group's willingness to be brutally honest went right out the window.

By the end of the meeting, Liza possessed a greater understanding of why writers drink.

🦋

"What's up with you and our resident writer?"

The question caused Kendall to miss the nail and hammer his finger. Smothering a string of profanities, he pegged his helper with a hard glare. "Nothing is up," he lied.

Aadi chuckled. "Looked like something on movie night."

Kendall was starting to regret agreeing to help the doc replace the damaged lattice around the bottom of his house. "You were supposed to be watching the movie, not the audience."

"That walk on the beach afterward is what got folks talking."

He stopped midswing. "What does that mean?"

Dark eyes twinkled. "The natives are restless, son. You can't take a stroll with a pretty woman in front of half the population and not expect a little chatter."

The hammer slid into the hook on his tool belt, and Kendall descended the ladder. "It's break time." Crossing to the cooler, he snagged a bottle of water and took a seat on a large rock. That he and Liza were the source of gossip shouldn't have been surprising, but that didn't mean he had to like it.

The doctor grabbed himself a water and settled on the next rock over. "If it's any consolation, the talk is positive. The locals love her, and we both know that's no small feat."

Kendall knew his neighbors well enough to know where their minds were going. "She's temporary, Aadi. Liza is here to do a job for Ray, and then she's gone."

After a moment's hesitation, he said, "That doesn't have to be the case. Maybe, with the right incentive, she'd be willing to stick around."

The same thought had occurred to Kendall the night before, but he knew all too well that a city girl like Liza wouldn't be happy on the island long term. He'd vowed long ago never to create the same situation his father had, and coercing Liza to upend her life would be doing exactly that.

"I know the incentive you're suggesting, and you're running that flag up the wrong pole. We barely know each other, and I'm not looking for a leg shackle anytime soon."

"Come on. You're what, thirty-seven?"

"Thirty-four," Kendall corrected.

"Well, then. What are you waiting for?" Aadi turned to face him. "I knew Sacchi ten years before I came to my senses and asked her on a date. Six months later, we were married. That's ten years wasted. Now that she's gone, I'd give anything to have those years back." Tapping Kendall on the knee, he added, "Life is to be lived, my friend. Live it!"

A powerful speech, if a bit premature. "I've barely known her ten days. What if she's a terrible cook? What if she has smelly feet? Or bites her toenails?"

Aadi drew back. "I had a cousin who did that. Disgusting habit."

Kendall had been joking, but okay. "She's already said she doesn't like dogs. That's a deal breaker right there."

"Francine says Amos loves her."

"He does." And she seemed to love him right back. "But what does a dog know?"

"Oftentimes, much more than people." Aadi rose from his rock. "Whatever you do is your business. I'm merely suggesting that when an opportunity lands at your door, you should let it in." Slipping the half-empty bottle back in the cooler, he reached for a new piece of lattice. "Advice over. Back to work."

Finishing off the cold drink, Kendall let Aadi's words drift through his mind. As Francine had reminded him, Ray couldn't live forever. When he was gone, which hopefully wouldn't happen for years to come, what would Kendall's next chapter be?

He'd like to have a family of his own, and Mom had been hinting about grandchildren for years. But the atmosphere he'd grown up in kept him gun-shy in that area. At least while he was still tied to the island.

After tossing his bottle in the recycle bin, Kendall hauled himself up the ladder, doubtful that Liza would be receptive to Aadi's suggestion. But maybe it *was* time to start thinking about his future in a more substantial way.

Chapter 14

"Why would she do that? She would never have done that!"

Marcelo threw his hands in the air for the third time, each instance in response to someone else in the group disagreeing with his interpretation of the book. At the moment, he was taking issue with the way Liza's main character behaved during the climax of the story.

"How do you know she wouldn't have done it?" Daniel asked. He hadn't contributed much to the conversation, so Liza had started to think he hadn't read the book at all. "It's not like you're in her head or something."

Liza tried not to flinch at that statement. She hadn't actually enjoyed the discussion, since several of her shortcomings as a writer had been conferred and debated, but she had learned a great deal about how readers both connected with and became emotionally invested in a story.

"What do you think reading is?" Bernadette turned to her husband, brow drawn. "We're in their heads the whole time."

"I know," Marcelo replied, ignoring Bernadette's comment, "because right at the beginning we learn that she's nonconfrontational. Growing up in foster care has taught her to keep her head down and not make waves."

"But she's grown by this point," Carrie interjected, renewing Liza's faith in the group. "That's the whole point. She's grown through every obstacle that's come her way, and her character is changing. So when that nasty old lady tries to shove her around, Penelope is ready. She's found her backbone."

Yes! Liza wanted to shout, biting down on the inside of her cheek to contain the urge. So far, she'd managed not to interject herself into the conversation and planned to keep it that way.

"I agree with Carrie," Kathy said, causing Marcelo to fume louder. "If she'd stood up for herself in the first half, I'd have said she was acting out of character, but this is the big blow-up moment. She's the hero of the book, and that's the time Penelope needed to step up." Turning to Liza, she added, "Are we right?"

Six pairs of eyes turned her way, and Liza's throat tightened. She didn't want to take sides, since every reader's experience was unique and valid, yet she couldn't outright refuse to answer. And then there was the fact that the majority was right. At least in what she'd intended for the character and the story as a whole.

"It's true," she began, clearing her throat to buy time, "that Penelope's character has evolved by this point in the story." Liza tried to read their faces, as if their expressions might offer her a way out of this. "But if Marcelo didn't recognize that growth, then I didn't do my job to make her evolution clear. That means he's correct for the story as he read it, and the rest of you are also right in how you interpreted the book."

There. A nice diplomatic response that didn't put anyone in the wrong. Except herself.

"Bullshit," Tabby snapped. "Every bit of that girl's development and growth is on the page. If Marcelo missed it, that's his fault, not yours."

Like a figurative grenade lobbed into the center of the gathering, Tabby's words caused an explosion of voices. Liza looked at Francine for a clue as to what to do, but the hostess only grinned, as if she were enjoying the cacophony echoing off her bare walls.

Bodies were on their feet in seconds, and Marcelo made the mistake of facing off with Tabby, who no doubt could defend herself, but Kathy took exception to the way the smaller man wiggled a finger in her sister's face. Personal space was invaded, and before Liza knew it, the young man's glasses were askew, though only because he'd tripped over one of the ottomans in the melee.

"That does it for this week!" Francine yelled above the fray, startling Liza and silencing the crowd.

As if they hadn't been on the brink of physical combat, they all returned to their seats, faces serene and completely at ease. If she hadn't witnessed the change herself, Liza never would have believed a disagreement could dissipate so quickly.

"I'll post the poll for next month's book choice within a week," Francine announced in a more level voice, "so if you have a suggestion, be sure and email it to me. Now let's thank the fabulous L. R. Teller for joining us today and giving us such an amazing book to discuss."

Liza rose along with everyone else to accept handshakes, hugs, and profuse praise for her work. Something she took with a grain of salt after spending the last hour absorbing the occasional less-than-complimentary commentary.

The last to share his goodbye was Marcelo, who leaned in to whisper, "I saw the character growth. I guess I just related to her a little too much and was putting myself in her place."

Tears threatened as she gave the lovely young man a gentle squeeze. "You have the strength, too," she whispered back, grateful for the gift he'd just given her.

His smile was timid, but it was there. With a nod, he followed the others to the front door, and Liza dropped back onto the sofa, exhausted and relieved all at once.

Francine returned from seeing her friends off, hands clapping and a satisfied smile on her lips. "Thank you for making me queen of the book club." She plopped down next to Liza with a contented sigh. "Feels good to be the queen."

Liza searched for a sliver of her earlier indignation, but the victorious look on her new friend's face made the last hour worth the blows her ego had taken. "I'm happy I could help, but a little warning would have been nice."

"Would you have come if I'd told you the truth?"

A tough question to answer now that she'd survived the ordeal. Knowing what she knew now, not coming would have meant missing out on some useful information. Tidbits she could use going forward. That was, if she ever managed to write another work of fiction.

"How about if I just say I'm glad I came?"

Francine nodded in understanding. "I'll take that."

As the hostess rose to gather the remnants of the meeting—napkins, small plates, and empty wineglasses—Liza followed suit, taking the opportunity to pose the question she'd wanted to ask since first walking into the house.

"Why don't you display your beautiful artwork on your walls?"

Francine paused with three glasses in one hand. "For the same reason you didn't want to be part of this discussion. We're too critical of our own work." Crossing to the kitchen, she unloaded the used dishes onto the island. "If I hang a piece, all I'll see is the flaws. And then I'll want to fix them, and there will be more flaws . . . It's a vicious circle that would lead to madness, if I let it."

Liza understood the explanation perfectly. Allowing Vanessa to send her book off to publishers in order to sell it had been ridiculously difficult. Especially when Liza knew that the manuscript wasn't perfect. Even today, the flaws haunted her, and that was after three rounds of edits, a copyedit, and two proof passes. All from professionals with whom she held no personal connection that would cause them to lie about how good or bad the book truly was.

There were also the thousands of copies sold and hundreds of positive reviews posted on various distribution sites. Even with all that positive reinforcement, Liza wished she could go back and tweak here or polish there.

"That makes perfect sense," she replied, feeling a kinship with Francine that she'd never experienced before. Liza was glad that Ray Wallis had brought her to this island. Though she'd only expected to return home with a book to write and maybe a minor tan, this adventure had brought friends into her life—something she sorely lacked back home.

☙

Kendall's efforts to ponder his future had turned into a battle to keep Liza off his mind.

For the first time in years, he'd contemplated a life focused around something other than protecting Ray Wallis. Unlike his situation sixteen years ago, when he'd been a bright-eyed eighteen-year-old ignorant of what had brought his family to the island, Kendall now possessed a bank account that rendered his options limitless.

Since his income came from the island rentals, which were managed by Larimore, there was no need to find an occupation. In fact, he didn't even need to live on the island. That left him to imagine moving elsewhere, and Kendall formulated a mental list of options.

Charleston, so he could keep an eye on the rentals and come back whenever he wanted. New York, to be close to his mom and the extended family he rarely saw. Or he could go big. The tropics, the mountains, the West Coast. But no matter where he imagined himself, one specific detail stayed the same.

Liza.

Whenever he imagined himself in a new place, she was there. Smiling. Teasing. Provoking. He tried shaking her from his mind, reminding himself that she wasn't supposed to be part of the picture, but there she was, igniting a new possibility. One that would allow Kendall to break his own rule and see if he and Liza could be more than friends.

But all these possibilities hinged on one painful event—Ray Wallis's passing. And even though Kendall had done no more than entertain vague ideas about a life after Ray, he still felt guilty. Especially after the call from Aadi around lunchtime, who'd made a courtesy stop by Ray's that morning after Liza had grown concerned about the older man's health.

Aadi hadn't mentioned anything specific that was wrong with Ray but had suggested that Kendall check on him more often . . . and that Liza might need a break from being his constant caretaker. Suggestions that led Kendall to the place where he currently stood.

"Oh," Liza said, eyes wide when she opened the door. "Hello."

"Hi." Kendall snapped for Amos to stay. If this was a bad time, he didn't want the dog disturbing their work. "Am I interrupting one of your interviews?"

She leaned against the door. "Ray was about to tell me about the day he met his wife."

"Oh." Kendall had never had to call before visiting Ray, but he should have today. "I'll come back later."

"Have you heard the story?" she asked.

Ray had never talked about his life before the island. At least not with Kendall. "No, I haven't. But I don't want to get in the way."

Liza opened the door wider. "Don't be silly. Come on in."

Amos obeyed the order immediately, darting past Liza and into the house. Kendall took his time and followed her to the table.

They hadn't seen each other since the afternoon she'd been at his house. The visit had been going better than he'd hoped, until Liza had made the connection between his family and Ray, reminding him of the secrets that complicated their connection. In a way, Kendall wished

Ray would tell her everything, so he'd no longer have to dance around the subject.

At the same time, he knew the damage that revealing those secrets could do. Unless Ray was right, and the threat that had driven him to take such drastic measures no longer existed.

"Look who's here," she said, causing Ray to spin around.

Watery blue eyes lit up. "There's my boy. Where've you been?"

Kendall gave the old man's shoulder a squeeze. "I had some repairs to catch up on." A true statement, though he'd also had some thinking to do.

"As I said," Liza cut in, "Ray was just about to tell me about his sweetheart." She lifted a small recorder and pressed a red button. "This is the day Ray Wallis met his wife," she said into the tiny gadget, and then nodded for Ray to begin as Kendall settled quietly into the chair at the end of the table.

"I didn't want to go to the zoo that day," Ray began, "but Sam Levitt's date was bringing a friend, and he offered me ten bucks if I'd keep the girl busy." Fuzzy brows arched. "Ten dollars was a lot of money back then."

"I know it was." Liza checked the recorder to make sure it was running.

"When we got there, Sam couldn't find his girl," Ray said. "They were supposed to be by the elephants, but we didn't see them. Then we walked by a fountain, and sitting at the edge of the water was the prettiest girl you ever saw. Dark curls, big brown eyes, and a smile that could stop a runaway train." He sat back with a dreamy look. "She stole my heart, right then and there."

Ray's words brought to mind the day Kendall had discovered Liza at the ferry landing. Not that he'd fallen in love on sight. That was stupid. But there had been something that made him want to learn more about her.

Until he'd found out who she really was, and then he'd become a royal jerk.

"Did the girl feel the same way about you?" Liza asked, chin resting in her palm as she gave Ray her full attention.

"You bet she did. I'm not much to look at now, but I was a handsome devil in my day."

Kendall chuckled, enjoying seeing Ray so animated. He looked better than he had since the scary day on the beach.

"You're still quite handsome," Liza assured her subject. "Does this mean poor Sam lost his wingman?"

Ray's grin widened. "That's the best part. Essie was the girl I was there to meet." Smacking the table, he cackled. "How about that? If I'd turned down that ten dollars, I'd have missed out on the best girl in the world."

Liza laughed, her exuberance matching Ray's. "Essie, huh?"

Ray sighed with a hand pressed to his chest. "My Essie. She was the only girl for me from that moment on. We'd have gotten married right away, but her father wanted more for his little girl than an unemployed suitor living in a forty-five-dollar-a-month rental above a dry cleaners."

Forty-five dollars a month? That would hardly buy a tank of gas these days. And that had been New York City. When Kendall had last visited his mom, his taxi from the airport had been more than that.

"You didn't have a job?" Liza asked, rolling past the cheap-rental part.

Ray shrugged. "So many of us cashed in our GI Bills after the war that, come 1950, there were more of us than there were people hiring. I did odd jobs around the cleaners, but that wasn't going to provide a good home for my girl, so I knocked on every door I could to find something full-time. Took three more months before I could afford a nicer place, but by the end of the year, I put a ring on Essie's finger, and we were well on our way."

Liza's expression softened, and something fluttered in Kendall's chest. He rubbed his breastbone, telling himself it was only indigestion from the frozen pizza he'd eaten the night before.

"And she was willing to wait?" the writer asked.

Eyes alight, Ray sat up a little straighter in his chair. "There were others prowling around, trying to coax her away from me, but my Essie was a patient girl. She knew when I promised to make myself worthy of her, my word was good."

"And her father? Did he come around?"

Ray jammed a gnarled finger into the polished wood. "That man never did like me. Said I was too bold for my own good, and unreliable, too. I showed him. Until the day he died, I never asked him for a penny. Essie always had a solid roof over her head and all the pretty dresses she wanted, too. Unreliable, my foot."

"Good for you," Liza cheered.

"Did your grandmother ever tell you how she met your grandfather?" Ray asked. The question seemed odd to Kendall, but Liza answered.

"I wish." She sighed. "My grandfather died when I was barely two, and his loss devastated her. The whole family, really. Mom said that when she met my father, the Tellers gathered every Saturday for dinner. But after my grandfather died, the gatherings stopped."

She set the recorder on the table and looked up. "I asked Granny Teller about him once, the summer after my freshman year of high school. I'd never even seen a picture of him, and I was curious what he looked like. You'd have thought I'd suggested exhuming his body, the way she reacted."

Ray stared at his knuckles silently, but Kendall asked, "Was she angry?"

"No." Liza's lips turned down. "She burst into tears. My father reprimanded me never to ask about him again." With a shake of her head, she added, "So I didn't."

"Then she never remarried?" Ray asked, eyes still downcast.

"Goodness, no. Granny Teller mourned her husband until the day she died." Slender fingers brushed a curl off her forehead. "A few months before she passed, she did tell me that she was happy she'd get to see her Eli again." The older man seemed to wither in his chair, and Liza leaned forward. "Ray, are you okay?" She glanced at her watch. "I'm so sorry. We went past your rest time."

Kendall rose from his chair. "Let's get you to bed."

"No need. I can do it," he said, waving the aid away.

Despite the stubborn man's best efforts, he couldn't lift himself off the chair. Kendall eased him up while pulling the chair farther from the table, and Ray didn't put up a fight. A quick glance to his left revealed deep concern in Liza's eyes. Ray had obviously not been as healthy as Kendall assumed.

"There we go. Nice and easy," he said, lowering Ray onto the bed once Liza had pulled back the covers.

Amos jumped onto the bed, and Kendall shooed him off as Ray leaned back. When his head hit the pillow, his bright-yellow hat fell to the floor, and shaky hands snapped to cover his bare scalp as Liza retrieved the fallen fedora.

"What happened?" she asked, drawing Kendall's attention to the bloodstained gauze beneath Ray's hands. "When did you bump your head?"

Ray snatched the hat from her fingers and tried to cover the injury. "A few days ago. It's fine."

Fine, my ass, Kendall thought. "Who put that bandage on you?" The tape was applied too straight for Ray to have done it himself.

"Franny came over," he replied, bottom lip pushed out like a petulant child. "Neither of you were around."

She and Kendall exchanged doubtful glances. "Are you sure you're all right?" she asked. "It looks as if it's been bleeding."

"There's no need to fuss." Ray swatted her hand away. "Old folks bump their heads. It happens."

They obviously weren't going to get the truth. Kendall nodded toward the open doorway. "Get some rest, then. Liza and I will be in the kitchen if you need us."

Amos whined to get on the bed, but Kendall snapped his fingers and pointed at the door. The dog obeyed and followed Liza out of the room. It was time to get some answers on what was really going on with Ray.

Chapter 15

Liza leaned against the island, a thumbnail locked between her teeth. She should have called Kendall sooner, but she'd promised Ray she wouldn't.

"How often does he get weak like that?" Kendall asked as soon as he was far enough from the bedroom door not to be overheard.

She crossed her arms and braced for an angry response. "He was doing okay until Wednesday. When I came back from Francine's, I found him struggling to navigate the step in from the back deck."

Despite his protests, Liza had needed to help Ray into the house, but he'd brushed her off before shuffling into his bedroom under his own power. The next day, Ray had assured her that he was fine, yet she had been with him for two weeks now and had witnessed the steady decline for herself.

A call to Francine the day before had resulted in a visit from Aadi that morning. He'd brought fresh strawberries, claiming he'd thought Ray might enjoy them. A slight fib, or so Liza assumed, but she'd been grateful for the unscheduled checkup.

Like a car that stopped making the wonky sound as soon as the mechanic was close by, Ray had appeared bright and alert, capable of dancing a jig, or so he'd claimed. Not until the doctor left did he let the weakness show.

Damn stubborn man.

"Was that the only time you've had to help him get around?" The question was direct, but not accusatory.

She nodded. "It is, but he's been getting tired earlier and earlier this week. And that's with the daily naps. The first week I was here, we watched the sunset from the deck together every night, but now he barely makes it through dinner before he needs to lie down." Feeling bad for not telling him sooner, Liza added, "I would have said something, but Ray didn't want you to worry over nothing."

"This doesn't look like nothing to me." He sighed, mouth pinched with concern. "I don't like that bump on his head."

Neither did Liza. "I talked to Francine yesterday, but she didn't mention helping him with any bandages." Odd, considering the call had been about Ray's health. "Do you really think she'd help him and not tell us?"

Kendall rubbed a hand along his jaw, and Liza noticed the lack of his ever-present stubble. In fact, Kendall wasn't wearing his normal uniform of T-shirt, jeans, and boots, either. Well, he still wore jeans, but these weren't stained and worn like usual. The well-fitting denim was dark, clean, and complemented the body inside them nicely.

Very nicely. Liza clamped down on the naughty thoughts swirling through her brain. She'd been thinking about Kendall a lot since Monday, but not in such carnal tones. No, she'd been thinking of him more as a man she could get to know. Someone she wouldn't mind being more than friends with.

Despite their contentious start, Kendall had proved himself a caring man. The first and most obvious indicator was his relationship with Amos. Liza may not know much about dogs, but she'd been told more than once since arriving on the island that canines were known for their ability to distinguish the good guys from the bad. The pit bull clearly saw Kendall as one of the good guys.

Then there was Kendall's connection with Ray. He clearly cared about the man, treating him as if they were family. In fact, he and Ray were more like relatives than Liza and her father, who were bound by blood. A depressing thought that she still hoped to rectify, given more time.

More than once, Kendall had shown concern, and even devotion, for her headstrong host, often against the older man's will. Even his objections to Liza's writing Ray's story had been born of concern. Beneath a taciturn and temperamental facade, Kendall James was a considerate, generous, and protective man who any woman would be lucky to have.

Including Liza.

"I'm sorry you aren't getting as much time with him," she said, realizing how much she'd monopolized Ray since her arrival. "If you want to stick around until he wakes up, I'll work upstairs so you can talk alone."

"Actually," he said, sliding his hands into his pockets, "I came to see both of you."

A warmth blossomed in her belly. "You came to see me?"

"You've been on the island two weeks now. I thought you might like dinner in a real restaurant again."

Now that he mentioned it, a break would be nice. Not that she didn't enjoy the quiet, but she also missed the hum and hustle of the real world. But this wasn't the best time to leave Ray alone.

Liza pointed toward Ray's bedroom door. "I'm not sure that's a good idea."

Broad shoulders rolled beneath a pressed gray button-down. "Yeah, well . . . I didn't know Ray was this fragile before coming over." Kendall studied the floor before lifting his chin to meet her eyes. "I could have Larimore come over. Just long enough for us to grab a bite to eat."

She didn't know Larimore well, but if Kendall trusted him, then so did Liza. "That would be nice. Do you think he'd mind?" It *was* a Friday night, after all.

"Larimore's a good guy." Kendall pulled his cell phone from his back pocket. "He won't mind."

That he'd thought about her enough to give up his Friday night on her behalf was further proof of Kendall's generous nature. Every person she'd encountered on the island had nothing but positive things to say about their resident handyman. A thought made her realize the irony of the situation. Liza found herself on an island filled with the extravagantly wealthy, and she was falling for the one person who didn't fit that description.

Not that she minded. A smile crossed her lips as she watched Kendall lift the phone to his ear. She wouldn't know what to do with a millionaire anyway.

❦

"Do you think he'll be okay?" Liza asked as they made their way to the ferry landing.

While they'd waited for Larimore to arrive, she'd run upstairs to change—despite Kendall's assurance that they weren't going anywhere fancy—and returned in the same dress she'd worn the day of her arrival. Since she knew how he felt about the garment, he couldn't help but wonder if she'd donned it on purpose.

"I asked Aadi the same thing," Kendall replied, checking the mirror and finding it odd not to see Amos drooling back. Since Morgan's frowned on canine visitors, they'd left the dog with Larimore. "He says people lucky enough to get to their nineties often hit a wall. As if their bodies realize how old they are and suddenly slow down."

"Have you ever taken him to one of his doctor visits?" she asked.

"Not for a while. Francine took over the task about six months ago. Ray said he liked her driving better than mine, so she kept taking him."

Liza snorted. "If you drive a car the way you drive a cart, I don't blame him."

"Har, har," he said, tossing a half smile her way. "You're a regular comedian."

She shook her head as the wind blew a curl over her eyes. "Not usually. I mean, I think smart-alecky comments all the time, but I don't typically say them out loud." Blue eyes turned his way. "You're just so fun to agitate."

If she kept looking at Kendall that way, he'd let her agitate him all she wanted.

"I'm not going to know what to do with a full menu to choose from," Liza said, holding the hem of her dress down with one hand. "After this trip, I'll never again take restaurants for granted."

The comment reminded him of his mother's main complaint about the island—the lack of simple amenities. Kendall had never seen the issue, since Isle of Palms was only twenty minutes away. When Mom had lived in Charleston, they'd traveled twice as long, often in bumper-to-bumper traffic, to reach a destination.

He'd rather do twenty minutes on a ferry than forty on a crowded interstate.

"You know you can head over to the city any time, right?" he asked, feeling defensive.

Liza's smile remained in place as she held her chin high in the breeze. "I know, but then I'd miss the serenity of the island. Since I'm only here for two more weeks, I want to soak in as much as I can before going back to the chaos of New York."

Her response soothed his indignation and served as a reminder that their time together had an end date. Unless, like Ray's Essie, Liza might be patient enough to wait until Kendall was free to live elsewhere.

Sunlight streamed through the trees as they approached the landing. Kendall had called ahead to make sure the smaller boat would be waiting. After finding an empty parking spot, he escorted Liza down the walkway to find Chester waiting on them.

"A private boat?" Liza asked as they approached the smiling boat captain.

"No, this is just the one we use when there are fewer passengers." He held her hand as she climbed aboard the swaying vessel. "Watch your step." Both feet aboard, she waited for Kendall to get on. "Do you want to sit inside or up at the front?" he asked.

Swiping the hair from her eyes, she replied, "Inside would be better."

"Works for me."

As she disappeared inside, Chester cut off Kendall's entry. "Larimore called with a suggestion." The gray beard twitched as he winked. "Said you can thank him later."

Thank him for what? Kendall started to ask, but a cry from inside provided the answer.

"Champagne?" he heard Liza say, and rolled his eyes as the captain shuffled off to his post.

Kendall couldn't imagine where Chester had found the bubbly on such short notice, but he wouldn't put it past Larimore to have recruited other conspirators for his mission. First Aadi's gentle nudge, and now this. Shaking his head, Kendall stepped into the boat's interior, the prospect of moving away from his meddling neighbors growing more attractive by the minute.

❦

This was starting to feel like an honest-to-goodness date.

Liza couldn't remember the last time she'd had one but knew for certain it had not included a relaxing ferry ride and champagne.

Though, according to Kendall, the fancy drink had supposedly been a lucky break at the expense of a honeymooning couple who had canceled their reservation earlier in the day. She hoped because they hadn't wanted to leave the bedroom and not due to trouble in paradise.

They made the twenty-minute ride sipping bubbly and watching the scenery roll by. Sometimes open water, sometimes densely forested islands, but every shifting image as beautiful as the one before. Despite the mostly enclosed cabin, the wind still whipped through Liza's hair, cooling her cheeks and calming her worries.

"This is a lovely ride," she said, laying her head against the back of the cushioned bench seat. "The other ferry isn't nearly this comfortable."

Sitting across from her, Kendall swirled the drink around his plastic cup, seemingly distracted. "No, it isn't."

Assuming he was still concerned about Ray, she tried to distract him. "Is this a nice place we're going to?"

"Pretty nice, yeah."

His eyes lingered on the horizon, while his mind floated somewhere else.

"Do you take all your dates there?" Liza asked, hoping to snap him back to the moment.

Kendall turned her way, eyes narrowed, and she added, "I just wanted to see if you were paying attention. I know this isn't a date."

With slow movements, he slid the drink into a cupholder to his right and scooted forward on the seat. "We could make it a date."

Liza couldn't tell if he was teasing her. "Are you serious?"

He held her gaze. "Yeah, I'm serious."

The possible ramifications of her next response raced through Liza's mind, providing an endless array of reasons why crossing this line would be a bad idea. But as she stared into Kendall's eyes, recognizing the vulnerability that matched her own, she chose to ignore her head and listen to her heart.

"Okay, then. We're on a date."

His smile was slow and sensual as one capable hand reached her way. "In that case, you should come sit over here."

Tamping down the flutter of nerves lighting through her system, Liza slid her palm against his and joined her date on the opposite bench, snuggling close as one strong arm slid across her shoulders.

🦋

They were on a date. Not how Kendall had pictured the evening going, but he certainly wasn't about to complain.

She'd caught him off guard with the four-letter word, but then he'd picked up the inkling of interest in her expressive face. Not the lust that had darkened her eyes the night in Ray's kitchen, but something different. Something more.

When Liza had taken him up on the offer, Kendall felt as if he'd won a prize. And then she'd pressed against his side, and the world seemed to snap into place. As if the missing puzzle piece had been found.

A dangerous idea that he'd shoved to the back of his mind, in favor of simply enjoying the night ahead. Once they reached Isle of Palms, Liza headed for the tree-covered parking lot adjacent to the landing, but Kendall tugged her to the right.

"Aren't we driving?" she asked.

He pointed to the restaurant thirty yards away. "We're here."

She smiled with brows arched. "That's convenient."

Inside Morgan's, they were seated immediately, the hostess taking their drink orders before leaving them to peruse the menu.

"I'm starving, and this all looks so good."

"Is Ray not feeding you?"

She turned a page. "He wasn't hungry today, so we worked through lunch." Lowering the menu, Liza said, "Did you know that Ray ran with the bulls?"

That was news to Kendall. "Sounds like a stupid thing to do."

"Not to Ray. He makes it sounds like a great, joyous adventure." The menu lifted again. "Of course, he talks about everything that way. I've never met anyone with so much enthusiasm for life. He raved about eating crepes in Paris, pizza in Naples, and schnitzel in Frankfurt."

Kendall chuckled. "No wonder you're hungry."

"I'm serious. Why would a man so in love with life and adventure spend thirty years on Haven Island?"

For the love of something else was the true answer, but he wasn't at liberty to share that information. "Maybe he'd had enough adventure and wanted something more peaceful."

Liza considered the possibility. "I guess. He *was* in his sixties by the time he came here."

The waiter arrived to take their orders. Liza went with sliced ahi tuna to start, and the fried flounder for an entree. Kendall stuck with the usual—gator bites and the flounder po'boy.

"That might be the most southern meal I've ever heard anyone order," she whispered as the server walked away. "Please tell me gator bites are not really alligator."

"Yes, they are. And don't knock 'em until you've tried 'em."

"I'll stick with my tuna, thanks. Can I ask you something?"

Afraid another fib on Ray's account would be needed, Kendall braced himself. "Go for it."

"Is Aadi Patel single?"

Not the question he expected. "Yeah, why? Am I failing at this date thing already?"

A blush danced up her cheeks. "You're doing fine," she said, spreading the napkin in her lap. "I'm asking because I think Aadi and Francine are dating."

Now that was a new development. "What gives you that idea?"

Liza leaned forward and twirled the straw in her soda. "When I called Francine to tell her about Ray's episode the other night, it was late, and I could have sworn I heard Aadi's voice in the background."

Less than conclusive evidence. "She could have been watching television."

"I thought that, too, but when he showed up this morning to check on Ray, he smelled like Francine." She whispered that last part like a southern woman sharing gossip in church. "Like he'd used her soap or something."

If her assumption was correct, Kendall and Liza would not be dominating the gossip lines for long.

"Then I say good for them."

Her face lit up. "Right? They'd make an adorable couple. Francine is a sweetheart, despite what she pulled on Wednesday, and Aadi seems very nice."

Kendall paused with his beer halfway to his lips. "What happened on Wednesday?"

"Oh," she said, rolling her eyes, "let me share this fun story."

Liza recounted the Haven Island book-club meeting with full hand gestures and a detailed list of every disparaging word that was said about her book. Kendall had no doubt the conversation included plenty of positive comments as well, but Liza didn't share any of those.

"Could have been worse," he said once she'd run out of air.

"How?"

Kendall took his drink and set down the beer. "They could have hated it."

Liza's mouth snapped shut. "I just told you all the negative things they said. How do you know they didn't hate it?"

This was an easy one. "Because Francine would not have invited you to an all-out roasting of your book, *and* you dismissed three positive comments while telling that story."

"I what?"

"Bernadette loved it, but . . . ," he repeated, counting on his fingers. "Kathy said she couldn't put it down, but . . ." Kendall ticked off. "And Carrie let her kids run amok because she was too engrossed in the book to put it down. I don't remember how you dismissed that one, but I can spot a pattern when I see one. You, Liza Teller, cannot take a compliment."

Crossing her arms on the table, she slid a finger around the rim of her glass. "I can take a compliment."

"Okay, then." He went for the obvious. "You're beautiful."

Pink lips flattened. "Very funny."

"I'm not trying to be funny. You are beautiful."

The blush inched up her slender neck. "I'm okay-looking. On a good day."

Kendall sat back. "I rest my case."

"Come on," she said, defending herself. "You could have called me smart or kind or generous. Instead, you went with looks. That says more about you than it does about me, my friend."

She could deflect all she wanted, but Kendall wasn't giving up. "Why don't you think you're beautiful?"

"I didn't say—"

"*Okay-looking* is not the same as *beautiful*."

Glancing around to their fellow diners, she made a circle with one finger, eventually landing on her nose.

"You don't like your nose?" he guessed.

"Now you're getting it."

Kendall set down the beer and leaned forward. "Liza, there's nothing wrong with your nose."

She scoffed. "Easy for you to say. You don't have to wear it."

It wasn't the smallest nose he'd ever seen, but the centerpiece fit with her other features. "I like it."

"Well, I don't."

Trying a different approach, he said, "Fair enough. I don't like my ears."

Liza laughed, as he'd hoped she would. "There's nothing wrong with your ears."

"Look closely." Kendall tucked his hair back and kept his head straight.

Blue eyes narrowed as she studied him, and he knew the moment she saw it. "One is higher than the other."

He quickly covered them again. "Yep."

"Oh, Kendall. That isn't even noticeable."

"It is when you have a crew cut." He'd been tortured on the playground as a kid. Nicknamed Sloth at an early age after the character in *The Goonies*. And in a lady's company, he wouldn't repeat the jokes he'd gotten in the military. "So you don't like your nose, and I don't like my ears. That makes us even."

"Not even close," she argued. "I can't grow my hair long enough to cover my nose."

"Sure you can."

Her laughter drew the attention of other diners. "I could do what that pop singer does and hide my face behind wigs."

Kendall didn't know who she meant, but he went with it. "There you go. Problem solved."

The waiter arrived with their appetizers, and Liza caught her breath. Kendall liked her this way. Relaxed with an easy smile. Even a bit audacious, with the right encouragement. But what he really liked was how he felt when he was with her. A sense of peace mixed with the sudden urge to do better. To *be* better.

Once the waiter left, Liza cut into her starter but seemed to sense him watching her. "What?" she asked, checking for something on her face.

"You're good for me, Teller."

She blushed yet again, and the smile brightened her eyes. "That's a compliment I'm happy to accept."

Progress made, Kendall dug into his gator.

Chapter 16

Kendall James was living proof that first impressions could be overcome.

Dinner had passed with pleasant conversation and enough laughter to leave Liza's cheeks aching. Between the humorous stories about his fellow islanders and the earnest compliments on her appearance, Kendall had charmed her into almost forgetting his earlier behavior.

They'd shared a little more champagne on the ferry ride back, though just enough to tickle her tongue and not put her to sleep. After the filling meal, she was already feeling sleepy. But the best part of the evening had been the moonlit stroll along the water behind Ray's house.

At first, she'd been reluctant to venture into the dark—that is, until Kendall retrieved a flashlight from Ray's storage room and showed her there was nothing to fear. A gallant thing to do, but not nearly as gallant as how he'd carried her to the beach.

She'd removed her sandals and left them at the bottom of the stairs leading to her apartment, still trepidatious about what she might encounter in the brush between the house and the edge of the sand. When a twig snapped, causing her to leap backward after a single step, Kendall swept her into his arms, eliciting a yelp from Liza as she struggled to keep from flashing her panties to the world.

Clinging to his neck, she enjoyed the ride, feeling as if she were being saved by a dragon-slaying knight. Liza had never thought much of the damsels in distress portrayed so helplessly in books and movies, but cradled in Kendall's strong arms, she began to think those damsels were onto something.

Once they'd cleared the brush, he set her gently on her feet, keeping her hand in his as they strolled toward the water. Though not quite as bright as the week before, the moonlight reflecting off the waves was enough to illuminate their path, turning the sand a glistening shade of silver.

"As far as dates go," she said, "this one easily ranks in the top five."

"Top five? I was shooting for top three."

Liza squeezed his arm. "We can't score it too high. Then there's no room at the top for the next one."

Kendall moved a shell out of her way with his boot. "So there's going to be a next one?"

She hoped so. "That's up to you."

Without hesitation, he asked, "What are you doing tomorrow night?"

"Hmmm . . . A typical Saturday night would be painting my toenails while watching a *House Hunters* marathon," she answered honestly. "Do you have a better idea?"

Stopping at the water's edge, he pulled her against him, locking his hands at the small of her back. "I can think of a few things, though I bet you look sexy painting your toenails."

He did know how to make a girl blush. "If you really want to earn bonus points," she teased, "you could let me paint *your* toenails. I have an adorable shade of pink that would go perfectly with those work boots of yours."

Laughter rolled through his chest, stirring the night creatures from their hiding places. "If I agree to that, what do I get to do to you?"

A weighted question that brought several ideas to mind. None that she had the courage to mutter aloud. "What do you *want* to do to me?"

"Everything," he breathed, before locking his mouth over hers.

In an instant, Liza was lost. Kendall lifted her off the ground, and she wrapped her arms tightly around his neck, desperate for an anchor in the storm. His lips were sweet and hot, pecan pie mixed with raw need, and Liza would never look at dessert the same way again.

She whimpered when his mouth left hers to drop a trail of love bites across her jawline. Fingers deep in his hair, her toes curled when he nibbled her earlobe and whispered something she was too lost in desire to comprehend. Liza moaned as she tugged on his thick locks, and Kendall understood her plea.

Lips met once more, his tongue licking and teasing until one word echoed through her mind. *More.* More touch. More taste.

More Kendall.

Lungs burning, they both came up for air, panting as if they'd sprinted down the beach. Pressing his forehead to hers, he held her tight, her feet still hovering above the sand.

"I've been dying to do that."

Since the night she'd discovered him shirtless in the kitchen, so had she.

"I'm glad you did. I wasn't going to survive much longer, either."

His chuckle forced her to hold on tighter. "Good to know we're on the same page."

Liza slid a finger over his dimple. "Kendall?"

"Hmmm?" he mumbled.

"You can put me down now." Without warning, he twisted her sideways and slid his arm beneath her knees. "I said down, not up."

"Quiet, Teller. You're ruining the moment."

She squealed with laughter, tossed her head back, and spotted a sea of stars above. "Such a beautiful sky."

Kendall ducked a low branch to stop beneath the hanging palmettos. "Not as beautiful as you."

Staring into heavily lashed eyes lit only by the light of the moon, Liza's heart landed at Kendall's feet, leaving her incapable of stopping the flood of emotions crashing through her defenses. When they reached the house, instead of setting her down, he carried her all the way up the stairs.

At her door, he dropped Liza slowly to her feet before pulling her close. "Was that a yes on tomorrow?"

That was a yes on *more* than tomorrow, but she knew better than to say so. "Yes, it was."

"Good to know." Opening his hand to caress her cheek, Kendall brushed his nose across hers. "Your place or mine?"

Flattening her palms against his chest, she replied, "For what?"

His lips brushed hers, stealing her ability to think. "Tomorrow night."

"Oh." Liza tried to form a coherent answer, but when strong hands cupped her bottom, she tugged on his belt loops, urging him closer as her lips found the warm flesh beneath his ear.

Kendall lifted her high, pressing her back against the door, and on instinct, she locked her legs around his hips to grind against his erection.

Before she knew it, Liza had unbuttoned his shirt to trace her tongue down his neck. Her hands explored the dark fur dotting his chest, and she imagined how it would feel against her bare breasts. Muscled arms braced against the door behind her, Kendall let her have her way until his every muscle pulled tight with restraint.

"Baby, I can't take much more."

The strain in his voice brought Liza to her senses. "I'm sorry," she said, lowering her legs to the floor. "I got carried away."

He drew in a harsh breath, shaking his head. "You can get carried away anytime, but if we don't stop now, I won't be able to walk down those stairs."

Liza refastened the buttons. "I'm not feeling so steady myself."

Kendall tipped her chin up, and the care in his eyes touched something deep in her chest. "Tomorrow," he whispered, placing a soft kiss on the end of her nose.

Her heartbeat quickened as Liza began to wonder if she'd made a gross miscalculation. She knew she was leaving, and so did he. So what were they doing starting something that was destined to end?

Ray's words came back to her. *Stole my heart, right then and there.*

Liza lowered her head, and Kendall tensed, as if feeling her withdrawal. "Are you okay?"

She nodded, offering what she hoped was a convincing smile. "I am, but I think I'd better go in now." Liza needed to think, and she couldn't do so objectively with Kendall standing so temptingly near.

Warm breath rustled her curls as he sighed. "Yeah. Okay. I should go let Larimore know we're back anyway. Tomorrow, then?"

"Yes. Tomorrow."

Feeling as if she'd been cracked wide open, Liza watched Kendall make his way down the stairs and wave from the cart before driving around to the front of the house. After racing down to retrieve her forgotten sandals, she made her way inside as a reckless idea crept in.

Did she really have to leave?

Dropping to the sofa, she stared at the shoes in her hand, contemplating the answer. In New York was her father. The man she'd barely begun to know, who most days still felt like a stranger. There was also Vanessa and Granny's little apartment.

Granny's apartment. Not hers. The place had never truly felt like Liza's.

In New York, there was noise and pressure and . . . loneliness. A reality she rarely acknowledged, convinced that in time the feeling would fade. If she just waited long enough, her life would magically change.

Maybe that change had come in the form of an extraordinary little island.

Hopping to her feet, she rushed into the bedroom. Casting the sandals aside, she surveyed the options in her closet. Within minutes, a handful of dresses lay in a heap on the bed, each dismissed for one reason or another.

And then she spotted it. The dress she almost hadn't packed. Shorter and tighter than all the others, the simple sleeveless white sheath fit her body like a glove. Large blue-and-purple flowers blossomed across the bottom, accentuating the thigh-revealing scalloped hem.

Flipping the garment around, she remembered the day she'd tried it on. Due to the low positioning of the zipper, the dress left Liza's entire back exposed, turning her into a sex kitten she hadn't recognized in the mirror. But then Vanessa had looked up from her phone, gasped with approval, and refused to let Liza leave the store without it.

Carefully returning the dress to the closet, Liza took a deep breath, both frightened and exhilarated at the idea of spending the night with Kendall. Though he hadn't in any way implied that sex was an expected part of their date, she doubted he'd turn her down if she offered.

Shifting her glance to the dress-covered bed behind her, there was no question where the date would take place. Having sex with Kendall one floor above Ray was not going to happen. But then there was once again the issue of leaving Ray alone.

Liza checked the clock. A call to Francine would have to wait until morning. With luck, her new friend would be nice enough to play babysitter, though Ray would undoubtedly argue that he didn't need one.

Chapter 17

"I've got good news and better news," said Larimore when Kendall answered his phone, still groggy from a restless night.

He hadn't been kidding when he'd said he couldn't walk down the stairs. The drive home had been painful at best, and the lukewarm shower he'd taken before bed hadn't offered much relief. Lying awake, he'd replayed the night over and over in his mind, unable to decipher exactly what had shifted at the end.

"What time is it?" he asked, sitting up to lean against his headboard.

"An hour past time for your morning jog. Are you sick?"

Kendall didn't figure *sexually frustrated* fit in the same category as the common cold. As he checked the exact time on his phone, Amos bounded into the room and leaped on the bed, all his weight landing on an important part of his owner's anatomy.

"Jesus, dog. Watch what you're doing."

"Skipped your run *and* you're cranky. Someone didn't get laid last night."

"Hey," he snapped. "Not cool, dude."

Larimore took the reprimand in stride. "Crass on my part. Apologies. Now for the good news. We have a second offer on the house."

Lifting the hair from his eyes, Kendall lumbered to the back door to let Amos out. "How could we have a second offer when the place isn't even on the market?"

"The private-island business is hopping, buddy. But that's only the *good* news."

Aware of his friend's love of the dramatic, Kendall followed his cue. "What's the better news?"

"The second offer is a quarter million higher than the first one."

Good thing Kendall hadn't been standing far from the table. Falling into a chair, he did the math in his head. "That's crazy money."

The happy agent laughed. "Crazy *good*. I'm going to see if the first couple is willing to compete, but I wanted to update you first. You're about to be a whole lot richer, my friend."

Kendall didn't care much about money, but he'd also never been handed two million dollars all at once.

"Keep me posted."

"Will do."

The phone went dead as Kendall watched his dog toss a rubber dog toy into the air. The toy snapped in two, and Amos nudged both pieces with his nose, as if unsure which one to toss again.

"Don't worry, buddy. We can buy you another one."

Dropping the cell on the table, he crossed to the sink to start the coffee. He didn't drink the stuff daily, but today he needed the hit of caffeine. Before the pot could percolate, the phone buzzed on the table.

"That was fast." Assuming the first couple had backed out of the deal, Kendall picked up without checking the screen. "So we're down to one."

"One what?" replied a voice Kendall hadn't heard in months. "Is that how you answer a phone, young man?" Aunt Clarice was an advanced-level ballbuster, and she never missed an opportunity to bust his.

"Sorry. I thought you were someone else." Unlike with his friend, Kendall didn't feel comfortable talking to his mother's baby sister while wearing nothing but his boxer briefs. "Can you hold on a minute?"

"I'm only calling long distance from New York City. Sure. Put me on hold."

Kendall looked around for a quick fix. Returning to the table, he sat down and draped a kitchen towel over his lap.

"Never mind. How are you doing?"

"Better than your poor mother, and that's why I'm calling."

He bolted from the chair, ignoring the discarded towel. "What's wrong?"

"Relax, son. She's okay. For now."

These cryptic responses were getting him nowhere. "Clarice, tell me what's going on."

The older woman mumbled for her dogs to be quiet before returning to the call. "She had some sort of episode while playing cards. The other ladies thought she was having a heart attack and called 911. Thankfully, there was no heart attack, but the doctors found a murmur."

Again, Kendall sat. "What does that mean?"

"We don't know yet. She sees a cardiologist on Monday."

"When did this happen?"

"Last night. And if you called your mother more often, you'd know what night she plays cards."

Kendall wasn't in the mood for a lecture. "Where is she now?"

Clarice didn't answer right away. "They're keeping her in the hospital to run tests over the weekend. I asked if she wanted me to call last night, but she said not to bother you."

Damn stubborn woman. "You should have called."

"Well, I'm calling now." Never one to mince words, Clarice laid out her true feelings. "My sister gave up her home for whatever is so important on that godforsaken island. I don't know what you do down there, but it's a crying shame when a mother doesn't see the need in letting her own son know she's sick."

The line clicked dead, and Kendall pressed the phone against his forehead. He was not neglecting his mother, dammit. They talked every

Sunday, and at the end of every conversation, he asked if she needed anything. And like following a script, she assured him that she was fine and didn't need a thing.

Now he had to wonder how often that response had been a lie.

Amos scratched at the back door, jarring Kendall back to the present. Moving more from habit than conscious effort, he let the dog in, shut off the coffeepot, and fired off a text to his aunt asking for the name of the hospital. No response came.

Rubbing a hand over his face, he carried the phone to the bedroom, hoping he'd have an answer by the time he finished his shower.

❦

By Saturday morning, Ray appeared to have made a full recovery. Liza had slept like a baby and woke early, ready for breakfast. An empty milk jug sent her tiptoeing downstairs to fill her bowl, only to find her host dressed and soft-shoeing his way around the kitchen.

"You're looking much better today," she said.

"I feel better, too." He touched his hat brim in greeting. "You've got a pretty glow about you this morning, Liza Ruth. Does that mean dinner went well?"

"Dinner went very well, thank you." Remembering Ray had retired to the bedroom before Kendall had invited her to dinner, she asked, "How do you know about that?"

"Larimore," Ray replied, retrieving the eggs from the fridge.

Then Ray hadn't slept through the evening. That was a good sign. Setting her bowl on the island, Liza leaned her elbows on the smooth surface. "How's your head?"

"Oh, that's fine," Ray said, cracking eggs into a bowl. "Did I tell you about the time I had crepes at a lovely little café in Paris?"

He'd conveyed the story the day before. "We talked about that yesterday, remember?"

Bushy gray brows furrowed for only a second before he said, "That's right. No wonder I woke up craving them." With a flick of his wrist, he tossed a broken shell into the trash. "I've still got it."

Ray must have been such a fun dad. When Liza had asked if he had children, she'd learned that he had one son, but the two were estranged. She'd expressed hope they might resolve their differences, but Ray had been certain there was no chance of a reconciliation. Hopefully, he was wrong about that.

She watched him crack five more eggs and marveled at his renewed appetite. His impressive recovery eased her mind about leaving him for the evening. In fact, she decided she wouldn't mind having the day to relax and do a little primping before her date.

Since many of Ray's neighbors came to the island only on weekends, there was the possibility he might take the day off from their interviews in order to entertain.

"Is anyone coming over today?" she asked.

He drew a whisk from the utensil holder beside the stove. "Didn't I tell you?"

"Tell me what?" she asked.

"Jack and Wilma Forester are coming for breakfast. They'll be here any minute."

Liza rose off the stool. "No, you didn't tell me. Why didn't you warn me when I came down in my pajamas?"

He took in her outfit. "You look fine."

She looked like she'd just gotten out of bed, which she had.

When Liza darted from the kitchen, Ray called after her. "Where are you going?"

"To get dressed," she replied from halfway up the stairs. "I haven't even brushed my teeth!"

Hustling through the house, she stubbed her toe on an accent table and nearly fell into the screen door leading to her apartment. Hopping into her kitchen on one foot, Liza knocked the empty milk jug off the counter, spilling what little was left across the floor.

"For heaven's sake." Keeping her injured toe off the ground, she hobbled to the paper towels and yanked, bringing the entire roll off the dispenser. The towels unraveled into the living room, her pinkie-toe throbbed, and her nose still hurt from where she'd smacked the door.

This kind of start to the day did not bode well for her evening.

Liza dropped to the hardwood, ripped off two paper towels, and wiped up the milk. Once the mess had been cleaned, she lay back, hoping that a brief pause would reset her world. Eyes closed, she breathed deeply, letting the pain in her foot subside and praying that things would only improve from here.

❦

Kendall's day did not get any better.

The call with his mom ended the same way every other conversation did—son offering to help, and mother insisting that she didn't need it. When he offered to fly up in time for the cardiologist appointment on Monday, she argued that he shouldn't spend the money. When Kendall pressed, assuring her he could afford the flight, she implied that he would only be in the way.

Sometimes he preferred Clarice's more direct approach to his mother's brush-offs.

Exhausted, Kendall gave up, but he sent his aunt a text to call him the minute they spoke to the doctor. If the news was bad, he'd catch the first flight out of Charleston whether his mother liked it or not.

Following the downhill trend, his dryer stopped drying, Amos busted a lamp while chasing his own tail, and Kendall nearly had a heart attack of his own when a wayward bird slammed into his sliding glass door. The carnage had been especially gruesome, making the cleanup an experience he'd be happy never to repeat.

The one positive had been his call to Liza.

"Hello?" she answered, her voice alone brightening his day.

"Hey. It's Kendall."

"Oh, hi."

He'd hoped for more enthusiasm after last night. "How is Ray?"

"Better," she said. "I found him dancing around the kitchen this morning."

"Dancing?" He hadn't even been able to stand on his own not twenty-four hours ago.

"I was surprised, too, but he was like a new man. Bright-eyed and whipping up breakfast for the Foresters."

"Jack and Wilma are here?"

"I think that's what he called them. Then a Mr. Drummand came for lunch, and he's hosting someone else this evening, but I forget the name." Liza's tone was clipped, as if Kendall were bothering her. He was about to let her go when she said, "Dang it."

"Are you okay?"

A sigh carried down the line. "Not really. Have you ever had a day when everything went wrong?"

Funny she should ask. "I can relate to that, yeah."

"At this point, I wouldn't be surprised if a meteor took me out. The headline would read 'Extreme Klutz Dies of Bad Luck.'"

Kendall smiled for the first time that day. "How about we skip the meteor and I make you dinner?"

"You cook?" she asked, sounding as if he'd said he could fly. At least he'd finally earned her full attention.

"I'm a thirty-four-year-old bachelor. Of course I cook."

Sufficiently contrite, Liza said, "I guess I shouldn't assume that all men live on frozen dinners and takeout."

"Takeout is hard to come by around here."

"Good point." Papers rustled on the other end. "I'm organizing some notes while Ray prepares for his guest—or will be when I get this recorder to work—but I can set them aside whenever. What time should I come over?"

He checked the clock on the stove. "How about forty-five minutes?" That gave him enough time to marinate the shrimp and get the pasta on to cook.

"From now?" she squeaked.

Good thing he hadn't gone with his first thought and said *right away*. "Too soon?"

"Um . . . no. Forty-five minutes is fine." More rustling ensued before he heard a thud.

"What was that?"

"I dropped my laptop." Sounding hurried, she said, "I need to jump in the shower if I'm going to be there in less than an hour."

"No rush. Come over when you're ready." He supposed it couldn't hurt to drop the pasta once she got there. Cooking *with* her might be even better than cooking *for* her. More time for a proper hello that way.

"No, no. I can do this." Another thud. "Son of a—"

Kendall had never heard Liza use language like that. "Are you trying to kill that computer?"

"That was my bag," she said, clearly spoken through clenched teeth. "Who needs ten working toes anyway, right?"

Next time he'd let her pick the time. "I'll have an ice pack ready when you get here."

"Thanks. I'm going to need it."

Liza hung up without saying goodbye, leaving Kendall staring at his phone. "Maybe my day hasn't been so bad, after all." The moment the words crossed his lips, a crash sounded from the bedroom. "Come on!" he yelled, charging off to see what Amos had done now.

Chapter 18

"So help me, cart, if you even think about breaking down, I will not be responsible for my actions."

Liza had made it to the end of Ray's driveway before the blasted thing had stalled out. Assuming that golf carts worked the same as anything else, she turned it off, waited several seconds, and turned it back on again. The motor fired right up, and to her relief, the cart rolled into motion the moment she pressed the gas.

Torn between reaching Kendall's at his requested time and preserving her date-night look, she drove at a moderate-enough pace for the wind to chill her cheeks but not whip her curls into a mess. At her destination, Liza parked in front of the garage door, just as Kendall had nearly a week ago, and exited the cart.

After running a quick hand through her hair to dislodge the few tangles caused by the drive over, she hurried up the stairs, giving the time a quick check on her phone. Only five minutes late. Not bad considering how high up her thighs she'd had to shave.

Pausing at the door for one last deep breath, she knocked three times, instantly insecure about her outfit choice. What if Kendall was wearing shorts and a ratty old T-shirt? Liza would feel like an idiot, looking as if she'd dressed for a night out in Manhattan.

Not that she spent many nights out in Manhattan. Or any, for that matter.

Before she could beat a hasty retreat, her date opened the door wearing dark jeans and a black button-down shirt with the sleeves rolled to his elbows, revealing muscled forearms that did funny things to her insides.

What was it about those flexing muscles that pushed a girl's buttons? Whatever it was, Kendall had it in abundance.

The part of his ensemble she hadn't expected was the full-length apron hanging from neck to knees, reading IF YOU'RE GOOD, I'LL LET YOU LICK MY BEATERS.

"Nice apron," she said, forgetting any concerns about her own choice of clothing. "That's an enticing offer."

Mouth gaping, Kendall stood motionless in the doorway, offering neither a greeting nor an invite to come in.

"I got ready as fast as I could," she said. "I hope my timing didn't mess up dinner."

"Yes," he said. "I mean, no. You're right on time."

Liza couldn't tell whether he liked the dress or not, but feared she'd gone too far.

"Can I come in?" she asked.

"I have a better idea."

Instead of stepping aside to let her pass, Kendall joined her on the porch, strong hands caressing her face as his lips lowered to hers. In contrast to the feverish kisses of the night before, this one built slowly, with long, drawn-out moments of perfection that muddled her senses and turned her limbs to jelly.

Drawing back, he flashed a wickedly sexy grin. "You're gorgeous."

Relief weakened her knees even more. "Thank you. I was hoping you'd like it."

"*Like* is an understatement." A timer went off inside, and Kendall ushered her in, catching his first glimpse of the back of the dress. Or lack thereof. "Damn," he whispered, a trace of awe in his voice. Grasping her hips, he pulled her back against him as the timer beeped again.

"Shouldn't you get that?" Liza asked, slanting her head as he kissed her neck.

Kendall buried his face in her shoulder. "You even smell fantastic."

Speaking of smells. "Is something burning?"

"Shit." Sliding around her, he raced to the kitchen, lifting a pan off the stove with one hand and turning the timer off with the other. "Looks okay," he said, surveying the contents of the frying pan. "A little singe on the shrimp, but not too bad."

"Shrimp, huh?" Liza inspected the other items on the stove. "Does that go in the pasta?"

"Yes, ma'am. Toss it all together, add a little Parmesan, and we're ready to eat."

Now that the pan was off the heat, a more tantalizing smell filled the air. "Quite impressive, Mr. James. What other talents are you hiding?"

Placing a quick kiss on her lips, he murmured, "I make a pretty good cheesy omelet."

An excellent reason to stay for breakfast. "I'd love to try it sometime." *Sometime* being in about twelve hours.

Working the kitchen like a pro, Kendall set the frying pan on a back burner, drained the pasta, combined the ingredients with a practiced hand, and sprinkled cheese over the delicious-looking concoction.

"Dinner is served."

She turned to find the table already set, tall candles burning in the center and napkins folded neatly on the plates. Crossing to take her seat, she spotted Amos looking pitiful on the other side of the glass door.

"Should I let him in?" she asked, surprised she hadn't noticed his absence before now.

"Absolutely not."

"But the coyotes . . ."

"Don't come this close to the water." He placed the pasta dish on the table. "That dog has broken two lamps today. His ass can stay outside."

Liza tried to ignore the exiled beast, but he kept watching her with those pleading puppy-dog eyes. Her heart couldn't take it. "Kendall, I can't eat with him looking so sad and dejected. Look at him. He's totally calm. I'm sure he'll be good now."

Her host carried two bottles of soda to the table. "What happened to the woman who wouldn't get in a golf cart with that animal?"

That woman had changed quite a bit over the last two weeks. "Come on, Kendall. Look at his sweet face."

As if he knew redemption was in sight, Amos lifted his head, tilted it to one side, and rolled his expressive brows in an obvious display of repentance.

Kendall set the drinks on the table and ran a hand through his hair. "If I let him in, no feeding him under the table. He's spoiled enough as it is."

Schooling her features, Liza said, "Would I do that?"

"Hell yes. Don't think I don't know what you give him when I'm not around."

A little ham wasn't going to hurt anyone. "I don't know what you're talking about."

"Sure you don't." Kendall opened the door, and an excited Amos ran straight for Liza. She greeted him with a thorough scratch behind the ears before his owner ushered him from the room. "Come on, boy. You can stay in the bedroom until after dinner."

Liza felt good about her victory on the dog's behalf and settled into her chair feeling even better about the night ahead. So far, she'd managed to reach Kendall's house without any catastrophes, and the dress had been a success. Now to make it through the impending meal without wearing her food.

When Kendall returned, apron now removed, he caught her stealing a piece of shrimp from the bowl. "Good, isn't it?" he asked, joining her at the table as if they did this every day. "Take as much as you want."

Careful not to knock over a candle, she scooped a spoonful of pasta onto her plate before handing over the ladle and accepting the basket of bread he passed her way.

"That's all you're taking?" Kendall asked, heaping two helpings onto his own plate.

"This is enough," she said, preferring not to eat herself into a coma before endeavoring to seduce her dinner-mate. Liza had never seduced anyone in her life, and even thinking about trying to do so was making her nervous. The one time she could have used a little liquid courage and she found herself staring down a glass of soda. "I'm surprised you aren't serving wine."

Loading up his fork, Kendall replied, "You don't like wine."

Liza froze. "How do you know that?"

Her dinner partner shrugged. "You didn't have any on movie night, despite having a dozen bottles to choose from, and you didn't order any last night."

Quite observant of him. "Thank you for noticing."

"I also noticed the faces you made that first night at Ray's when he served you a glass."

Oh no. "Was it that obvious?"

One corner of his mouth curled up as he twirled pasta around his fork. "If you'd puckered any harder, I was afraid you were going to swallow your lips."

Well, crap. "That means I must have looked like an idiot at all those cocktail parties."

"Cocktail parties?"

Liza pushed a shrimp around her plate. "When my book came out, Vanessa—that's my agent—dragged me to half a dozen cocktail parties where everyone drank wine and talked about wine and waxed poetic about wine. At the first party, I walked around with a glass of water, and they all gawked at me as if I'd spit in the canapés."

"So you walked around with a glass of wine."

She pointed with her fork. "Exactly. A glass I *pretended* to drink, which resulted in my being parched by the end of the evening, but at least I was no longer the outcast with uncivilized tastes."

Kendall shook his head. "I'd rather be the outcast." Easy for him to say. He wasn't a debut author trying to earn credibility with the New York literati. Setting down his fork, he asked, "What's the point, anyway?"

Now he'd lost her. "The point of what?"

"Trying to fit in. You're obviously better than those pretentious assholes. Where do they get off making you feel like a turd in the punch bowl?" Not exactly how Liza had phrased it, but just as accurate.

Initially taken aback by his reaction, she belatedly realized he was angry on her behalf. How incredibly sweet.

"No one had outright insulted me. And maybe if I'd been more confident, I'd have tolerated the judgmental looks and stuck with the water. So really, I'm the problem here."

"You are not the problem."

Liza begged to differ, but Kendall said, "You haven't pretended to like the stuff here. Not since that first night, anyway. That makes the snobs at those parties the problem."

Liza had to admit, he had a point. She'd felt the pressure to fit in, in New York. Here on Haven, she didn't feel pressure at all.

"Some of them were nice," she felt the need to add, as a few of the individuals she'd met *had* been very kind. "But there *were* a lot of pretentious people at those parties. And I bet I wasn't the only guest there who didn't like wine."

"I'd be surprised if you were. I can't stand the stuff."

Liza had been well aware that she felt different on Haven than she had in the city, but she'd failed to recognize how different. Here, she could breathe, and not only because of the clean air. In the three short days since the book-club meeting, Liza had jotted down nearly a dozen plot ideas, and she was actually excited about several of them.

It was as if the fog that had settled over her brain had finally cleared. Throughout the day, as she'd worked on Ray's memoir, Liza had found herself stopping several times, drawn by one shiny new idea or another. Her fingers itched to dive into one in particular, igniting an excitement she'd feared might never return.

Trying to be practical, Liza took a breath and reminded herself that two weeks on Haven Island wasn't nearly long enough to make the kind of decision she was considering. What if she was wrong? What if she moved, and in three months, she hated it? Or couldn't write in the new setting any more than she could write in New York?

"There's a cookout up at the Welcome Center next Saturday," Kendall said, eyes on his food. "Nothing too fancy. Burgers and dogs, and a little dancing in the evening." Brown eyes met hers. "Want to go with me?"

Liza had been around the natives long enough to know that she'd be welcome at such an event with or without Kendall's invitation. But the invitation meant something. It meant letting everyone he knew and cared about know that they were venturing beyond friendship.

Just like that, Liza's doubts fell away.

"I'd like that," she replied, holding his warm gaze. "Thanks for asking."

Kendall grinned and his shoulders visibly relaxed. "Good." He returned his attention to his meal, repeating, "That's good."

🦋

"Thank you for the delicious meal," Liza murmured as Kendall loaded the dishwasher. She carried the large serving dish and basket of bread to the counter. "If you point me to the storage bowls, I'll empty this dish for you."

"Bottom shelf of the pantry. Right side." As she moved gracefully across his kitchen, Kendall hoped she wouldn't be in a hurry to leave. He only had two more weeks to give her a reason to wait for him. To wait until he was free.

"This one?" she asked, holding a glass bowl with a dark-blue lid.

"That works."

They worked in silence, side by side, arms brushing now and then. Appreciative smiles were exchanged. When she stepped closer to rinse the heavy bowl, Kendall gave in to temptation and dropped a kiss on the delicate skin beneath her ear. Liza bit her bottom lip but didn't respond, and he opted not to push his luck.

Once the dishwasher was loaded, she asked, "Should I let Amos out of the bedroom?"

Kendall had been too distracted by the beautiful woman in his kitchen to remember his troublesome dog. "Yeah, go ahead and let him out."

She slipped from the room, taking her subtle scent with her, and Kendall took the opportunity to tighten his control. The last thing he needed was for her to think he was only after one thing. Like getting her out of that dress and driving into her until she screamed his name.

"Not helping, dumbass."

"What was that?" Liza asked, opening the sliding glass door for Amos.

"Nothing," Kendall replied, sounding like a twelve-year-old caught with a dirty magazine.

Liza pointed toward the door. "Do you mind if I step outside? I know you can't see the sunset from here, but I've grown to love this time of the evening, when the air cools and all the creatures fill the silence."

Kendall could use a cool breeze himself. "I'll come out with you."

Instead of going out before him, she waited and took his hand to step out together. Amos had already located his favorite toy—a colorful stretch of rope with a small tire on the end—and was tossing it in the air.

"He's a happy dog," she said, stopping at the edge of the porch. "That's a testament to you." Liza turned his way. "You're a good man, Kendall."

Warmed by the sentiment, he squeezed her hand. "That's not what you were saying a couple of weeks ago."

Her laughter mixed with the night sounds, as natural in the setting as any of the others. "Very true. I just needed a little more time to get to know you." His sentiment exactly. "You know, you forgot an important part of dinner."

Kendall ran through the meal, trying to think of what he'd overlooked. "What was that?"

Closing the space between them, Liza wound her arms around his neck and rose up on her tiptoes. "Dessert."

◆

The moment Liza pressed her lips to his, Kendall pushed her back against the wooden post, his body hot and hard against hers as he drove her mad with his touch. Gentle hands explored her back and hips and every curve in between. The dress shifted higher when he pressed a denim-clad thigh between hers.

Their tongues entwined, sucking and licking, both of them giving as much as taking, but when Liza slipped the hem of his shirt from his jeans, Kendall pulled away.

"Are you sure you want to do this?" he asked, breathing heavy but holding his body in check.

"Yes," she gasped, sliding her hands beneath the soft cotton. "Yes."

Thankfully, Kendall didn't need any further convincing. When they reached his bedroom, Amos whimpered in protest as the door slammed in his face.

"That wasn't very nice," Liza teased, struggling with the buttons of his shirt. Impatient, Kendall tugged the black button-down over his head and tossed it into the corner. Like the night she'd found him half-naked in Ray's kitchen, her body tightened with need. "You're so perfect," she whispered, aching to feel him against her, skin on skin.

Eyes dark with desire, Kendall ignored the compliment, pulling her to him and reaching around to find the zipper on her dress. But instead of freeing her from the garment, he searched her gaze. "We don't have to do this, Liza. This isn't why I brought you here."

She appreciated his need to have her full consent, but right now, Liza needed him to move things along. Cupping his face in her hands, she pressed a kiss to his lips. "I want you, Kendall. All of you."

As if she'd found the magic words, Kendall kissed her back, his arms tightening before he finally loosened the dress, which fell forward off Liza's shoulders. His thumb rubbed across one nipple, and her body rocked.

"Is that good?" he asked. She nodded, unable to speak. "What about this?" Slowly, Kendall bent to lick her nipple, hands firm against her bottom, holding her core against his erection.

"Oh God." Liza's head dropped back, the curls tickling the small of her back.

Kendall sucked harder, heightening the pressure pooling between her legs. Running on instinct, she ground against him, mindless with overwhelming need. When he slid her thong aside to caress her wet folds, Liza's body tensed with instant release, forcing her to cling to his shoulders or land in a heap at his feet.

Lungs burning, she rode out the last shivers of orgasm seconds before Kendall shifted just enough to let the dress fall away. Left with nothing but her lacy thong, Liza expected to feel vulnerable and exposed, but instead she felt cherished. Powerful. Sated.

"You're very good at this," she purred.

"I can do better."

Kendall walked forward, urging her along until a soft material touched the backs of her knees. Still amazed she'd had her first orgasm before they'd even reached the bed, she sat down and scooted back, but before he could join her, she rose to kneel before him.

"Not so fast." Reaching for the button on his jeans, she held his gaze. "These need to come off."

"I'm good with that."

Liza lowered the zipper as he'd done for her and tugged the denim over his hips, taking his gray boxer briefs, too. What she revealed took her breath away as Kendall stood before her, hard and pulsing and igniting her arousal once more.

"You approve?" he asked.

Lowering to the bed, she laid her head on a pillow and smiled. "Wholeheartedly."

He removed his jeans the rest of the way before crawling up to join her. Kneeling between her feet, he removed her thong and kissed his way from her toes to her navel. By the time he reached her breasts, Liza was a whimpering mess.

"Those whimpers are driving me crazy," he said against her collarbone. When he settled hard and hot between her thighs, whimpers turned to moans. "That's even better."

Liza was only vaguely aware of his movements as Kendall reached for the nightstand, mostly because his other hand had reached her clit, and his talented fingers were driving her close to the precipice once again. Knees bent, she waited impatiently as he slid the condom into place and braced above her.

Eyes locked, he entered her, hot and hard and way too goddamn slow.

"Kendall, please."

"What, baby?" he asked, voice hoarse as he withdrew.

She clamped her hands on his ass. "All of it. I need all of it."

"Yes, ma'am."

Loosening the reins on his control, Kendall gave Liza exactly what she'd asked for. Hard and fast, deeper with every thrust until she cried out his name. Fire lit through her veins as she sank her teeth into her bottom lip, arching her hips as mind-numbing pleasure shot through her limbs. Liza's body shattered beneath him, and before she'd crested the last wave, Kendall growled with his own release, muscles taut, taking them both through the storm.

Chapter 19

Kendall's day hadn't started this well in a long time. Maybe ever.

Blonde curls splayed across his arm as Liza's cheek rested on his chest. His body still hummed with satisfaction, yet the whisper of her breath across his sternum provoked a carnal response he doubted the sheets would hide for long.

Amazing sex wasn't a new experience for Kendall, but burying himself in Liza shot well past amazing. Considering she'd screamed his name no less than three times, he felt confident she approved of his performance.

Kendall planned to let her sleep, but when Liza stretched, a purr escaping her lips, he kissed the top of her head. "Morning, baby." Shifting his weight, Kendall lifted her to lie atop him, his dick jumping in response, and her eyes opened wide.

"Good morning to you," she drawled, dropping a smooth thigh over his hip.

Cupping her bottom, he nipped at her lower lip. "You up for another round?" The other thigh rubbed the length of him as she nipped him back.

"Not if I want to walk out of this room at some point."

"Who said you have to leave?" The question took Kendall by surprise, especially coming from his own lips, but Liza didn't flinch.

"Finishing the interviews with Ray while lying naked in your bed would be more than a little awkward." Flicking his nipple with her tongue, she said, "But there are other ways to take care of this." Grasping his dick, she slid farther down his torso until her chin rested at his navel. "Should I show you?"

Warm lips caressed his abs before she pressed his dick between her breasts. Kendall nodded his approval as his hands clutched her hair.

"Is that a yes?" she murmured, gliding him up and down her cleavage.

Kendall groaned, and Liza progressed to massaging his balls while sliding her tongue down his shaft. His hips drove up as his body locked, every muscle anticipating what would come next. She took the opportunity to fondle his ass, taking him in, surrounding him to the hilt.

He told himself to lie still. To let her have her way. But his control hung by a string as she sucked him hard, sliding her nails down his inner thighs. Kendall lifted, mindless with desire as every nerve in his body vibrated on a razor's edge. The quiver started behind his knees, rolled into his groin, and exploded like a lightning strike, blasting through his limbs as if he'd touched a live wire.

Sparks still rippled through his system as Liza crawled back up his body, dropping a series of kisses along the way.

"Feel better now?" she asked, kissing his chin.

Wrapping her in his arms, he didn't know whether to laugh or cry. "Like I've been gutted and set on fire, but in a good way." Her giggle made him smile. "Thank you," he mumbled, rolling to his side and tossing a leg over hers.

Cuddling into his chest, she whispered, "Any time."

🦋

Once they were finally out of bed and dressed, which took several more hours, the day took a turn for the worse.

"The battery's dead," Kendall declared when Liza's cart refused to start. "I should have come down and plugged it in."

Though she'd planned to spend the night in Kendall's bed, she hadn't counted on staying half the next day. Not that she regretted a single moment of the last twenty-four hours, but Liza was now without a cart and in desperate need of a shower.

Kendall had offered his, of course, but she also needed clean clothes, and those were at her place. Why she hadn't packed a bag, Liza couldn't say, but she wouldn't make that mistake again.

"I'll run you home while the battery charges," Kendall said, playing her knight in shining armor once again.

"Thank you. If you let me know when it's fixed, I'll find someone to bring me back for it later."

He looked as if she'd insulted his manhood. "Why would you call someone else? I'll come back for you when it's ready."

To think she'd considered him an ogre two weeks ago. "That works, too."

Matter settled, Kendall led her to his cart around the side of the house. With her shoes in her hand, Liza took extra care to watch where she stepped, catching the subtle movement of what looked like an inno-cent stick seconds before the strike came.

Screaming, she leaped to the side, landing on a sharp rock that made her cry out in pain.

"What?" Kendall said, watching her hop on one foot as she tried to spot her attacker.

"A snake! Didn't you see that? It nearly bit me." Too freaked out to think, she jumped onto the seat of the cart, gripping the shoes to her chest. "Amos, get back! Where did the damn thing go?"

If she hadn't been scared out of her mind, Liza might have tem-pered her reaction. But a close encounter with a snake seemed like probable cause to *lose her shit*.

"Liza, it's okay." Kendall tried to examine her feet. "Did he get you?"

"Don't step there!" She pointed to the spot the snake had been. "Are you trying to get yourself killed? You can't die and leave me alone with that monster. What the hell is wrong with you?"

To her utter amazement, he laughed at her. "Honey, it's okay. You probably scared the snake more than he scared you."

Liza stomped on the seat. "Does that look possible to you?"

Kendall held up his hands. "Okay. Look." Scanning the area, he picked up a stick, and Liza nearly screamed at him again. Thankfully, this one really was a stick, and he used it to scrape the area where she'd pointed. "No snake. See? He's long gone."

She didn't believe him. What if the sneaky thing was under the cart, waiting for a second chance to strike?

"Keep looking."

"But it's—"

"Keep looking!"

Pinching the bridge of his nose, Kendall took a deep breath. "If he were still here, Amos would have let us know by now."

Clinging to the roof of the cart, she remained skeptical. "Are you sure?"

Nodding, he moved closer. "Come down from there."

"I'm never coming down again." He could drive her like this, and she'd leap off to land on her steps. No more touching the ground.

Scraping a hand down his face, Kendall's eyes dropped to her feet. "Babe, you're bleeding."

Liza glanced down to see red splotches all over the seat. "What—?" Lifting her foot, she spotted a dark gash across her heel. "I'm bleeding!"

"We need to get you back inside." Kendall swept her off the cart and into his arms. They were halfway to the stairs before she thought to cover her private area, which she was once again flashing to the world. "You can't walk around out here without shoes on. What's wrong with you?"

Right. A snake tries to bite her and she was supposed to be calm. A little blood, and Kendall got to be Mr. Panic Attack.

"I'm fine," Liza insisted. "My foot doesn't even hurt." That might have been the adrenaline talking, but she really couldn't feel it.

"You're bleeding, dammit."

Yeah. She got that. Kendall carried her into the house and charged into his bedroom, setting her down gently before rushing into the bathroom. He returned seconds later with a first-aid kit and emptied the contents onto the bed next to her.

After ripping a packet open with his teeth, he lifted her foot and dabbed at it with a moist cloth. Liza hissed when the pain shot up her leg.

"I'm sorry, baby, but we have to get this clean."

Liza endured his ministrations, flinching as little as possible. When he felt confident that the wound was clear of debris, he gently applied a bandage.

Doctoring over, he knelt on the floor in front of her. "Is there a snake phobia you want to tell me about?"

This was *not* a matter of *her* withholding pertinent information. "Is there a snake population you *failed to mention?*"

Kendall set the kit aside and sat down gingerly beside her, brushing a curl off her cheek. "We're in the South Carolina Lowcountry. I thought snakes were a given."

"I didn't get that memo." Now that the frenzy was over, the pain she hadn't noticed before made itself known. "I'm not having a very good weekend," she said, dropping back on the bed.

"Really?" he asked, clearly offended.

Liza waved her hand in the air. "Except for that, of course. That was great. But yesterday I sprained two toes, spilled milk across my kitchen floor, destroyed a paper-towel holder, and nearly broke my brand-new laptop." She lifted her damaged foot. "Now this. I really am afraid of what might happen next."

Taking pity on her, Kendall rose from the bed and extended a hand. "Next is a nice hot bath while I find you something else to put on.

When you get out, we'll dig into the chocolate ice cream in the freezer, and by the time we're done with that, your cart should be ready to go."

He really was perfect. "You're my hero, Kendall James."

Lifting her off the bed, he helped her hobble into the bathroom. "Anything for a damsel in distress."

🦋

The house felt empty. One day. That's all it had taken for Liza Teller to turn his life upside down.

Not that they hadn't been leading up to this since the night she'd arrived. Kendall knew now what he hadn't been able to admit the day he spotted her on that ferry landing. The way she'd smiled. The way his chest had tightened and the hairs stood up on the back of his neck. His heart had recognized what he'd stumbled into even if his head hadn't.

"Let me get this straight," Larimore said. "This is Aadi's fault?"

Kendall was going to need another beer if this kept up.

"Not his fault, but he's the one who put the idea in my head." Not completely accurate, but who knows how long this development would have taken without Aadi's uninvited nudge.

"By telling you to have sex with Liza Teller?"

Make that six more beers. Leaning forward, he tried talking slower. "Aadi never mentioned Liza." Or did he? Kendall couldn't remember. "He pointed out that I'm not getting any younger, and that if I want more from life than watching Amos lick his balls, I should probably get my ass up and do something."

Larimore pondered that statement for a minute. "Seems like sound advice. So you did something. You did the writer. I'm still not seeing the problem here."

"We're talking about my life," Kendall corrected. "Not my weekend."

The blank stare returned.

"Liza is leaving in a couple of weeks. She was never supposed to be a permanent option."

Kendall could almost see the wheels turning.

"Oh, shit." Finally. The light dawned. "She's the one?"

"She might be," he hedged, knowing full well that she was. "But Liza lives in New York, and I live here."

"You're talking to a real estate agent, buddy. People move all the time. Say the word and I'll find you an agent in the city with one phone call."

"I can't leave the island. Not yet, anyway."

"Then ask her to move here," Larimore suggested.

That was the last thing Kendall would do. "That isn't going to happen. Especially after that snake encounter this afternoon."

"Snake?" Larimore scanned the ground around his lawn chair. "I hate those damn things."

"Apparently, so does Liza. She thought one came at her over by the garage." He still wasn't convinced that she saw anything more than a twig, but Kendall wasn't about to tell her that. "I thought she was going to rip my arm off, and while hopping around, she ended up stepping on something sharp. The cut wasn't bad enough for stitches, but she'll be hobbling for a few days."

"Sounds painful. But remind me again why you can't go to her?"

"She's working on her notes for Ray's book tonight."

Larimore rolled his eyes. "Now who can't keep up? I mean, why can't you leave the island? Not that I'd be happy to see you go, but there's nothing keeping you here. I can handle the rentals, and with the money from the sale, you'd have plenty of cash on hand to get a nice place."

It wasn't that easy. "Ray is here."

"Ray has Francine and Aadi and two dozen other locals to watch out for him. New York has Liza *and* your mom. I'm not saying set sail tomorrow, but come on, man. This is a no-brainer."

Kendall actually agreed with his friend's assessment. All but the part about someone else taking care of Ray. He may have looked good to

Liza the day before, but his health had been too erratic to pretend the man wasn't on the decline.

"This is all premature, anyway," Kendall said, determined not to get ahead of himself. "For all I know, I'm just a vacation fling she can tell her friends about."

Larimore leaned back in his chair and closed his eyes. "I wouldn't mind being somebody's vacation fling."

Though his friend didn't live the same hermit life Kendall did, he'd been in a dry spell since the first of the year. "I hear there's a group of ladies staying over on lot twenty-nine."

With a sigh, Larimore shook his head. "They're all married. I checked."

Kendall tapped his friend on the leg. "Sorry, buddy. Maybe next week."

Chapter 20

Life was funny sometimes.

Though Liza had intended to spend her evening setting up a time line for Ray's memoir based on the notes she had so far, her brain would not cooperate. Instead, she'd spent the last hour playing with her new plot ideas.

The concept with the most promise was the black comedy inspired by the twins, Kathy and Tabby. But then she'd been drawn to the plight of a single mother fighting to survive with four kids and a deadbeat ex—an idea that had the potential to spawn a series, provided Liza littered the story with other strong women looking for their own happy ending.

The plot that surprised her was the murder mystery, involving a book club, a bespectacled librarian with a mean side, and an author who uses clues from classic literature to solve crimes. Grimacing, she scratched out *bespectacled*, partly to avoid giving Marcelo the impression she'd turned him into a villain.

Whether she could pull off a mystery or not was yet to be seen, but even if she didn't pursue that particular plot, Liza wanted to read the story badly enough that she contemplated passing the idea on to Vanessa for a client who might do the book justice. No pun intended.

As if these weren't enough to get her started, somewhere between dinner with Kendall—followed by other more energetic activities—and being hobbled by the snake encounter, her list of ideas had doubled. Good in one way but bad in another.

Good that she might actually manage to save her fiction-writing career. Bad when she was supposed to be focused on the book currently under construction.

"I have provisions for the invalid!" called Francine through the open door leading to Ray's part of the house. Liza had been leaving the door open to hear if Ray called for her. Or, heaven forbid, she heard a noise that might be him falling and needing help. Though how she would hobble down the stairs in a hurry, she wasn't sure.

"You didn't have to do that," Liza replied, not meaning a single word coming out of her mouth. She'd already resisted the urge to call Kendall to ask if he'd bring her chocolate, hesitant to take advantage of their new, more intimate status to send him out on a honey-do errand. "But I'm grateful you did."

She lowered her foot off the chair she'd been using as a stool, intending to meet her benefactor at the kitchen island.

"Don't move, young lady. I have strict orders to make sure you keep that foot up and your butt in a chair."

"I told Ray I was fine," Liza argued. "He shouldn't have called you."

"Ray didn't call me." Francine smiled like the Cheshire Cat. "Kendall did."

Just the mention of his name sent heat dancing up Liza's cheeks. "Kendall called you?"

An array of candy bars, chips, soda, and ice cream was pulled from the brown paper bag. "Yes, ma'am. And he was explicit in his instructions. Foot elevated. Butt planted. Woman pampered. In that order." Adding a bottle of wine to the collection of snacks, she added, "This is for me." Sliding the ice cream into the freezer, Francine said, "If I didn't know better, I'd think Mr. James has a thing for you."

Liza wasn't fooled. "The whole island knows, don't they?" And she wasn't talking about her injury.

"It's all anyone can talk about." Francine tossed a bag of chocolate peanut butter candies onto the table as she took a seat. "Speculation began on movie night, when the audience behind you was more fascinated by Kendall playing with your hair than Bogey and Bergman."

Liza reached for her curls. "Kendall played with my hair?"

"Twirled that curl for a good half hour. Doreen claims that at one point he leaned in and took a sniff." Francine ripped open the candies. "But that hasn't been corroborated."

Liza closed the laptop, not sure whether to be flattered or creeped out. "You people need hobbies." She snagged the bag of chocolates Francine slid her way. "How would you feel if a gaggle of busybodies was gossiping about the intimate details of your love life?"

The older woman rolled her eyes. "There isn't much to talk about there."

"Really?" Liza unwrapped a candy. "You don't think they'd be interested to know that you and Aadi Patel are an item?"

Francine froze. "What are you talking about?"

Suspicion confirmed. "I heard him in the background when I called you about Ray's failing health."

"Dang. I told him to stop talking."

"He also smelled like you the next morning, and I doubt he uses lavender-scented shampoo at home."

The bag of candy was pulled out of Liza's reach. "What do you want, Teller?"

That chocolate, for starters. "Francine, why don't you want people to know? I think it's cute."

The playful expression left her face. "Aadi's wife was a big part of this community until she passed away three years ago. Everyone loved Sacchi. Heck, *I* loved Sacchi. But I'm nothing like her."

Liza read between the lines. "In other words, you aren't what? As worthy? As deserving?"

"As right for Aadi," she replied with a sad smile. "He's kind and smart and thinks I'm being absolutely ridiculous about all this, but I'm not ready to face the jury just yet."

Now Liza knew how absurd her cocktail-party story must have sounded. "Screw the jury."

Francine's eyes went wide. "What?"

"Who cares what anyone else thinks?" Kendall was clearly rubbing off on her. "Do you like Aadi?" Liza asked.

"Well, yes, but—"

"I assume he likes you?"

"He says he does."

"Then to hell with everyone else," Liza declared, smacking her hand on the table for emphasis.

Francine stared in stunned silence for several seconds before bursting out laughing. "Where did that come from?"

Excellent question. "I'm not sure," she replied, rubbing her stinging hand. "But I'm right. And so is Aadi. You're being ridiculous."

"Maybe I am." She slid the chocolates back to Liza. "There's a cookout at the Welcome Center this weekend. I assume you and Kendall will be attending together?" Liza nodded. "Then perhaps I'll have a certain tall, dark, and brilliant doctor on my arm."

Clapping her hands, Liza cheered. "That's the spirit! Speaking of Kendall, do you know if my cart is here yet?" The battery hadn't been charged enough for her to bring the vehicle home the day before, and Liza wanted to see a man about a house.

"That's the other thing I'm supposed to tell you." Francine rose from her chair and fetched a glass from one of the kitchen cupboards. "Your cart is dead."

"My cart *was* dead," Liza corrected, "but it should be charged by now."

Francine popped the cork on her wine. "It wasn't the battery, after all. Kendall worked on it all morning, and he can't figure it out. I'm pretty sure he's just going to buy you a new one."

Surely he wouldn't. "He can't buy me a new golf cart."

"Why not?" she asked, filling her glass and then bringing the wine with her to the table.

"Because carts can't be cheap. I'm sure Ray will let me use his."

The older woman lingered behind a chair. "What do you think Kendall does around here?"

Liza never had gotten a clear answer on that. "Handyman stuff, I guess. Odd jobs for whoever needs him."

"So you think he doesn't have a lot of money?"

"Not as much as everyone else, no." Doubts creeped in. "Why are you looking at me like that?"

Lips pursed, Francine took her seat. "Darling, Kendall James is one of the wealthiest men on this island. He owns nearly a dozen rental properties, which is twice as many as anyone else. Do you know how much a rental goes for around here?"

Guessing, she said, "A few hundred?"

"Try a few thousand. A week. Twice that for the bigger units."

"But . . . but he has the smallest house."

"By choice, not necessity." Francine lifted her glass into the air. "And from what I hear, the one he's selling isn't going for chump change, either."

Though math was not her forte, Liza did some quick calculations in her mind and came up with a staggering sum. Even a rough estimate put him at seven figures a year.

Too stunned to be tactful, she said the first thing that came to mind.

"Holy shit. I'm dating a millionaire."

Due to Liza's sore foot, navigating her way down to Ray's part of the house wasn't the easiest task, but the show had to go on. After two days of rest that only shifted the pain from her foot to her bottom, Ray took the initiative to come to her. Liza had voiced concern about him climbing the stairs, only to be reprimanded that he might be as old as dirt, but he could still get around just fine.

His words. Not hers. And not the case the previous week, but she'd kept that reminder to herself.

They'd spent Wednesday morning moving from Ray's newlywed days, which had involved transitioning from being young idealists to exhausted parents, through the birth of his son and the growth of his accounting career, all of which took place in the turbulent 1960s.

For Ray's generation, such an enormous amount of social and emotional change in a relatively short span of time had threatened everything they understood about their world. What had been a given the decade before was no longer acceptable, and the future they'd envisioned, honed through the eyes of their parents, simply didn't exist.

Writing this phase of Ray's life would present the greatest challenge, because Liza's perspective, looking back on the time period, differed greatly from that of the man who'd lived through it. Progress that brought long-overdue sweeping changes for society as a whole had felt like an attack on Ray's way of life. Conveying his experiences and opinions without adding her own modern commentary was going to be a fine line to walk.

"We're up to the '70s, then?" Ray asked, clearing their lunch dishes and refilling Liza's soda glass. She'd assured him the lunch mess could wait, but he'd insisted.

"We are." She checked her trusty recorder to see that the light was still green. Once it turned red, she'd need to plug it in. "Your accounting business is up and running, and by this point your son is a teenager?"

Despite Ray's previous insistence that nothing would be off-limits, he'd made the last minute decision not to go into detail about his son. Since their relationship was already strained, Liza agreed that this was likely for the best.

"Yes, that's right. I'm not sure how much you know about the '70s," Ray began, "but the economy wasn't great."

Not a decade she'd thoroughly researched, but Liza knew that issues like inflation, unemployment, and soaring interest rates had hindered economic growth in the decade. "I've read about some of it, yes."

"The bread and butter of my business were the mom-and-pop operations that had been serving New Yorkers for decades. When those businesses starting going under, so did mine."

A frightening predicament to be in. "What did you do to stay afloat?"

Ray kept his eyes down, holding silent for several seconds. He resembled Amos when he'd gotten in trouble for leaping over Kendall's coffee table. Ashamed and apologetic. "I had to make some hard decisions."

A sense of dread rolled up Liza's spine. "By hard, you mean . . . ?"

The older man crossed his arms. "I had to take whatever clients I could get. The mortgage wasn't going to pay itself, and your . . ." He stuttered and then shook his head. "My son wanted to go to college. I needed to bring in money from somewhere."

He made it sound as if . . . Liza recalled Kendall's vague comments. "Ray, did you get involved in something illegal?"

The fedora shifted as he shook his head. "The only people making money in those days were the mob. They gave me the ability to take care of my business and my family, and all I had to do was make the books look legit." He lifted his hands up and down as if he were weighing the options. "The money came through a plumbing-supply business, nightclubs, even convenience stores. I kept the books, and everything ran smoothly."

Liza couldn't believe her ears. Ray, a mobster? This kind, gentle spirit who'd served his country, adored his wife, and charmed every person he met was a bona fide criminal? He had to be joking.

"Are you sure they were mobsters?" she asked, convinced no one would believe this plot twist if she wrote it in a novel.

Ray had the wherewithal to look offended. "You know when you work for the Mafia, Liza. Dark suits. Enforcers. Black sedans parked outside your house at all hours, just to remind you that they're always watching."

When he put it that way, he wasn't so much a mobster as an intimidated employee.

"Weren't you afraid of getting caught by the authorities?"

"At that time in New York City, the mob *was* the authorities. They had everybody in their pockets. Police. Politicians. And the men in the mob were a hell of a lot scarier than any Goody Two-shoes with a badge."

Ray sounded like a character out of *Goodfellas*. "Even more reason not to get involved. Did Essie know what you were doing?"

Pale lips curled into a snarl. "Not until the late '80s, when the old dons started to die out and the next generation didn't know how to keep their heads down. Those young punks didn't know the meaning of the word *honor*."

Liza marveled at the man before her, feeling as if she were interviewing a complete stranger. Instead of expressing relief that the criminals who'd always been watching him, as he'd put it, were dying off or being caught and prosecuted, Ray sounded angry that his lucrative clients were being condemned.

"Wait," she said, realizing he'd jumped a decade. "You worked for these people for twenty years?"

"Eighteen," he replied, as if wanting to get the details right. "Until I landed on the Feds' radar in '89. They came calling, offering me a lighter sentence if I'd turn on my bosses."

"So you did it," she said, relieved that the hero of her story was about to be redeemed. "You turned them in."

Ray rose from his chair. "I don't want to talk anymore today."

Liza tried to rise, but pain shot up her leg when her heel hit the floor. "We can't stop now. Ray, what did you do?"

He shook his head like a toddler refusing to eat his brussels sprouts. "I need to lie down. I don't feel good." Shuffling from the apartment, he pulled the door shut behind him, leaving Liza gaping at the table, stunned and distressed.

Did he turn them in or not? Of course, he did, she assured herself. If Ray hadn't cooperated with the authorities, they wouldn't be having this conversation today.

Would they?

Liza cursed her injured foot for keeping her from bounding down the stairs. She needed Ray to tell her the rest of the story. Except she knew from experience that Ray didn't talk about anything until he was ready. That's why it had taken two full weeks to get this far. And he still had three more decades to share.

After switching off the recorder, Liza closed her laptop, replaying the startling revelations in her mind. Ray said the authorities came knocking in 1989. That was . . .

"Holy freaking crap," she mumbled. That was thirty years ago. The day she'd arrived, Ray had said he'd been on the island for thirty years, as of this fall. And according to Kendall, the James family had come with him. Was Kendall's father involved in this mess? How could he *not* be if he'd worked for Ray and then followed him here?

Was this the secret that Kendall kept hinting at? Did she dare ask him?

No, Liza thought. Not yet. Not until she knew the rest of the story. She had to make sure Kendall's father wasn't the bad guy in all this. Or *a* bad guy, she corrected, since Ray had already placed himself in that category. Not that laundering money ranked as high as murder in the grand scheme of things, but still.

Ray Wallis worked for the mob. And in all probability, so had Kendall's father. The implications raced through Liza's mind. For Ray. For Kendall. For all of them if she wrote this book.

"Good Lord." She breathed deeply, staring at her recording. "He put that on tape."

Chapter 21

Between failing to fix the cart and the unreturned calls to Aunt Clarice, Kendall was not in the mood for company. The only reason he let Larimore in at all was because he was there on business.

"Unfortunately, we didn't get the bidding war I'd hoped for," he said, strolling to the kitchen, oblivious to Kendall's dark mood. "But the higher offer still stands, so if you're ready to do this, we have some details to finalize."

Retrieving two beers from the fridge, Kendall set one on the table in front of the agent before letting Amos in the back door. "You read. I'll nod."

"That'll work."

As Larimore read through the list of inane details, Kendall filled Amos's bowl, unloaded the dishwasher, and wondered who he had to bribe to get a new cart delivered to the island. He'd tried every dealer in Charleston—all three of them—and gotten quotes of two weeks or more. Liza would be gone by then, but in the meantime, she still needed to get around. And Ray could use the backup in case his gave out. Not that he drove himself around much anymore, but he needed the option.

"The final offer is two point two million."

The number caught Kendall's attention. "I thought you said two even."

"That was before we threw in the furniture and the carts that go with the rental." Flipping a page, he continued. "The buyer wants to close as quickly as possible, and after making sure their financing would hold up, I agreed to the terms."

As quickly as possible meant that in a matter of weeks, the house his dad had built would no longer be his. Kendall's gut turned as he fought the urge to call the whole thing off. He'd taken what he wanted. The rest was just wood and nails.

Larimore spread the papers on the table and held out his pen. "Sign and initial next to all the little tabs, and the deal is done."

After drying his hands on a towel, Kendall reached for the pen as the phone in his pocket buzzed. Checking the cell, he said, "I need to take this." Before accepting the call, he stepped onto the back porch. If this was bad news, he wanted to take it alone.

"Hey, Clarice. How's she doing?"

"She isn't nearly as annoyed as she should be after that high-and-mighty doctor made us wait all damn day."

Kendall paced the length of the porch. "What did he say? Does she need surgery?"

"That's the good news. He says the murmur isn't long enough to indicate a major problem. They want her to get tested every six months, but they're releasing her today, so we're busting out of here soon."

Tension eased from his neck. "Thank God. Let me talk to her for a minute."

"Do I hear a please in there somewhere?"

"Please," he mumbled, digging deep for patience.

"That's better. Here she is." Clarice barked out orders about not damaging the flowers as she passed the phone over.

"I told you there was nothing to worry about," his mother said in greeting. "I'm perfectly fine."

"You still have a heart murmur, Mom. Make sure you keep up with those tests."

"As if Clarice would let me miss one." She had him there. "Thank you for the pretty flowers, son, but you didn't need to do that."

"Sure I did. I'm glad you like them." Glancing into the kitchen, he said, "I wanted to let you know that I'll be sending a good bit of money up there soon."

"I've told you before—"

"I'm selling the house, Mom. Dad would want you to have the money."

Silence lingered on the other end. "You're selling the house that Christopher built?"

"I am. It's going for a good price, so you can do whatever you want with the money."

Kendall already made sure his mother didn't want for anything, but this would put a nice chunk in her account. He hoped she'd use it to take that long trip to Europe she'd always talked about.

"I don't know what to say, Kendall. I know you love that house."

"You don't have to say anything, Mom. Dad built it for you. It's only right that you should have the money from it."

In a rare acknowledgment of the past, she murmured, "He never understood that it wasn't a house that I wanted."

Clearing the lump in his throat, Kendall wished that the house could have been enough. "You let Clarice take good care of you, and I'll call in a couple of days."

"I love you, son."

"Love you, too."

Kendall stayed on the porch for several minutes after the call ended, wishing his mom wasn't eight hundred miles away.

Chapter 22

Saturday dawned ugly and gray, with a downpour that Liza feared would wash out the Welcome Center cookout. Knowing Francine's plan for the day, she wanted everything to be perfect, and the sun did not let her down. By noon, the clouds were gone, replaced by sunny skies, mild temperatures, and the typical warm ocean breeze that had stirred her curls every day since she'd arrived.

Despite still walking like a drunken penguin, Liza couldn't help but smile, because other than the fact that she would be leaving the island in less than a week, everything was right in her world.

Kendall had come to see her several times, and contrary to what Francine had suggested, he had not bought her a brand-new golf cart. He did, however, bring Liza a slice of pecan pie from Morgan's, which she'd devoured in a very unladylike fashion.

During Kendall's many visits, there was no repeat of the previous weekend's activities since Liza could not get past the idea of having sex while Ray was downstairs. There was also the issue of keeping Ray's secret. Or her own secret. Hell, Liza didn't know what she was keeping from whom at this point.

If she shared Ray's confession with Kendall, and the mob connection was news to him, she'd not only be breaking Ray's confidence, but conceivably, she'd also be revealing to one of the most upstanding men she knew that his father had been a criminal.

Liza could not have that on her conscience. Not when she already had the anxiety of sending an old man to prison. That was, if he hadn't made the right choice thirty years ago. She'd hoped that Ray would put her out of her misery on Thursday morning, but he'd refused to even come out of his room. By lunchtime on Friday, she'd begun to really worry, but upon knocking on his door, Liza had found the room empty.

He'd failed to mention an early doctor's appointment, which she hadn't learned about until Friday evening when she'd returned from spending the day with Kendall. Ray had been on his way to bed, and in response to her inquiry about where he'd been, he said, "At the doctor," and then disappeared into his room.

Hoping Ray felt well enough to attend the cookout, as he loved nothing more than a social gathering, Liza hobbled down the stairs to check on him. Despite what she'd learned about him, he was still the sweet man who'd brought her into his home with a ready smile and endless generosity. She was still struggling to reconcile the man she'd come to care about with the Mafia accountant she now knew him to be.

"Ray?" she called, searching in the usual places. He wasn't in the kitchen or on the back deck. "Ray?" Liza called again, making sure he wasn't out front before checking his room.

Easing the bedroom door open, she found an empty bed and nearly spun to look elsewhere before she spotted Ray in a chair by the window. "Are you feeling okay?" she asked.

He didn't turn or answer her question. "Come in, Liza Ruth. There's something I need to tell you."

This seemed like an odd time to finish his story, since Kendall would arrive any minute to take them to the cookout, but Liza wasn't about to put him off. She only wished she had her recorder.

"Are you sure you don't want to talk at the table?" That way she could grab pen and paper from the kitchen drawer to take notes. This was not the part she wanted to get wrong.

His expressionless face turned her way. "We've reached the end of our road."

If he was trying to be ominous, he was doing a damn fine job. Liza tried to read his expression, and for a moment, she feared he was canceling the project without ever giving her the ending.

"What do you mean *the end of our road?*"

"Do you see that picture over there?" Ray pointed to the dresser on the other side of his bed. "The one to the left of the mirror."

A beam of sunlight cut across the image, creating a glare. "The one in the silver frame?"

"Yes, that one." His hand dropped into his lap. "Will you bring it over here to the light?"

Honoring the request, Liza rounded the bed and retrieved the framed photo without looking at it. "Here you go."

Ray shook his head. "I want *you* to look at it."

"Okay." Shifting so the light wouldn't reflect off the glass, she was shocked to see a familiar face. "This is my grandmother." Unable to look away, she said, "You knew my grandmother?"

He nodded. "That's the last picture I have of her."

Liza didn't understand. "But how could you know Grandma Teller? I asked if you knew my family, and you said you didn't."

As the breath left his lungs, the old man seemed to shrink into his chair. "I lied. I wanted as much time with you as I could get."

"You wanted time with me?" This didn't make any sense. She wouldn't have abandoned the project just because Ray knew her family. "Your knowing my family wouldn't have caused a problem. That isn't a conflict of interest that would force me off the project."

Studying the picture again, she traced a finger over her grandmother's kind face before realizing the size of the photo. An eight by ten, and it looked to have been taken around the time Liza was born, which would have been right before her grandfather passed away. "Please tell me you didn't have an affair with my grandmother."

"You remind me of her," he said, ignoring her question. "Strong and beautiful. And the writing. Essie loved to write stories."

Liza stopped breathing, and the picture crashed to the floor. "My grandmother's name was Ruth. What kind of a cruel joke is this?" She backed away, nearly falling over when her knee caught the bed.

Ray rose to his feet, shaky and clinging to the windowsill. "Her name was Ruth Ester Rabinowitz Teller, and she was my wife. Liza, I'm your grandfather."

No. That couldn't be true.

"My grandfather died when I was a baby. He left behind a wife and a son who loved him." Liza refused to even consider what Ray was saying. "My grandmother mourned her husband until the day she died, and she's buried beside him."

"Honey, I had to do it." Ray's hands shook, and he took a step away from the window. "To protect them, I had to let them go. I had to disappear or they would have killed us all."

"People don't disappear!" she yelled, tears blurring her vision. "Who? Who would have killed them? The mob? The scum that you brought into their lives?"

He reached for her, but Liza leaped out of his reach. All those years. He stole all those years from the people who loved him. The people he was supposed to care about.

"Listen. You have to listen to me."

"I've been listening to you for weeks, and now you tell me this? All those questions about my family, pretending that I was talking about a bunch of strangers." What kind of monster could look his own granddaughter in the eyes and not tell her who he was? "I've listened enough. Now I'm going home."

The moment Kendall walked in the house, he knew something was wrong.

"Ray?" he called. "Liza? Where is everybody?"

They should have been ready and waiting to leave for the cookout. Kendall checked the deck first and was about to dash up the stairs to find Liza when Amos whimpered from the entrance to Ray's bedroom.

Kendall's chest tightened with dread. "What is it, boy? What'd you find?"

At the open doorway, Kendall was relieved to find the bed empty. "He isn't there, buddy."

Amos whined again and moved to the end of the bed. Kendall followed him.

"Ray!" Dashing around the bed, he reached the man slumped on the floor, a broken picture frame in his hands.

"It's okay now. Let me take care of that."

Rocking forward and back, the old man shook his head like a petulant child. "I ruined everything. I thought she would understand. I thought I could make her understand."

"She'll come around. You just surprised her." Kendall assumed they were talking about Liza, though he couldn't fathom why she'd leave a defenseless old man crumpled on his bedroom floor. "Careful now. Don't cut yourself."

Watery eyes stared up at Kendall. "I should have waited. I should have told her at the very end."

The very end of what?

"Lean on my shoulder. We need to get you onto the bed." Gently lifting the frail man, Kendall caught a glimpse of the face in the picture. There was something familiar about her. Once they were both sitting on the bed, he asked, "Who is this, Ray?"

"That's my Essie," he replied, watery eyes locked on the picture. "Liza Ruth looks so much like her, doesn't she?"

Kendall hadn't known anything about Ray's life before he'd come to the island, except for the events that had driven him there in the first place. Looking closer, he saw the resemblance.

"Ray, why would Liza look like your wife?"

"Because Liza is my granddaughter."

Fearing Ray had had a stroke or some kind of mental break, Kendall leaned forward to catch his gaze. "Liza is a woman who came here to write your memoir. She isn't your granddaughter. You're confused."

But Ray didn't look confused or out of his mind. He looked heartbroken. "She's my granddaughter, Kendall. And now she's leaving me."

🦋

The more Liza rubbed her eyes, the more the tears came. By the time she'd reached her apartment, her cheeks were soaked. and her vision was blurred. Without stopping to think, she pulled her suitcases from the closet and started throwing things in. There was no time to fold or organize. She had to go. She had to get off this stupid island.

Sweeping her belongings from the bathroom sink, she hobbled into the bedroom and tossed them into the smaller case. Another brush of her cheeks and she reached the clothes hamper in the corner and dumped it on the bed. At the bottom, she found the dress she'd worn to Kendall's the night they'd made love.

As if she'd been punched in the gut, Liza toppled over, burying her face in the discarded garments.

"Liza?" she heard Kendall call.

Bolting upright, she grabbed a towel to dry her eyes. A useless effort, as the tears continued to fall.

"Liza!" he yelled, panic clear in his voice.

"I'm here." She exited the bedroom but didn't go to him. Liza didn't trust anyone at this point, and her heart ached with the fear that Kendall had known. That he'd kept this from her.

Kendall rushed toward her, and Liza shifted to the right, putting the kitchen table between them. "Baby, please."

No. He didn't get to do that.

"Did you know?" she asked, voice low and raw.

He shook his head. "I had no idea." Kendall took another step, and she held up a hand to stop him. "I swear," he added. "I didn't know."

"You kept telling me Ray had secrets." Liza hiccupped. "You said there were things I didn't know. But you did."

Strong hands gripped the back of a chair. "I knew that Ray got into trouble. I knew that he got mixed up with the wrong people, and to save his family, he ran away. Liza, I swear by all that's holy, I had no idea he was your grandfather."

Relief flooded through her, but Kendall's innocence didn't change the situation. Liza still had to go. Unless . . .

She swallowed, willing herself to be strong. "I can't stay here."

Kendall's face contorted as a hand swiped through his hair. "Then Ray was right. You're leaving?"

Liza nodded, a voice in her head begging him.

Ask me to stay.

"I understand." Dark lashes dipped as his eyes dropped to the table. "I'll take you to the ferry."

"No." The word ripped from her throat as her knees threatened to buckle. "No," Liza said again, chin quivering. "I'll have Francine take me. It's better that way."

Better than Kendall seeing her fall apart.

"Liza," Kendall whispered, but she cut him off.

"Please. I need to finish packing if I'm going to catch the next ferry."

His mouth opened, but no words came out. Instead, he nodded before leaving the apartment, the door clicking softly closed behind him.

Taking deep breaths, Liza stayed where she was, willing her heart to keep beating. Willing her feet to carry on. To carry her back to New York, where she clearly belonged. If only he'd said the words, then she would be moving across the island instead of leaving it behind. But the words hadn't come.

At least now she knew. She knew the secrets her benefactor had been hiding, and that the man she'd fallen hopelessly in love with didn't love her back.

Chapter 23

If Kendall was going to lose Liza, he was going to know the reason why.

Ray had moved to the back deck, and Kendall prowled the narrow landing, anger and frustration boiling in his gut. "Why didn't you tell me?"

"I couldn't tell you before I told her," he replied, as if that made some kind of sense.

"You've had her here for three weeks. What were you waiting for?"

Eyes locked somewhere in the distance, Ray scratched beneath his hat. "I had to wait. I needed her to know me first. I thought if she knew me, she'd understand."

Kendall had known Ray all of his life, and he didn't understand any of this. "You let your family think you were dead?"

"I had to. It was the only way."

Doubtful. "Did Dad know about this?" Kendall couldn't imagine his father helping anyone dupe his entire family in such a cruel way.

"Christopher knew everything," the older man replied, hands gripping the arms of the rocker. "He even helped me plan the explosion."

"Hold up." This was starting to sound like a bad movie script. "What explosion?"

"The one the Carpetti family killed me with. Or would have, if I hadn't done it first." Finally meeting Kendall's eyes, he added, "As my driver, Christopher would have died, too. I saved us both."

"Jesus," Kendall muttered, struggling to believe the far-fetched tale. Although owing Ray his life explained his father's unflinching loyalty to the man. "Did Dad know who was after you?"

"Of course he did. He worked for them, too."

Now wait a damn minute. "I thought he was *your driver*."

Ray had the nerve to roll his eyes, as if Kendall were being purposely difficult. "He was my driver, but only because the family assigned him to me."

"No." Kendall refused to believe his father had worked for a crime boss. "Dad did not work for the Mafia."

"Well, someone was paying him, and it wasn't me." Ray rubbed his forehead. "When the FBI came knocking, threatening to put me away unless I testified against the Carpettis, I tried to convince them to take my records and say they got them in a raid or . . ." He waved a hand in the air. "I don't know. However they get stuff like that. They said they could protect me, but I'd been around long enough to know that if I agreed to testify, I'd be dead within a week."

None of this matched the story Kendall had been told. "Dad said you went to the Feds, not the other way around."

A sheepish look crossed Ray's wrinkled face. "I'm not surprised. Things were moving quickly. There wasn't a lot of time to hash out the details."

In other words, Ray had let his driver believe the best of him. *Nice.*

"The day Christopher told me that they were sending someone else to change the oil in the car, I knew. Christopher had always changed it before. There was no choice after that. To save both our lives, I knew we needed a place to disappear. If I left without him, they'd know he tipped me off. And if I'd tried to take my family and run . . ." Ray shook his head. "No one ran from the Carpettis. At least not for long."

Though he didn't like it, Kendall had to admit that the story made sense. "So you landed here."

Another nod. "I remembered an old army buddy talking about an island his family owned. They used it for hunting and fishing but hadn't done much with it. Lucky for us, he was ready to sell, and I had a good bit of money banked in an offshore account."

Offshore accounts. *Holy hell.*

Kendall dropped into a rocker. "What about the people you left behind? Did you consider them at all?"

Ray spun in his chair. "Everything I did was for them. To protect them. To keep them alive."

"By letting them think you were dead. You heard what Liza said. Her grandmother was devastated."

Rounded shoulders drooped. "She was devastated, but she was alive."

Barely, to hear Liza tell it. Whatever Kendall's father's sins might have been, at least he hadn't abandoned his family. Processing what he'd heard, Kendall watched a bird flit from branch to branch. So Ray had faked his own death, and his father's, too.

Wait.

"So your real name is Teller?"

"That's right. Elijah Teller."

"Then what the hell is *my* real name?"

As if this was funny, Ray chuckled. "Relax. Christopher James was a common enough name—we didn't see the point in changing it. Besides, your dad was a driver, not an enforcer or an informant. They wouldn't waste their time looking for him or his family."

Releasing the breath he hadn't realized he'd been holding, Kendall leaned back in the chair. "Did Mom know all of this? Did she know the real reason we came here?"

Ray pushed himself out of the chair. "You'll have to ask her that. I don't know what your father told her." Shuffling past Kendall's chair, he said, "I'm going to my room. Let me know if Liza comes back."

He couldn't really believe she'd come back. Not after being manipulated and lied to. Dragged eight hundred miles from home under false pretenses and then blindsided with an undead grandfather.

Kendall had wanted to ask her to wait. Beg her to give him some time. But how was he supposed to say, "Wait until your grandfather dies again; then we can be together"? Besides being incredibly morbid, it didn't seem like the right move to remind her of Ray's betrayal in that moment.

Asking her to stay was never an option. He knew how that would turn out, and repeating his parents' mistakes was the one thing Kendall would not do.

Eyes closed, he saw her face, puffy and red, streaked with tears. His hands, balled into fists, felt as if they were tied to the chair beneath them. They might as well have been, because despite all Kendall had learned about Ray, he still couldn't abandon him. Couldn't break the promise he'd made to his father all those years ago.

Kendall wasn't choosing Ray over Liza, but he didn't know how to tell her that. If only he could be in two places at the same time. He'd follow Liza anywhere she wanted to go. New York. Nantucket. New Zealand, for all he cared. He just couldn't follow her . . . yet.

🦋

This day just kept getting worse.

This morning, everything had been right in Kendall's world. His mom was doing great. The cart he'd ordered was finally going to be delivered. And by sundown, Liza would be back in his bed, where he planned to keep her for as long as possible.

How could shit go so wrong so fast?

"How could you keep a secret like that?" Francine demanded as Kendall paced her living room. "That poor woman just had the shock of her life. Can you even imagine what she's trying to process right now?"

A lecture was not what he needed. "I told you. I didn't know he was her grandfather. I barely knew about the Mafia part."

"Excuse me?" Aadi said, speaking up for the first time. "Ray was a mobster?"

"Not exactly."

Debating how much to tell, Kendall assessed his audience and assumed that whatever he revealed would stay between them. Then again, all this could end up on bookshelves soon, so what did it matter now?

"Back in the '70s and '80s, Ray was an accountant for the mob. He flipped to the Feds, or was being forced to—that part of the story is still a bit fuzzy—and ran off before the bad guys could take him out. By ran off, I mean he faked his own death." Kendall wasn't ready to share his father's role in the deception, so he skipped to the end. "The only part I knew about was that he'd turned over evidence, left town, and changed his name. I was barely a toddler when it all happened, and they kept me in the dark until I left for the army."

"So you *did* know," Francine accused.

A muscle ticked along Kendall's jaw, and he shot her an impatient look. "One more time. I never knew Ray's real name, and I had no idea he was related to Liza until today."

Silence fell over the room as doctor and artist stared unseeing, absorbing the story more fit for Hollywood than Haven Island. Kendall understood the dazed expressions. He was still dazed himself.

Carrying her wineglass to the sofa, Francine dropped onto the stark white cushion. "Well, that changes everything." A bit of an understatement. "What do we do now?" she asked.

"Nothing," Aadi said. "Ray Wallis, regardless of *who* he is or *what* he's done, is dying."

Francine frowned. "True. At his age, there's no telling how much time he has left."

The doctor rose to his feet. "Months at the most. More likely, weeks."

"What are you saying?" Kendall closed the distance between them. "You can't know that."

Weary eyes met his. "Ray has an aggressive form of melanoma. By the time he sought treatment, it was too late. I'm guessing that's why he brought Liza here. He wanted to see her before he died."

Words failed as Francine gasped from behind him. "But I took him to all those doctor appointments. We were there just yesterday. Why didn't they tell me?"

"They needed his permission to do that, honey. Ray didn't want anyone to know."

"But you knew," Kendall growled, infuriated. "Why didn't you tell us?"

Aadi didn't flinch. "I guess we all helped him keep his secrets."

A beat passed before Francine mumbled, "His head. They brought me in and showed me how to change the bandage. Ray said he had a mole removed and didn't want anyone else to know." She looked up with wide eyes. "I thought he was just being vain, so I kept quiet."

Ray had made them all unwitting accomplices.

"What about Liza?" Francine asked. "She needs to know."

"Do you think that's fair?" Aadi said. "She's hardly had time to deal with him being alive, and now we're going to tell her that he's dying? That's a lot to put on a person."

Kendall didn't want to put any more weight on Liza's shoulders, but Francine was right. She deserved to know. "Are you sure he only has weeks to live?"

The doctor locked his hands behind his back. "I recognize palliative medicines when I see them. The day Ray fainted on the beach, I convinced him to give his doctor permission to share his condition. The oncologist was pretty certain, but doctors aren't God. We can never know for sure."

"So he could have months," Kendall said, clinging to whatever hope he could find.

Aadi's eyes cut to Francine before coming back to Kendall. "It's possible, yes. But unlikely."

Could they afford to gamble? Hold off on telling Liza until she'd had time to process what she already knew? There was a chance, if Kendall told her now, that she wouldn't believe him. Why should she? Ray had lied to her from the moment she'd entered his home. Who's to say he wouldn't lie again to get her back?

"I say we wait."

"But—" Francine started.

"Trust me," Kendall said. "We keep this between us until the time is right."

Aadi agreed and Francine nodded reluctantly. They would keep one more secret. But this time, for Liza's sake, not Ray's.

❦

By the time her plane touched down at JFK, Liza almost wished her face would fall off. Despite her best efforts, she had not been able to stem the flow of tears during her long journey home.

"You look like hell," Vanessa said when Liza emerged from baggage claim.

That meant she looked better than she felt. "It's been a long day. I don't want to talk about it."

The trunk slammed shut. "Are you kidding me? You called me from the Charleston airport, sobbing so hard I thought I was talking to a walrus."

"I'll tell you everything, I promise." Liza's bottom lip quivered. "Just not now."

Visibly annoyed, the agent relented. "Fine. Then let's go." She dashed around to the driver's side, not noticing her passenger's lack of movement until she'd climbed inside the Lexus. Lowering the passenger window, Vanessa waved impatiently. "What are you waiting for?"

In addition to the throbbing around her eyes, Liza's heel felt as if she'd driven a nail through it.

"I can't walk."

"But you walked out here."

"I can't." Dots entered her vision. "Please . . ."

Within seconds, Vanessa was propping her up, struggling to get her passenger in the car. A horn blew loudly from the car behind them. "Shove it up your ass!" the native New Yorker yelled in reply. "Stupid jerk."

The moment Liza's bottom hit the leather seat, exhaustion and a killer headache combined to take her down. The next thing she remembered was waking up in her own bed, water and pain medication on the nightstand, and a note from her agent that read CALL ME.

Squinting against the intruding sunlight, she checked her alarm clock. Eight fifty-two. Her plane had landed shortly after six in the evening, which meant she'd slept for close to twelve hours. No wonder her face felt better. Ignoring the water, she limped into the kitchen, desperate for coffee, only to find the cupboards bare.

Oh yeah. Stocking the shelves had been unnecessary when she wouldn't be home for a month.

Dragging a chair away from her tiny two-person table, Liza plopped down, contemplating her new reality. No way in hell was she writing Ray's memoir. Though he wasn't Ray anymore. He was Elijah Teller, her long-deceased grandfather. Which was the exact reason she wouldn't be writing his book. Because there was no book.

Three weeks of her life spent believing that she was there to do a job. A job she'd already been well compensated for. Liza dropped her head onto her folded arms. She'd have to give that money back. And if he wouldn't take it, she'd give it to charity, but she couldn't keep it. Regardless of the fact that it was all she had.

Sitting up, Liza told herself there had to be something redeemable about Ray . . . Rebranding him as Elijah in her mind was going to be difficult. There had to be some good in him for Grandma Teller to have loved him so much. She wouldn't have devoted her life to a manipulative, selfish man.

But she had. Her husband had abandoned her. Abandoned his entire family.

To protect them.

Liza didn't want to give him the benefit of the doubt. She didn't want to justify his actions in her mind. All she wanted was to go back to the way things had been. Before Elijah had made his confession. Before Kendall had let her go.

"No," she said, bolting from the chair and regretting the forceful stomp immediately. "I'm not ready to forgive him. Either of them."

What she needed was a plan. Without the advance money for the memoir, Liza was back to being broke. But she had a notebook full of plots, and if she needed to take a job until one of them paid off, she would do it.

In order to plan, she needed coffee. Hitching herself from the room, Liza waddled down the hall toward her room, pretending she had everything under control.

Chapter 24

Showered and dressed, Liza dabbed at the swollen bags below her eyes—why did women always cry in the shower?—before exiting her bathroom. Discarding the tennis shoes that reminded her of Haven Island, she dragged an old pair of sneakers from the back of her closet and carried them down the hall toward the kitchen.

Halfway there, her front door flew open, and Liza screamed like a banshee.

"What is wrong with you?" Vanessa snapped. "Are you trying to give me a heart attack?"

Give her *a heart attack?*

"Have you ever heard of knocking?" Liza asked, lungs heaving.

The agent dropped Liza's spare keys into the bowl on the entry table. "Since you never called, I assumed you were still sleeping." She held out a white paper cup. "Here. I come bearing gifts."

Bless her.

"I'm really sorry about last night," Liza said, leading Vanessa into the kitchen. "Did I fall asleep in your car?"

"Out cold. I nearly drove straight to the ER, but then you snored. That seemed like a sign you'd survive." Making herself at home, Vanessa settled at the table, crossed her denim-clad legs, and pinned Liza with a steady gaze as a Coach purse hit the floor. "Now spill. Why are you home a week early?"

Liza's mother had always said that putting off the bad never made the good come any quicker. Not seeing anything good on her horizon, Liza leaped headfirst into the bad.

"I won't be writing the memoir."

A three-inch pump hit the floor. "You have to write the memoir. We signed an agreement."

They'd signed an agreement with Ray Wallis, a man who didn't exist. "The client provided false information. There is no agreement."

The willowy brunette bounded to her feet. "What false information? Liza, I sold this book to Sudberry Publishing. They're expecting a completed manuscript by Labor Day. The contract is in the works right now."

How the . . .

"What do you mean you sold the book?"

"I mean, I sold the book. That's my job, remember? You write them, and I sell them."

"But there *is no book.*"

Vanessa plucked a manila folder from the tote beside her chair. "You sent me notes, remember? The entire book is outlined." She waved the folder in the air. "How could there not be a book when you sent all this?"

Panic seized Liza's heart as her stomach churned. "I didn't know the truth when I sent those." Her hands began to shake, so she set the coffee on the counter, splashing hot latte on the laminate. "The man in those pages doesn't exist."

Green eyes narrowed. "You mean none of this happened?"

"No. I mean, yes, all of it happened. Maybe. But . . . things are different now."

Jimmy Choos clicked across linoleum, stopping inches from Liza's bare toes. "I'm trying to help you here, Liza, but you need to meet me halfway. You are in the business of writing books. Because I believe in your ability to do that, I've put my name and reputation behind finding a home for those books. That won't work for either of us if you don't actually write *a book*."

Eyes misting, Liza swallowed hard against the weight of failure turning her stomach.

"Then I guess we can't work together anymore, because I can't write Ray Wallis's book."

Vanessa spun away, pacing like an angry mama tiger. "Okay, then. Not this book. The advance Sudberry offered was piddly—seeing as you don't have a substantial track record yet—so we'll cancel the contract. You can write a different book." Vanessa stopped pacing and turned hopeful eyes to her client. "Please tell me there's another book."

"There is," Liza said, "but I don't know when it will be finished." Vanessa's refusal to give up on her reinforced Liza's determination to stop being a deadweight around the woman's neck. "In the meantime, I need you to send the advance money back to Mr. Wallis. I'm going to find a job to pay the bills, and if I ever write a book worthy of being published, I'll let you know."

"Liza Ruth Teller, I have never given back money in my entire career. You say the client hired you under false pretenses. If that's the case, and he has failed to uphold his part of the agreement, then that money is yours."

Breathing through the pain in her chest, Liza kept her gaze steady. "I can't keep the money."

"Why?" Vanessa asked, throwing her hands in the air. "Why can't you keep the money?"

Liza locked a white-knuckle grip on the edge of her counter. "Because Ray Wallis is my dead grandfather."

"Come on, Mr. Kendall. Uncle Bradley says you should come light the bottle rockets."

"Maybe later."

The six-year-old crossed his arms and stomped off down the beach.

"Pout all you want, kid. Life is full of disappointments."

A fact that Kendall knew all too well. He'd done a lot of thinking since the day Ray came clean. About his father. And how his life might have been different if Christopher James had never met Elijah Teller. But mostly, he thought about Liza.

"Are you going to kill that twelve-pack on your own or pass some around?"

Kendall squinted up at the good doctor. "Have at it. There's plenty to go around."

Larimore was supposed to join him, but a pretty divorcée staying at forty-two B had made him a better offer.

With a sigh, Aadi lowered to the sand beside Kendall's chair. "How's Ray?"

"He's hanging in there. Some days are better than others." Now that Kendall knew the truth, he accompanied Ray to all of his doctor's appointments, and they'd drawn up official documents to give him medical power of attorney, should the need arise.

Aadi spun the top off a longneck. "Where's Amos today?"

The man was dancing around something, and Kendall had a good idea he knew what. "Home. He doesn't like fireworks."

"Right. That makes sense." A weighted pause before Aadi finally got to the point. "Francine thinks you should call Liza."

Kendall had hoped that she might call him. Liza reaching out first would be a strong indication that she'd come to terms with Ray's true identity. And so long as Ray showed signs of getting stronger, he felt comfortable giving her time to get there.

"We all agreed, Aadi. It hasn't even been a week."

"That's one less week she has with him."

A truth that only complicated things further. Kendall was trying to do what was best for everyone, but at the top of that list was Liza.

"Aadi, everything Ray put her through was for selfish reasons. I don't blame him for wanting to see her, but the way he did it wasn't fair to Liza. And putting this on her before the rest sinks in isn't fair, either. We need to wait."

The older man rolled the wet bottle across his knee. "I can't help thinking about Sacchi . . ."

"I get it, man. But this is different. Ray made his choice a long time ago. Liza had the right to make hers."

With a nod, the contemplative man rose to his feet. "I hadn't thought of it that way."

Kendall had thought of it every way imaginable. Every night, he stared at his cell phone, debating whether or not to call. Whether to buy a plane ticket and go after her. Whether to walk away and let Liza get on with her life.

And then the sun cut through the sky, and he still didn't have any answers.

As Aadi strolled off down the beach, Kendall sought a distraction from the noise inside his head. Dragging out his cell phone, he called his mom.

"Happy Fourth, son. How are you doing today?"

Kendall closed his eyes as the knot in his gut loosened. "Happy Fourth, Mom. Things are good. Are you over at Clarice's for the cookout?"

"Not yet. Your cousin Davis is picking me up in about an hour." As if she could sense his tension through the phone, she said, "What is it, Kendall? What's wrong?"

"Can I ask you something, Mom?"

"Of course. You can ask me anything."

He hoped that was true. "What did Dad do when we lived in New York?" The line hummed as Kendall's heart beat in his ears. "Who did he work for?"

A long sigh echoed from the other end. "Let me guess—Ray Wallis finally started talking."

Kendall exited the chair and strolled back toward the trees. "His name isn't Ray, but you know that."

"Yes, I do. How much has he told you?"

"Enough." More than Kendall wanted to hear. "Is the Carpetti part true? Was Dad part of the mob?"

A bitter laugh floated down the line. "Your father was a lot of things, but a mobster was not one of them."

The muscles in his chest relaxed, and Kendall took his first deep breath in days. "Then he didn't work for the Carpetti family?"

A beat passed. "He did, but not the way you think."

How many ways could someone work for a crime syndicate? "Either he worked for them or he didn't. Which is it?"

"If we're going to have this conversation, I need to sit down." The background noise from the TV grew quiet. "We needed money," she started. "Everything was behind—the car payments, the rent. I told him my parents would give us a loan, but Christopher was too proud for that. He went out every day looking for work, and when a man in a suit offered him a thousand dollars a week to do odd jobs, your father said yes."

Kendall would have been immediately suspicious. "That's a lot of money for odd jobs."

"That's what I said, but, bless his heart, your father was as naive as he was stubborn."

Kendall smiled at the Southernism. She may have left South Carolina, but she'd taken the language with her. "So how did odd jobs lead to driving a car for Elijah Teller?"

"It was a natural progression, I guess. He started out doing basic maintenance-type work, on buildings first and then on different people's cars. A few months in, someone handed him an envelope full of cash and told him to go buy himself a nice suit. The next day, he was Elijah's driver."

"How much did you know about the events that brought us down here?"

"Not enough," she answered emphatically. "For one, I didn't know until we got there that the old man was part of the package. As for the island, your father made it sound like paradise, as I'm sure Ray had painted it out to be. The second I stepped foot on that sand, I was ready to go home. But Christopher was all in. I think in some twisted way, it reminded him of the farm he'd grown up on back in Kansas."

"Dad grew up in Kansas?" How did Kendall not know this?

"He did. That's one of the things I liked about him. He wasn't anything like the city boys I'd always dated. Christopher was . . . softer, I guess. Though he'd hate to hear me say that."

Soft was not a word Kendall associated with his father. At six foot five, he'd loomed above most men, built many of the homes still standing on the island today, and never backed down from a fight. Then again, he only ever fought when someone smaller than he was needed defending.

"Anyway," his mom said, "I was not living in a shack, in fear every day that an alligator was going to eat my child, so we compromised and found a little rental in Charleston. The one thing I'll say for Ray is that he had the vision. He believed there was money to be made on that island, and the one promise he upheld was splitting the land with your father. You're in the position you are today thanks to the rare generosity of one of the most selfish and manipulative men I've ever met."

That Ray and Jacqueline James didn't like each other had always been obvious, but Kendall had never known the source of the animosity. Mom had never praised Ray or feigned any fondness for him, but she'd also never said a bad word about him. At least not in front of her son. Until now.

"When did you know about the fake explosion?"

A pause came from the other end. "Explosion?"

So Kendall hadn't been the only one left in the dark. "Dad helped Ray create an explosion that would make it look like they'd both been killed. That's why Ray changed his name when we got here. So the Mafia family he'd worked for couldn't hunt him down."

He could almost hear his mother's teeth grind. "God, that man was a fool. Christopher told me that Ray gambled with the wrong man's money, and if he found him, he'd take payment any way he could. That's why he refused to leave the old man's side. But there had been no mention of an explosion."

Money laundering and gambling weren't exactly the same thing, but there was a thin line of truth in this newest version of events. Amazing that two men could spread so many different versions of the same story and never get caught in the lies.

"After thirty years, we may never know exactly what happened." Ray hadn't volunteered any more details, and Kendall had to assume the people he'd run from were long gone. "But thanks for answering my questions."

"You're welcome, son. Though it sounds like you know more than I do."

One more question came to mind. "Mom, did you know Ray's family? Or Elijah's, I guess."

"I didn't really know them, but they invited us for a cookout once. Mrs. Teller was a sweet woman. Quiet, which was the complete opposite of her husband. His son was less friendly, but the daughter-in-law was nice. They had a little girl you played with."

Kendall sat up straighter in his chair.

"A little girl?"

"I don't remember her name, but she had a head full of blonde curls. And she clung to her mother's leg, as if she was afraid someone might steal her away. You did your best to coax her into the sandbox, and she finally sat on the edge, watching you build a fort." After a brief silence, she added, "I wonder what happened to her."

Ray happened to her. Kendall slid the top onto his cooler and stood to fold up his chair. "Have a good time at the cookout, and I'll call you next week."

"Kendall," she said, halting his movements, "you need to know that I don't regret marrying Christopher. He was a good man and a good father. And though it might not have always seemed like it, I did love him."

He hated to admit the truth, but he'd doubted that fact more than once during his life. "I'm happy to hear that, Mom. I know he loved you, too. Talk soon, okay?"

"Talk soon. Happy Fourth, buddy."

"Happy Fourth to you, too."

Ending the call, Kendall finished gathering his things and headed for his cart. The main fireworks display would start soon, and he didn't want Amos to be alone.

Chapter 25

Conveying the entire story of her Haven Island adventure had taken two hours, and though Liza had been careful not to mention Kendall except when absolutely necessary, Vanessa had not been fooled. Liza had then cried her way through the third hour amid empty coffee cups and greasy pizza boxes.

As if reading Liza's mind, Vanessa had said, "I can't believe he didn't ask you to stay."

Liza's sentiments exactly. Looking back, she saw the short, painful exchange as if she were floating above the scene, witnessing the words practically written across her forehead.

Ask me to stay.

Instead, Kendall had offered to help her leave. But as Liza played the encounter back again, she realized one important element she'd been too emotional to see at the time. It was an ending without an ending. There'd been no argument. No bitter fight or hateful words exchanged. Just *I'm leaving* and *Let me help you go.*

Not that Kendall had looked happy to send her off. In fact, her own pain had been reflected in his eyes. If only he'd said the words.

In the days after Liza's return, she took Vanessa's advice and buried herself in a new book. But contrary to how her mind had worked on the island, she found herself ignoring the new ideas and studying her notes on the memoir. Liza wanted to know if the things Ray had told her had been true. From the names of his parents, which she shamefully had never heard before, to his years in the service.

Research had always been Liza's favorite way to pass the time, and in this case, it served as a helpful distraction for her aching heart. If she was digging into Elijah Teller's past, she couldn't torture herself wondering what Kendall might be doing. If he missed her. If Amos missed her. She deeply missed them both.

Her first instinct had been to call her father, but she had to tread lightly. Liza had debated for days whether or not to reveal all and, in the end, decided that until she knew everything, she would tell the family nothing. To prevent arousing her father's suspicion, she called Aunt Julia, Ray's youngest sister and only living sibling.

One brother and two sisters, all younger. The clues had been so obvious. How had she missed them?

As the genealogist in the family, Julia could provide documents to prove or disprove the information Ray had shared. She would also, hopefully, be willing to discuss her brother's death. Something Liza had never heard her father do.

There was the added bonus that Julia was Liza's favorite member of the family. A younger, female version of Elijah, but less boastful and more likely to shine a spotlight on others instead of herself.

Within days, Liza had been engrossed in census records, marriage records, birth certificates, and obituaries. As far as she could tell, every detail Elijah had shared was accurate. A fact that revealed two things— Liza knew far too little about her own family history, and the memoir project may not have been a ruse.

Why go to the trouble? Why not put her off entirely, traipsing Liza about the island with one excuse or another about getting to the details later? Even on days when Elijah hadn't felt his best, he'd arrived at the table ready to talk. Another sign that he really *had* wanted her to write the book.

A conclusion that made her feel better about the proposal she planned to offer Vanessa.

A boom outside Liza's window drew her attention away from the mounds of printouts and notebooks spread out on her comforter. She'd forgotten. Today was a holiday. Another pop and the sky lit up, celebrating her country's independence. Watching the red-and-blue sizzling streams fill the air, she thought about Elijah going off to war.

A naive eighteen-year-old who'd never stepped foot outside New York City was handed a gun and shipped off to the other side of the world. Then she thought of Kendall in the same situation. Though not as naive as a boy who'd grown up in the '30s, he was still only a boy.

A kind, loving, unselfish boy who deserved happiness and laughter. Not tanks and body armor.

The fireworks finale kicked into high gear, filling the apartment with noise and the air with smoke. Liza pushed herself away from the window and brushed a tear off her cheek before pulling the laptop back onto her lap.

❧

July turned hot and muggy, with daily showers rolling into heavier storms several times during the previous week. Kendall hated this time of year. The wind off the water felt like a hair dryer blowing in his face, and even in the air-conditioning, he could barely get cool.

The rain led Amos to track mud through the house. After getting caught in a sudden downpour two days ago, the spoiled dog had squirmed past his towel-wielding owner and dashed straight to the bedroom to dry himself on the comforter.

Once the weather cleared, Kendall had been relieved to get back to work. If he was working, he couldn't think about Liza. As much. Though twice she'd invaded his mind and nearly cost him dearly. The first time had been when a tourist walked by a public marsh dock that Kendall was repairing. She'd been wearing the same scent as Liza, and when the perfume hit his senses, he'd missed the nail by more than an inch, nearly smashing his thumb to smithereens.

The second time, Kendall had been driving. Rounding the corner in front of the Welcome Center, he had spotted a cart parked on the side of the road. Blonde curls dancing in the breeze, the driver, a woman in a bright-blue dress, had been staring at her phone. Kendall's heart had stopped, but his cart hadn't, and he nearly plowed into a family of four. When a horn sounded, the blonde had looked up, revealing the face of a stranger, and Kendall had been forced to swerve to avoid the collision. If Amos had been with him, he no doubt would have landed in the female driver's lap.

Or worse, been truly injured.

After the last incident, Kendall realized that for the safety of himself and those around him, he needed to call Liza. What he would say was yet to be determined, but in the unlikelihood that she *did accept the call, he should probably come up with something. As Francine continued to insist, Liza deserved to know that her grandfather was dying, but Kendall wasn't to open up with that.*

Hi. How are you doing? Your grandfather is dying.

Definitely not the way to go, but he'd be damned if he knew what was. If he ever figured out what to say, Kendall considered the idea that she might want to talk to Ray. If that happened, he wanted to oblige her.

"Ray?" he called, letting himself in when no one answered the door. "Ray, are you here?"

He'd probably gone out—with Francine or one of the other locals who'd been helping keep an eye on him—and failed to pull the door closed behind him. That's what Kendall hoped, anyway, but some sixth sense pushed him to search the house.

"Hello?" he said louder, as Amos trotted into the kitchen and found something edible on the floor. The dog sniffed around for more crumbs while Kendall moved into the living room. "Is anyone here?"

No response came. Kendall checked Ray's room. The blankets were tossed back, but the room was empty. The hairs on the back of Kendall's neck stood up. This wasn't good. After a quick check of Ray's bathroom, he returned to the kitchen and noticed Amos sniffing around the back door. Stepping around the island, Kendall could only see the dog's back half in the doorway to the back deck.

"What is it, buddy?" Crossing to the door, he spotted Ray lying on the deck and Amos licking his forehead. "Amos, move!"

The dog obeyed but stayed close to the unconscious man. Checking for a pulse, Kendall reached for his cell, relieved to feel a faint beat beneath his fingertips. Selecting the rarely used number in his contacts, he tucked the phone against his ear and felt around Ray's head for any obvious injuries.

The instant someone answered the call, Kendall snapped out orders. "Emergency at Ray Wallis's house. Bring the medical truck, and get the ferry headed this way. And find Aadi Patel. He needs to get here now."

❦

This was why Liza rarely left her house. New York was just too . . . people-y.

Especially Manhattan, where she ventured only when Vanessa couldn't meet her closer to home. At least today, she had positive news to share. She hoped.

"Sorry for the delay," the agent said, leading Liza into her office. "I didn't expect that last call to take so long." After shifting a stack of folders off the center of her desk, she gave the client her full attention. "What's the verdict?"

Taking a deep breath, Liza squared her shoulders. "I'm going to write the memoir, but with compromises."

Dark brows shot up, and Vanessa leaned forward. "What does that mean? *Compromises.*"

Liza took a deep breath, assuring herself she was doing the right thing. "The original plan had been to tell the life story of Ray Wallis, from start to finish. That was, of course, before the man going by Ray Wallis became Elijah Teller."

Vanessa nodded. "I remember."

"Now that I know who he really is, I've been able to learn more about his life from the people who knew him. Well," she hedged, "from a person who knew him. My aunt Julia—that's Elijah's youngest sister—has filled in more of the years before Elijah left town. The man I've discovered does not deserve to have his story told."

Green eyes blinked several times. "But you just said you're going to write the book."

"I am. Stay with me." Liza continued the pitch as she'd rehearsed. "Elijah comes from immigrant parents and grew up in New York City during one of the most progressive eras in the city's history. At eighteen, he joined the military and entered World War II, serving in the Pacific. I know he kept a journal during that time, and I might be able to get ahold of it." Cooperating with her now was the least the man could do. "Regardless, his is a classic American story, and I believe I can turn the early years of his life into a compelling read."

Fingers steepled, Vanessa considered the idea. "What about the rest? What about the faked death and disappearing for three decades? That's where the story is."

Liza settled her hands in her lap. "Someone else will have to write that book, and I'm willing to share my research. But the story *I'm* writing will be about an ambitious Jewish boy who survived the Depression, defended his country, and met the love of his life on a blind date at the Bronx Zoo."

Lips pursed, Vanessa tapped a bright-red fingernail on her blotter. "Your mind is made up?"

"It is." Liza held her breath, awaiting the agent's response.

After what felt like an eternity, the agent finally shared a response. "Then let's run with it."

Liza could have cried with relief, but she didn't want to get too excited. She still intended to return Elijah's money, so piddly or not, she could use the advance from Sudberry.

"Do you think the publisher will agree?"

Vanessa waved the question away. "Leave that to me. Now I'm taking you to lunch. You look like you haven't eaten in a month."

Between stress over the book, and constant thoughts of Kendall, Liza hadn't been very hungry. "I'm not *that* thin."

"Yes, you are." She nudged Liza out of the office and closed the door behind her. "Hayley, I'm going to lunch. Reschedule my one o'clock, and move the three-thirty meeting to four."

"Yes, ma'am."

Liza didn't want to throw off her agent's day. "We can do lunch another time if you're busy."

With a hand on her shoulder, Vanessa pushed her forward. "Hayley will take care of everything. Besides, now that the book issue has been resolved, it's time we tackle your man problem."

Liza nearly stumbled over an invisible speed bump. "I don't have a man problem."

Striding into the Manhattan heat, Vanessa said, "Not for long, you don't."

🦋

Why were hospital waiting rooms always so damn uncomfortable? If there was any room in the world where comfort should be the number-one priority, the space where family and friends waited for their loved ones to live or die should be that room. They'd taken Ray back an hour ago. An hour of Kendall sitting alone, in some baby-blue plastic chair, with nothing to do but remember the last time he'd been in a hospital.

The night his father had passed away.

That was a short list when he thought about it. Lots of people would feel that only two hospital visits in eight years was a pretty good run. Then again, hospital visits didn't have to be a bad thing. Good things happened there, too. Life started there, after all. Children were born. Families were made.

"I'm sorry, Kendall. We headed this way as soon as we heard." Francine took the seat next to him, teetering on the edge. "Aadi is trying to get some information. Have they said anything?"

"Nothing."

"I feel horrible. We checked on him this morning, and he seemed fine. I just wanted to visit this new gallery downtown." She dropped her head in her hands. "We shouldn't have left the island."

Kendall put his arm around her. "You couldn't have known this would happen. We don't even know what it is yet. He'll probably wake up and start fussing that he wants to go home." Or maybe he would never wake up at all.

Sitting up, she pulled a tissue from her purse and wiped her nose. "I've talked to him a lot in the last couple weeks, and I can't figure out if it's his age, or the disease taking a toll, or if he's really as selfish as he sounds. But I'm convinced he thinks all those lies were harmless. Like he made some great sacrifice, and everyone he hurt should be grateful." Shaking her head, Francine met Kendall's gaze. "And I still can't help but care about him."

Maybe that's how he'd duped them for so long. By being too likable to ever be a bad guy.

Aadi entered the waiting room looking grim. "The doctor is on her way. The staff won't tell me anything."

"That's okay," Francine said, taking her partner's hand. "Thank you for trying."

The three sat in silence for several minutes, each lost in their own thoughts. Most likely imagining the worst. Kendall tried to be positive. Ray was a fighter. If anybody could make a comeback, it was him.

An African American woman with close-cropped hair and an air of authority stepped into the room. "I'm looking for the family of Ray Wallis?"

Kendall replied, "That's us."

The arched brow said she didn't believe him. Not that he blamed her. A five-foot-tall Chinese woman. A balding Indian man. And Kendall, with dark hair, dark eyes, and a frame easily triple her patient's size.

"Are any of you blood relatives?"

"Not to each other," Francine replied.

Kendall struggled to hide his smile.

Aadi stepped forward. "I'm afraid Mr. Wallis doesn't have any blood family around here. I'm Dr. Aadi Patel, retired, this is Kendall James and Francine Adams, and we're all very close with Ray."

"We're all he has," Francine added.

Softening, the doctor nodded. "I see. Are you all aware of Mr. Wallis's medical condition?"

"We know he has cancer," Kendall replied. "And I have medical power of attorney."

She held out a hand toward the chairs. "That will work." Once they were seated, the doctor shared the grim news. "The cancer is starting to affect Mr. Wallis's organs. We're doing what we can to keep him comfortable, but I'm afraid the rest is out of our hands."

Francine began to cry, and Aadi pulled her close. "Is there a chance he could recover enough to go home?"

"I'm sorry, but I don't believe so." Patting Francine's knee, she said, "I'm very sorry. If there's anyone out of town who might want to say goodbye, I suggest calling them right away. There isn't much time left."

Nodding, Kendall said, "I'll call her."

Chapter 26

The waitress arrived with their meals. A club salad for Vanessa and a ham and cheese on rye for Liza. When they were once again alone, Vanessa repeated her initial argument.

"I still say you should call this Kendall guy." She stabbed a tomato with her fork. "You obviously fell for him."

"I'm not ready yet."

The fork waved before Liza's nose. "You're a thirty-two-year-old broke writer living alone in your grandmother's old apartment—which still smells like her, by the way—who hates socializing and hasn't been in a relationship in over five years. He is, by your own admission, a gorgeous thirty-something millionaire who owns half of a private island, is incredible in bed, and wants *you*. How are you not ready?"

Well. When she put it that way. "I don't think he feels the same way I do," Liza said, airing her fear for the first time. "He could have stopped me from leaving, but he didn't."

"You mean he let you make your own decision? What a jerk." After plucking a shred of lettuce from her teeth, she added, "You should call him."

Liza really wanted to call him. "What would I say? 'Hey, I know things got awkward there at the end, but look me up the next time you're in New York.'"

Her agent had the nerve to visually consider this suggestion. "I'd offer to fly down there."

She wanted nothing more than to go back to the island, but Kendall had to want her there. "Haven isn't the kind of place where you make a surprise appearance."

As she picked up her sandwich for a bite, Liza's cell phone rang out a tropical tune from her purse.

"Maybe that's him," Vanessa said, dabbing dressing from the corner of her mouth.

"This isn't . . ." Liza stared at the glowing screen in stunned disbelief. "It's him."

Vanessa's fork hit the table. "No shit."

The phone continued to ring. "I don't know what to do."

"Answer it!" yelled Vanessa, nearly snorting avocado out her nose.

Eyes wide, Liza did as ordered. "Hello, Kendall." Her heart beat so loudly, she feared she wouldn't be able to hear his voice on the other end.

"Hi," Kendall said in his sweet, wonderful baritone. "I'm sorry to bother you."

"No. No, it's fine." Her lungs suddenly forgot how to function, and Liza fanned her face, desperate for air. "I don't mind. How are you?"

His sigh raised the hairs on her arms. "Liza, Ray took a turn. I don't know if that even matters to you at this point, but we thought you should know."

There was too much in that brief statement for her to process all at once. "I'm . . . Is . . . A turn? What does that mean?"

She could almost see him run a hand through his hair. "That scratch on his head wasn't a scratch. It's melanoma. The disease is pretty far along."

Another lie. Another secret. How many could one man keep?

Liza pushed back from the table, and Vanessa mouthed, "What is it?"

Ignoring the question, she turned to the side and leaned forward, head nearly to her knees. "There must be treatment options. What does Aadi say?"

"It's too late, hon. There's nothing they can do."

Heat rushed up her neck, and the food roiled in her stomach. "Are you sure? He kept bouncing back while I was there. Maybe he'll do that again."

Liza barely knew him, but the fear of losing Elijah before reconciling her feelings—before even getting to decide if she wanted him in her life—was a cruel injustice.

"We're sure." Kendall's breath filled the silence as Liza ran through every emotion imaginable. How could she feel so connected to a grandfather she barely knew? One who'd removed himself from her life before she'd even been old enough to remember him.

And still, Kendall waited. Patient. Loving. Supportive.

A tear slid down her cheek as she asked, "Where is he? Is he in a hospital?"

"Yeah. I can text you the information if you want."

Liza didn't know what she wanted. "That would be good, thank you."

There didn't seem to be anything else to say, but she couldn't bring herself to end the call. Listening to him breathe, she could close her eyes and pretend he was there. Beside her. Making everything right again.

"I guess I better go," he said.

She nodded before remembering he couldn't see her. "Thank you, Kendall. Thank you for calling."

He hesitated so long Liza thought he'd hung up. "I'm here, Liza. Anytime. I'm here."

The call beeped dead as she stared at the half-eaten sandwich on her plate, blurry from her tears.

"What happened?" Vanessa demanded. "What did he say?"

"It's my grandfather." Looking up, she met concerned green eyes. "He's dying."

Vanessa tossed her napkin on her plate and rounded the table. "Do you want to go see him? Do you want me to go with you?"

The offer made Liza cry harder, so she took a deep breath, using her own napkin to wipe her eyes. "I don't know. I need to think about it."

The other woman let out a long breath. "How much time does he have?"

Liza hadn't thought to ask, but based on Kendall's tone, not long. She had to tell the family. They needed to know.

"I have to go," she said, rising to her feet.

"Of course. I'll call Hayley to book the plane tickets right now. And we'll hire a private driver to get you from the airport."

Shaking her head, Liza pushed in her chair. "No, I don't mean that. I mean . . . I just need to go."

"Oh. Okay. Do you need money for a taxi?"

Shaking her head, Liza rushed through the tables and into the hot July sun, dreading the conversation ahead.

❦

"How did she take it?" Francine asked.

"Okay." Kendall rubbed the back of his neck, trying to purge the sound of Liza crying from his mind. "She didn't say much."

The longer Liza had taken to answer the call, the more he'd convinced himself that she wouldn't pick up. Kendall, Francine, and Aadi had debated what to do if she didn't take the call. No one felt good about sharing the cancer diagnosis through a text, but if Liza refused to talk, she'd have left them no choice.

And then she'd answered, and Kendall's heart had fallen to his knees.

Francine kept her eyes on the patient. "At least she answered. That's a good sign."

"Yeah. That's good." He'd have given anything to be spared the hurt in her voice. As Kendall had known she would, Liza had begun to forgive the man lying pale in a hospital bed. That's the only reason she would have broken down like that. "I sent the hospital info in a text, but I don't know if she'll come."

God, he hoped so. Even if only for a day or two. Kendall just needed to see her.

"Don't count her out yet, Kendall. No matter how hurt she is, he's still her grandfather."

He nodded. "I know."

The door slid silently open as Aadi returned from his mission. "Two more chairs are on the way, and I collected a list of menus for restaurants within walking distance of the hospital."

Other than the bed, the only furniture in the room had been one beige chair and a padded bench beneath the window. Since all three of them intended to stay, at least for the foreseeable future, Aadi had volunteered to apply his years of hospital experience to making their impending sit-in more comfortable.

"Did you make the call?" he asked. "Is Liza coming?"

"She knows his condition and where he is," Kendall replied. "The rest is up to her."

Francine straightened the blanket over Ray's chest. "I think she'll come. I just hope it won't be too late."

The weight of the situation had been hanging like a dense fog all afternoon, and the longer Ray remained unconscious, the more somber they all grew. At first, they'd tried staying positive. With more prodding, the doctor had admitted to a slim chance that Ray could rally and surprise them all. Slim was better than none, and they'd clung to that hope while waiting for him to be placed in a room.

But once they were finally allowed to see him, with tubes and cords attached to various parts of his body, reality had set in quickly. Ray Wallis would not be leaving this hospital. At least not alive.

As Francine leaned against Aadi's side, Kendall caught her rubbing her stomach. "You two go eat," he said. "I'll stay with him."

"Are you sure?" she asked. "What if . . ." Her eyes lingered on Ray's pale face.

"The doc said days, not hours," he reminded her. "Go on. I'll get something when you come back."

Aadi shot Kendall a grateful glance above Francine's head as he eased her out of the room. Alone with the man who'd shaped his life more than any other, he brushed a wisp of gray hair off Ray's forehead.

"This is a lot of drama, even for you, buddy." Clasping the old man's gnarled hand, Kendall willed him to open his eyes. "If you wanted round-the-clock attention, all you had to do was say so. We could have found a pretty nurse for you to waltz around the kitchen island."

No response.

"Come on, Ray. Open your eyes. Be the fighter I know you are."

Still nothing.

Jaw tight, Kendall turned to pull the one beige chair closer to the bed.

"Did you say 'pretty nurse'?" rasped the man on the bed, voice weak but steady.

Dropping the chair, he spun back around, afraid he'd imagined the words. "Ray? Are you with me, big guy?"

Dry lips smacked. "Seems that way. What happened?"

"You scared the hell of me, that's what happened." Watery eyes opened, squinting against the bright lights. Kendall pulled a chain behind the bed to cut off the strongest offender. "There you go, buddy. That's better."

Taking in his surroundings, Ray rubbed a hand over the large needle taped to the back of his left hand. His head fell slowly back to the pillow. "So this is it, huh? My last hurrah."

The calm acceptance tightened Kendall's chest. "Doesn't have to be. We can walk out that door anytime you're ready."

He shook his head, a subtle, almost imperceptible movement. "Not this time, son. Not this time."

Teeth clenched, Kendall ignored the burning in his eyes. "Don't you dare give up, old man. Not yet."

Pale-blue eyes met his. "Does Liza Ruth know? Does she know I'm here?"

Kendall nodded. "She knows."

"Do you think she'll come?"

Willing to give him any reason to hold on, he said, "She might."

Ray closed his eyes as the hint of a smile curved his lips. "I hope so."

So did Kendall.

❦

Liza arrived at the offices of Mitcham, Douglas, and Teller, Public Accountants with a knot in her stomach and her heart in her throat. For the entire cab ride over, she'd debated the best way to tell a man that his long-deceased father was still alive . . . but dying.

Rushing into the reception area, Liza still didn't have the answer.

"Hi, Martha," she greeted the receptionist. "Do you know if Dad is free?"

The older woman clicked a computer mouse as she checked her screen. "He has a meeting in fifteen minutes. Should I tell him you're here?"

Since Liza rarely visited the office, she didn't want him to worry that something was wrong. Then again, something *was* wrong. Very wrong.

"I'll just go on back. Thank you, though."

In the years since Liza had returned to New York, she'd invaded her father's workplace only a handful of times, and never uninvited. On those limited occasions, she'd never given much thought to how old the company was. In fact, the firm had been founded by Elijah Teller more than forty years ago and left to his son upon his death.

A death that never actually happened.

Rarely had the saying *Truth is stranger than fiction* been more accurate.

Approaching the door marked **EPHREM TELLER CPA**, Liza took several seconds to steady her nerves before knocking. Three quick raps on the door were met with a command to come in. Another deep breath and she crossed the point of no return.

"What a surprise," her father said, coming around the desk to give her an awkward hug. Liza held out hope that they'd someday get past the awkward stage. "Is everything all right? You don't usually show up without warning like this."

She couldn't tell if that was a reprimand or a simple inquiry. "I have something important I need to talk to you about."

"Can't it wait until tonight?" He checked his watch. "I have a meeting in a few minutes."

In all her life, Liza had never demanded anything from this man. Never inconvenienced him in any way. But what she needed to tell him now required a bit of inconvenience.

"No, I'm sorry, it can't wait." She took a seat, determined to get this over with.

Clearly perturbed, her father returned to his own chair. "Okay, what is it?"

Liza's determination faltered. She didn't know her father well enough to even guess how he was going to take this news. Remembering her own drawn-out experience, she decided on the direct approach.

"You remember why I've been out of town, right?"

"For one of those books of yours."

Annoyed at the way he made her work sound like a silly hobby, she replied, "Yes, for one of my books." Letting the slight go, she continued. "It turns out that the gentleman who hired me to tell his story isn't the person he portrayed himself to be."

"I'm sorry to hear that." He cast another quick glance at his watch. "I'm sure your agent can deal with any legal ramifications. And it's better to know now, when you can move on to something else." As if this was an obvious conclusion to their talk, he rose to his feet.

"Dad, sit down."

Brows drawn, the agitated accountant locked his hands on his hips. "Liza, I told you I have an appointment."

She fought for patience. "The appointment can wait. I'm trying to tell you something important. Something that affects our entire family."

"Why would a book you're no longer writing affect our family?"

Liza snapped to her feet. "Because the man who hired me is Elijah Teller."

Father and daughter stared in silence for several seconds. Heart racing, she tried to gauge her father's expression. Shock? Disbelief? Liza couldn't be sure.

And then he let out a breath, flattened his hands on the desk, and shook his head. "After all these years . . ." He slowly sat back down. "I can't believe he had the nerve to contact you."

The earth tilted beneath Liza's feet. "You knew," she muttered, lowering into her chair. "You knew he wasn't dead." Were there any men in her family who didn't lie with every breath?

"He wrote to me ten years ago, confessing everything and saying he wanted to come home."

Feeling dizzy, she locked her fingers on the arms of the chair. "What did you say?"

Eyes down, her father uttered the meanest words she'd ever heard. "I told him to stay dead."

"Why would you do that?" she cried, leaping from her chair. "He's your father. How could you turn him away like that?"

"He left us first," her dad argued. "Burying that man devastated your grandmother. For years, she would hardly even leave the house.

And then there was this mess." He waved a hand at his surroundings. "Criminals for clients. Fake books and offshore accounts. Once I cleaned house and convinced the FBI that we were no longer a Mafia affiliate, it still took years to make this a reputable operation."

The callousness disgusted her. "You didn't even give her a choice, did you? How could you steal that from her? How could you keep them apart like that?"

Nostrils flared. "He's the reason your mother took you away from me. His criminal activity, and the danger it brought to all of us, drove her away. I told her I could take care of my family, but the last brick through the window was too much." Rage swept through him as spittle accumulated at the corner of his mouth. "I lost my family because of him. He didn't deserve to have his back."

Liza stared at the stranger before her with Francine's words replaying in her ears . . . *his son wanted nothing to do with him.*

She didn't approve of what Elijah had done, but he was more family to Liza than this man had ever been. Remembering what her mother had told her on her eighteenth birthday, she took great pleasure in clearing up her *father's* illusions.

"Mom left you because you were selfish, mean, and could never love anyone as much as you loved yourself."

"That's a lie."

"That's the truth. And you didn't lose your family. You tossed us away like a child does an unwanted toy. I was right there!" Liza yelled. "Five hours away. All you had to do was drive five hours to see your only daughter, and you wouldn't do it."

Her father leaned forward, unmoved by her outburst. "Your mother never should have taken you away. I was here. Our home was here. I never should have had to drive anywhere to see my child." One finger drove into the top of the desk. "She should have had to bring you to me."

Liza went numb as she realized all the years she'd wasted on this man. Longing for his attention. Craving his approval. Convincing herself that someday he'd love her enough to want her in his life.

"A real father would have done anything to see his little girl. But then, you were never a real father."

Without another word, Liza walked away from Ephrem Teller for the last time.

Chapter 27

Two days after the doctor declared Ray Wallis a *dead man walking*, he made her half-right by walking out of the hospital. Well, technically, he *rolled* out, floating on a pharmaceutical cocktail that could fell an elephant, but he departed still breathing, and that was more than anyone had expected. Including Kendall.

Unfortunately, he was going home to die. But on his own terms, and on his own turf. Surrounded by the people he cared about. All except one.

Kendall never heard from Liza after that phone call at the hospital. No texts. Not even a cheap flower arrangement to say give 'em hell on the other side. Francine seemed the most disappointed. Up until the moment they loaded Ray into the ambulance for the slow ride back to the ferry, she'd truly believed that Liza would make an appearance.

On the other hand, Ray didn't seem bothered by the no-show at all. Unlike the rest of them, he didn't leap with anticipation every time someone knocked on the hospital-room door. He didn't even ask about his granddaughter. Kendall assumed that either Ray didn't remember their conversation or had accepted Liza's silent rejection.

But then he considered a third option. Maybe, in the back of his mind, Ray believed that she *was* coming. And just maybe, that belief was keeping him alive. How long that would last, Kendall didn't know, but whether a few hours or a few days more, he would gladly accept the extra time without complaint.

Establishing full hospice care in Ray's home had not been an easy feat. First, they'd struggled to find a provider willing to ship all the necessary supplies to the island. A logistical quagmire resolved in record time by an obscenely large check. Kendall would have paid more, if necessary. Then they'd needed qualified caretakers willing to live with Ray full-time until their services were no longer needed.

This task proved more difficult, as Kendall refused to hire just anyone. He'd spent three hours reviewing candidates, finally settling on two nurses—one male and one female. Both possessed impressive credentials and came highly recommended, but testimonials provided by family members of other patients they'd both served had clinched the deal. One claimed that nurse Oliver had kept her mother laughing until the end. Another mentioned nurse Lauren's endless patience and calming nature. All the elements Kendall wanted for Ray—laughter, patience, and peace.

The living room was transformed into the ritziest hospital room Kendall ever expected to see. The automated bed and machines that fed pain-dulling meds straight into Ray's veins could not be avoided. But thanks to Francine, nothing else looked sterile, beige, or uncomfortable. Colorful landscape paintings of every size filled the walls, bringing the outside in until it looked as if there were no walls at all. As if Ray lingered directly beneath the trees with the water a stone's throw away.

The patient slept most of the time, and when awake, spoke very little. But he smiled, flirting with Lauren with his eyes and appreciating Oliver's offbeat sense of humor. Haven Island residents and regulars paid daily visits, and Kendall knew Ray enjoyed the attention. To help him feel as much himself as possible, Aadi had altered a few of the trademark fedoras so they could perch atop his head without being knocked forward by the pillows.

Just over twenty-four hours into the new routine, Ray had felt well enough to spend an hour on the back deck. Lauren lined an Adirondack chair with blankets, and Oliver and Kendall carried Ray's frail and fading body out into the warm sunshine. With a thorough pillow fluff and a quick check of the ever-present medicine machine, the young nurse asked, "Are you good, Mr. Wallis?"

Waving her close with his gnarled fingers, he whispered, "My name is Mr. Teller. Elijah Abraham Teller."

Lauren nodded, her soothing smile never slipping. "That's a nice name. Are you comfortable, Mr. Teller?"

The old man grinned, nodding as his eyes closed, and Kendall made a mental note to slip a sizable bonus into the nurse's next paycheck.

Amos curled up at the foot of Ray's chair as Kendall lowered himself into a rocker. The dog hadn't left Ray's side, other than for the necessary trips outside, since they'd brought the patient home. The first night he'd whined until Oliver fetched a footstool that Amos then used to catapult himself onto the bed. His owner understood his dog's need to stay close, since he himself had taken to sleeping in a guest room instead of his own bed.

A heavy shower had passed through that morning, blessedly carrying off the blanket of humidity that had been suffocating the island for days. Enjoying the breeze left behind, Kendall watched a rare Wilson's plover snag a mud crab from the sand and flit off to savor his midday meal in the shade. From the corner of his eye, he saw Amos raise his head, body instantly alert, seconds before someone knocked on the door from inside.

Expecting another local, he turned to find Liza stepping onto the deck at the same time Amos leaped into motion. She bent to greet the excited animal, accepting a thorough face-soaking without complaint, before straightening to greet his owner.

Kendall rose from the chair, struck speechless by the sight of her, a dream he never expected to see again. If she *was* a dream, he hoped to God he never woke up.

❦

Liza had been chanting the same prayer over and over since boarding the plane in New York.

Please, don't let it be too late.

When Kendall didn't speak, she feared that's exactly what she was—too late. Thankful for Amos's weight against her leg, she managed to murmur a greeting.

"Hi." Inadequate, but the best she could do under the circumstances.

The large man nodded in response, holding silent. Feeling like a fool for believing that Kendall might be happy to see her, Liza turned her attention to the frail man between them. He was hooked to a blinking machine by a clear tube that disappeared beneath a heavy blue blanket tucked up close to his chin. Unaware of the tension snapping above his head, he slept peacefully, almost childlike in his expression.

"How is he?" she asked. "We went to the hospital, but they said he went home. Does that mean he's getting better?"

Kendall shook his head, still silent.

"Oh."

Liza had never watched a person die before. Other than growing winded more easily, Mom had been fine the week before she'd passed. Grandma Teller had been in the hospital only three days when she'd succumbed to an undiagnosed staph infection stemming from a routine procedure the month before. In both cases, Liza had arrived too late to say goodbye. She would not make that mistake again.

"Can he talk?" she asked, not planning to bombard Elijah with endless questions, but hoping to replace their last encounter with a more positive memory.

Kendall progressed from gestures to one-word answers. "Some."

Annoyed by his lack of communication, Liza moved closer to her grandfather. "I can see that you're surprised I'm here, but he is my grandfather, and I had a right to come."

"I know. That's why I called you."

So he *could* string together a full sentence. "Then why are you standing there with your arms crossed like a statue?"

"Because I'm fighting the urge to touch you."

The confession melted Liza's resolve to hide her true feelings. "Kendall, I—"

"Forget it. I shouldn't have said that."

He tried to charge past her, but Liza blocked his path. "Please, don't go," she said, heart beating out of her chest. "Not yet." Their eyes met, and she recognized every emotion he fought to hide—doubt, regret, longing, hope. She knew them all well. "We need to talk."

He slammed his hands in his pockets, nodding. "I can do that."

Standing a foot away from the man she'd dreamed about for weeks, Liza let his scent surround her. Fresh, strong, reassuring. Just like Kendall. Her courage strengthened as his eyes took her in, and she braced for the heat as one strong hand lifted toward her face.

"Is that my Liza Ruth?" rasped a shallow voice from behind her.

Amos barked as if to answer, and Liza laughed. "It's me, Ray. I'm here," she said, moving to kneel beside his chair. The name had slipped out, a habit from their time together.

"Not Ray," he murmured, watery eyes only half-open. "Elijah."

Her breath hitched. "How about Grandpa Teller?"

A flicker of his sweet smile curved her grandfather's chapped lips. "I've waited a long time to hear those words."

Liza would make sure he heard it many more times before he left this world. As his eyes drifted closed, she said, "Can you stay awake a little longer? I brought someone else to see you."

Fighting exhaustion, and probably whatever medication they were pumping into him, Elijah opened his eyes. "Who would come see me?"

Without answering, she rushed to the open door and waved. Hesitant but eager, Aunt Julia stepped onto the weathered deck. Liza caught Kendall's confused stare and mouthed, "His sister." When the older woman reached her brother, she fell apart.

"Julia?" Ray mumbled. "Is that you? I thought you were gone with the rest."

Too emotional to respond, Liza's aunt buried her face in her brother's chest, weeping uncontrollably. Knowing she'd done the right thing, Liza wiped away her own tears as Kendall led her inside.

❦

They walked in silence more than fifty yards down the beach with Amos running on ahead. Liza turned toward the water, sandals dangling from her slender finger, and Kendall stopped beside her.

"That's Elijah's younger sister," she finally said, watching the waves roll in. "I couldn't let him go without telling her."

A generous thing to do, but she could have brought every Teller in New York State so long as she came back. "I'm glad she was willing to come."

"Me, too." Head back, she closed her eyes. "I missed this wind."

Kendall missed her.

"No wind up in New York City?"

She smiled. "Not like this." Breathing deeply, she peered once again over the water. "I missed other things about this island. The quiet. The smell of salt in the air. You." His heart skipped a beat. "I missed you the most."

Now he had to be dreaming. "The most, huh?" he replied, keeping his tone light.

Liza shook her head. "No, that's a lie. I missed Amos the most." The blissful dog sprinted by with a large stick in his mouth. "But you were a close second," she added. They laughed together, some of the tension easing between them, but Kendall knew this was his best chance to make amends.

"I've missed you, too," he said, relieved to finally say the words.

Her expression sobered as she stared out over the water. "Then why didn't you ask me to stay?"

The question knocked the wind out of him, and it took him a long time to find the words. "I told you what my parents' marriage was like. I saw what happened when a person was asked to give up everything. I would never do that."

Turning, she faced Kendall head-on. "But I'm not your mother. I love this island."

"You say that now, but after a few months. A year. Things would change."

"No, they—"

"I planned to go with you," he said, cutting her off. "I'd already decided that I didn't have to stay here. I was going to move closer to you, and we could see if this would work, but I needed you to be patient, until Ray was . . . taken care of." Kendall couldn't bring himself to say *once Ray was gone*. "I was going to ask you to wait, but then Ray told you the truth, and everything blew up."

The confession poured out of him, heaped into the space between them with all the pent-up frustration that had been choking Kendall since the day she'd left.

Liza took a step closer. "You would leave Haven Island for me?"

Kendall nodded. "I'd do anything for you."

255

Taking another step, she held the curls back from her face and looked up into his eyes. "There's only one thing I want from you, Kendall."

Willing to honor any request, he said, "What is it?"

Slender fingers flattened over his heart. "Ask me to stay."

Cupping her face, he searched her eyes, unable to let the past go.

"There's nothing in New York for me," she said, dragging the hair out of her face. "Everything I want is right here on Haven Island. *This* is what I want, Kendall. *You* are all I want."

His breath hitched as her words sank in. "Are you sure? You have to be sure."

Soft lips curled into a smile as she nodded. "I'm sure."

Kendall pulled her into his arms, vowing to never let her go again. "Then stay, Liza. Stay with me."

🦋

On a warm July morning, in the shady corner of a quiet New York cemetery, Elijah Abraham Teller was laid to rest, permanently this time, beside the love of his life.

The lack of family in attendance was more than made up for by an abundance of friends who'd made the journey north to pay their last respects. Liza couldn't help but smile when Kendall leaned close to whisper, "He's up there bragging about this turnout to anyone who will listen."

Yes, he probably was. And she had no doubt that he was doing so with one arm wrapped tightly around his favorite girl.

The service was simple and solemn, and as the mourners proceeded to their cars, Liza supplied tissues to her bereft aunt, grateful for Kendall's foresight to bring extras. As the crowd thinned, Francine and Aadi lingered not far from the grave, waiting for the three stragglers to make their way to the car. Not until Kendall squeezed Liza's hand did she notice the solitary figure dressed in black waiting beside their rental car.

"Who is that?" she asked, squinting to make out the face.

"My mom," he replied.

Liza knew that Jacqueline James lived in the city, and they'd planned to pay her a visit before going home, but she'd had no idea the woman would attend the funeral. Based on Kendall's dazed expression, neither had he.

"Go on," she said. "I'll wait over here."

Never releasing her hand, Kendall turned to the couple who'd been with them through every trial of the last couple of weeks. "Could you guys take care of Aunt Julia for a minute?"

That he called her Aunt Julia made Liza love him a little bit more.

"Of course." Francine took over tissue duty as Kendall tightened his grip on Liza's hand.

"I need to warn you," he said as they respectfully skirted a line of graves, "Mom and Ray never got along."

Liza didn't know what to do with that information, but if he was trying to make her even more nervous about meeting his mother, mission accomplished. The first thing Liza noticed as they approached the statuesque brunette was the striking resemblance between mother and son. He may have gotten his overall size from his father, but the hair, mouth, and expressive brown eyes were all Jacqueline.

Releasing Liza's hand, Kendall skipped the greeting and wrapped his arms around his mom, burying his face in her neck like a little boy seeking the comfort only a mother could provide. Though Elijah had been her grandfather, she'd somehow failed to realize that in every way but blood, he'd filled that role in Kendall's life for more than thirty years. If anyone was family here, it was this stoic man who'd put his own grief aside to take care of everyone else. From making sure Elijah left the world with dignity and peace, to paying every penny of his funeral expenses.

Including the private jet that had carried him home.

"I know, son," she said, rubbing his broad back. "I know."

Kendall blew out a long breath as he pulled away, immediately retrieving Liza's hand. "Mom, this is Liza Teller, Elijah's granddaughter."

"I'm very sorry for your loss, Ms. Teller."

"Please," she replied, accepting the warm hand, "call me Liza. And thank you very much for coming. I know my grandfather would appreciate it."

Jacqueline chuckled. "He would be quite entertained by my presence, I'm sure. Old Elijah and I weren't the best of friends, but he was good to my boy, and for that I will always be grateful."

"He loved Kendall very much."

"And so do you, I hear."

Liza had never seen Kendall blush and cringe at the same time. "Yes, ma'am, I do."

"Good. Because I'd like to have grandchildren sometime soon."

Kendall winced as he pulled his mom against his side. "Okay, okay, okay. That's enough embarrassment for now." To Liza he said, "Ignore her. We are not talking babies anytime soon."

Thank goodness, because babies were not on her radar. At least not yet. Liza was still adjusting to living with a dog.

🦋

"What are you doing out here, babe?" Kendall flipped on the overhead light of Liza's New York apartment and padded into the living room, eyes half-shut. "It's two o'clock in the morning."

Liza looked up from the floor, photos in her hand and a sea of them scattered around her. "I found a box," she said, the quiver in her voice a sign that she'd been crying.

Feeling as if he'd stumbled into a minefield, Kendall joined her on the age-worn rug, struggling to determine if she was happy or sad about this finding. "A box of pictures?" Stupid question, but she had him at a disadvantage. Thirty seconds ago he'd been sound asleep.

"Look." Gently sliding a stack out of the way, she scooted closer. "This is Elijah in his uniform. He was so handsome."

Kendall had to agree with her. "He looks like a kid."

"He was." Liza turned the picture over. "This was taken less than six months after his high school graduation."

Though he'd joined up at the same age, Kendall felt protective of the boy in the picture. Like someone should have stepped in and said he was too young to go.

She handed him the old black-and-white photo to reach for another. "This is my favorite so far." Dropping her head onto his shoulder, Liza sniffled. "This is the day he and Grandma met at the Bronx Zoo. I love that they met on a blind date. Did he ever talk about her?"

"No, he didn't talk about his life before the island at all." Kendall now realized that must have been a survival tactic. He'd missed his family too much to talk about them. "How did you find these?"

Liza sat up and reached for a tissue on the table behind her. "I wanted to make sure I wasn't leaving anything important behind, and something told me to check the top of the closet." Since she was moving to the island and wanted to keep Grandma Teller's apartment in the family, they'd found a younger cousin who was happy to move in and take care of the place. "I pushed a chair over and found a shoebox at the back of the shelf."

Kendall picked up a handful by his foot. They were black-and-white photos with a scalloped edge all the way around. "Do you know who these people are?"

She leaned over to look. "I'm not sure, but that one looks like Julia, so maybe those are his sisters." Pointing to another, she said, "Wow. I bet those are my great-grandparents." The image showed a stone-faced couple standing in front of a large ship. "They came over from Poland in 1923, I think."

Kendall flipped the photo to find a date stamp of September 17, 1923. "I think you're right. This guy definitely looks like Elijah."

Liza cleared a space on the rug and took the photo from Kendall's hand. "We need to organize these. Put the oldest ones here, and we'll go by decade."

"Honey, we fly out in the morning. This could take all night." His words fell on deaf ears.

"That's why we have to do this now."

"But—"

"Kendall, I can't sleep knowing that all of this history is sitting in a box waiting to be rediscovered." Gathering the last snapshots in the bottom of the box, she froze, eyes locked on whatever she'd found.

"What?" he asked.

Eyes misty, she turned the picture his way. "You look just like him."

The picture showed Elijah Teller standing beside a black Cadillac and smiling up at a much taller man dressed in an ill-fitting suit. "That's my dad." Kendall held the picture as if it were a priceless treasure. "I've never seen a picture of him this young before."

"When I met your mom, I thought you looked like her, but, Kendall, that could be you standing beside Elijah."

"Yeah," he mumbled. "We looked a lot alike. Some people even thought we were brothers." Memories flooded back. Fishing. Throwing ball. Building things together. "Do you think there might be more of Dad in here?"

Liza smiled and kissed his cheek. "I don't know, but I'd be happy to help you look." Kendall kissed her hard on the lips before rolling to his feet. "Where are you going?" she asked.

"To make the coffee. We have a long night ahead."

When he reached the doorway to the kitchen, Liza called his name. "Kendall?"

He turned, expecting instructions on how to make her coffee. "Yeah, babe."

Huddled on the floor wearing baby-blue pajamas and surrounded by their shared history, she said, "I love you."

Kendall's heart swelled as he memorized every detail of the moment, from the emotion in her blue eyes to the color on the tips of her toes. Grateful for the man who'd brought her into his life, he smiled. "I love you, too, Liza."

ACKNOWLEDGMENTS

Though writing is a solitary endeavor, I couldn't possibly shape and mold these stories into being without the help of some amazing individuals. For this book, I have to thank Kim Law for helping me get the initial idea off the ground, and then swooping in during the editing phase and saving my sanity. I also have to thank my editor, Selina McLemore, for going above and beyond to help me whip a seriously flawed manuscript into a book I can be proud of.

As always, I'm grateful for my agent, Nalini Akolekar, who might be the most patient woman I know, and Megan Mulder, who pulls the levers behind the scenes that turn my stories into full-fledged books. And then there's my daughter, Isabelle—my cheerleader, my support, and the best thing that ever happened to me. Thanks for unloading the dishwasher, never complaining about all the fend-for-yourself meals, and scooping the litter boxes.

Haven Island is fully and affectionately based on Dewees Island, just off the coast of Charleston, South Carolina. When I stumbled upon the setting on a map and began researching, I couldn't believe there was an island with no paved streets, cars, stores, or restaurants. It seemed impossible in this day and age, but the place really does exist. I was fortunate to spend several days on the island, absorbing the peace and quiet, and I enjoyed bringing the beautiful setting to life on the page.

Portions of this book were written in Paris and London, and the opportunity to visit such amazing cities was a direct result of the generosity of readers. I am more grateful than I can possibly express and will do my best to keep writing stories that offer a laugh, a sigh, and a satisfying smile at the end.

ABOUT THE AUTHOR

Photo © 2017 Annastraya Photography

Terri Osburn is the *Wall Street Journal* bestselling author of contemporary romance with heart, hope, and lots of humor. She fell in love with the written word at a young age, and the genre of romance beckoned during her teen years. In 2007, she put pen to paper to write her own heart-melting love stories, including the Anchor Island series, the Ardent Springs series, and the Shooting Stars novels. Her work has been translated into five languages and has sold more than a million copies worldwide. Terri resides in middle Tennessee with her teenage daughter and a menagerie of high-maintenance pets. You can learn more about her by visiting her website at www.terriosburn.com.